Also by Robert McKean

The Catalog of Crooked Thoughts, NOVEL

I'll Be Here for You:

Diary of a Town

Robert McKean

Livingston Press
The University of West Alabama

ISBN 13: trade paper 978-1-60489-252-9
ISBN 13: hardcover 978-1-60489-253-6
ISBN 13: e-book 978-1-60489-254-3

Library of Congress Control Number 20200932320
Printed on acid-free paper
Printed in the United States of America by
Publishers Graphics

Hardcover binding by: HF Group
Typesetting and page layout: Sarah Coffey
Proofreading: Maddie Owen, Tricia Taylor, Jenna Frye, Tricia Taylor
Cover Design: Joe Taylor
Cover Photograph: Robert McKean

These stories appeared previously in the following journals: "However Innocently, However Unwittingly," *The Flexible Persona* (nominated for Pushcart Prize); "Tody Was a Seven," *34th Parallel;* "Velia Creaming Her Legs," *The MacGuffin;* "Ralphie's Clarinet," *The Kenyon Review;* "Placido Lombardi's Funeral," *Kestrel;* "Invisible Weaving," *BoomerLit Magazine;* "Mrs. Kattlove's Clerk," Finalist, *Adelaide Literary Award Anthology;* "Spare Parts & Bloody Bones," *The Front Range Review;* "Red Box, Red Box," *Kindred.*

I'll Be Here for You:

Diary of a Town

For my brothers, James and Joseph

*I say that we are wound
With mercy round and round
As if with air.*

—Gerard Manley Hopkins

Table of Contents

Ganaego, Pennsylvania

1971 — 2015

However Innocently,
However Unwittingly

Spring 2009

Heady things, humble things.

Her father's pet phrase, something the old man would mutter as he went about his housebound days in frayed slippers, whether he was parsing Virgil or cleaning the trap beneath a bathroom sink. It was, in fact, her father's coming-apart-at-the-seams slippers that Maddy was thinking about on her way to check in on him when, at the left-hand turn across traffic onto Linden Street at the T&V Supermarket she always dreaded making, she lost her nerve and caused the accident . . . well, the first accident.

"That's why I'm here," the police inspector who turned up at her house that evening explained. "The officers, you told them it was your fault? No disrespect . . ."—he consulted a tablet he withdrew from a pocket—"Mrs. Schoolcraft, but how do you figure you was to blame?"

The inspector, a tall, solemn black man, wore a light-colored suit as stiff as cardboard. Since he was not in uniform, he'd shown her a badge pinned to the inside of his wallet. Not that she could really see it. Why do officials display their IDs so quickly you never have time to read them?

"Ma'am?"

"I'm sorry." To steady her thoughts Maddy focused on the damp spots on his sleeve. "I was thinking of my father, I've been worried about him, and as I was inching forward to make the left there—you know, at the T&V?—I suddenly changed my mind. That's when he bumped me. I couldn't see—because of the rain—and I just stopped. I'm sorry, I'm not a very assertive driver."

The loose skin of the inspector's forehead drew up in pleats. "Still don't get it. We got all sorts of laws against driving recklessly, but not against driving cautiously." His voice took on a lecturing tone. "It's for the motorist behind, ma'am, to have control of his vehicle. The boy *did* hit you, that is correct, is it not? The woman behind him"—he consulted his tablet again—"said he got out of his car, looked at *your* car, then got back in his and swung around you to your right? Now, that's how it happened, am I not correct on that?"

She was forty-one, divorced. She worked at the community college as an administrator. People did not always regard her as a serious person, and here she was taking up the valuable time of the police. "I'm sorry," Maddy recanted, "I shouldn't have said that. Yes, he hit me, I mean it was only a tap, I'm sure there wouldn't have been anything for him to see back there, but he did exactly as you say. Is he going to be all right? He didn't die, did he? What about the truck driver?"

The vexing question of her guilt dispensed with, the inspector permitted himself to relax; his shoulders lowered, the muscles of his long face slackened. He stowed away his tablet. "The fellow in the truck? Oh, plenty shook up *and* he's lost his livelihood—that was his rig, he's a private contractor—but at least he walked away from it. As for the boy, it's pretty grim, but I've been told he's got a chance. And let me tell you, if he does pull through, he's going to be the luckiest kid in the world. By all rights he should be laid out tonight on a slab in the basement of Butterworth's Mortuary. He was thrown out on the road and got his face slashed, so *that* message he'll carry with him the rest of his life. But you, are *you* going to be all right, ma'am?"

No, not really. After the solicitous inspector left, Maddy made the ground beef and macaroni casserole that her son, home soon from his track meet, would wolf down in gulping mouthfuls. As she worked, she tried to erase from her imagination the scene before the T&V. She had not gone on to her father's. So violently was she shaking that, after the police had taken her puzzling statement and dismissed her, she could manage only to steer her car up Sutton Post Road and home—shaking that had gone on in the gray silence of her bedroom. The smeary windshield, her old Honda with its all-but useless wipers, the relentless procession of oncoming cars—how selfishly, how *unforgivingly,* people drive nowadays—her lurch forward and panic, jamming her brakes and then the slight jolt from behind. The young man leapt from his car in the pouring rain. He was shouting, revolving his arms. She heard his obscenities even before she rolled down her window to apologize. An apology he had no intention of accepting. As she turned to fetch her papers from the glove compartment, he screamed at her—called her a *cunt!* a word she hadn't heard in thirty years—and stalked back to his car. To fetch his papers? *No,* as Maddy watched in disbelief and went on re-watching in the theater of her mind, his car inexplicably spurted past hers onto the shoulder on her right, then swerved recklessly—and *yes,* that word of the inspector's was the proper one—across her front: taking his left anyway, the hell with her.

Without looking.

Her husband, former husband, an engineer for the power company, would no doubt have dispassionately explained the dynamics of such an event, two bodies traveling at great velocities attempting to occupy the same space at the same time, one a low-slung red sports car with spoked rims that flashed in the rain, the other a truck, one of those massive dump trucks you've begun to see more and more often. But no mathematical formulation of forces and counterforces on Dale's whiteboard could mitigate the shock of that impact, the enormous truck in a deafening shriek of rending metal and exploding glass crumpling and sweeping away, now on her left, the much dwarfed car.

The truck, it occurred to her, could have driven the boy's car into hers.

But it was her son who put a period to this disconcerting, jarring day. Sliding his gangly body with its oversized clownish feet into his chair at the dining room table, Ethan said, "There was an incredible wreck today—Terry Boswell."

"You *know* who it was? The boy?"

"Mom," Ethan spoke in impatience with his mother, "Terry Boswell's in my class!"

~ ~ ~

One lesson Maddy had fully absorbed in life was never to doubt her father. Now retired, but once beloved school teacher—Latin, French—Pop Warner coach, community-garden founder, pancake-breakfast and spaghetti-dinner organizer, chaperon for adults on tours to the Alhambra and for hormonal teenagers on senior trips to the nation's capital: Who knew how many travelers cheerful, unrufflable Albert Victorine had steered through the muddles that humans will inevitably make of things? But with his failing eyesight and periods of distraction, Maddy had begun to question her father's grasp, and walking in on him this afternoon brought her no reassurance.

What must have represented every scrap of clothing he owned, as well as whatever stray pieces remained of her mother's, was strewn across the sofa, the table, the floor: shirts, sweaters, socks, dresses, coats, scarves, hats, belts. It looked like the Mission after a two-for-one sale. And for the first few seconds when from the center of that disorder her poor wizened old papa blinked at her, perplexed, she feared it was even worse than it looked.

However Innocently, However Unwittingly

"Dad, what're you *doing?*"

"Simplifying?"

"You have everything everywhere?" She had taken the afternoon off to drive him to his appointment with the retinal specialist. She stepped over the tangle of clothes. "We'll have to put everything back—and we don't have time now."

"But I don't need all this, Madeline, really, I don't."

He looked down, as she did, at his slippered feet, the slippers whose tattered bindings had worried her yesterday. Nearby, a striped jersey lay, the kind of shirt that referees wear in sporting events. At least he was right about having too many things. Didn't they all have too many things? "Do you have a system?" she asked hopefully. "What you're keeping, what you're discarding? You do, don't you? You always have a system."

"I do." Albert brightened. "Anything with three or more colors goes."

"What do I smell? Something *burning?*"

The empty saucepot on the burner was glowing. It was nearly translucent; you could smell the metal—preparing to melt? Maddy turned off the gas and, using two potholders between her hands and the handle, doused the quivering pot under the cold-water tap. Great clouds of vapor rose up, fogging her glasses.

"Dad, we need to talk."

"We used to have one that whistled, well, screeched."

"Why don't I," she said, "make some tea for us? Then you need to get ready. You do remember you have an appointment, don't you?"

Her father looked around the kitchen he'd spent sixty years in. What did he see, what glimmered against those damaged retinas? Paths worn in the linoleum, rounded cabinet corners, paint on handles rubbed to wood? When her mother fell ill all too early in life, he had assumed household duties, becoming, no surprise, an inventive chef.

He gazed at her thoughtfully. "Should I change it to two colors? Your mother had a beautiful frock—of many colors. Stripes. You probably don't remember it, she wore it in the summer. She looked like a walking rainbow."

He'd been her best friend, perhaps her only friend. She had wanted to talk with him about yesterday. The accident continued to distress her, the shattering, convulsive violence of that impact, the image which she blessedly hadn't seen, but imagined, of a human face being flung against a pavement. From talking with Ethan, she gathered that Terry Boswell ran in a different crowd than the nerdy and jock crowds that Ethan bounced between, a fast, loose crowd. But *still:* It could have been Ethan. Not that Ethan was likely to burst from a car and begin hurling profanities at a stranger, but seventeen-year-olds were creatures of impulse. Editor of the school newspaper, basketball and track star, cycling enthusiast, Ethan would graduate in a month and intern again this summer for the *Citizen Chronicle,* the town newspaper. Her son's sports worried her, his cycling tours through the mountains, his nights out with his chums, even the long-legged girls he'd begun to date. Were girls any more responsible than boys? And come fall he would be off to college.

"Is this Terry Boswell some sort of spoiled rich boy?" she had asked. "Is that what you mean?"

"You hear stories. He got suspended for something last semester, I don't know."

He did know. She let it pass. "Did your father come to your meet?"

And this, Ethan could not dissemble. His eyes lingered vulnerably on hers, the soft eyes of a boy not yet a man, then fell away in sorrow and confusion. "Didn't see him, Mom."

Would it be embarrassing for Ethan if someone in school identified his mother as the person who had provoked Terry Boswell?

But now, this afternoon, was not the moment to burden her father with her troubles. The piles of clothes would have to wait until tomorrow, Saturday, but since she had fortuitously taken the entire afternoon off there was time to get him made presentable for his appointment. The doctor's office was nearby, in the assemblage of medical suites in a wing of the hospital. Reaching the suites required taking the elevator in the lobby and crossing a glass bridge. Albert had macular degeneration, the wet kind, and the consultations every six weeks were lengthy affairs. Before they could meet with the specialist, Albert had to be led away for dilation and returned to wait for the solution to take effect, then fetched again for a scan and returned, then finally summoned to an examination room. Most of the patients Dr. Giannetta saw were aged, the delicate machinery of the eye succumbing to time's ravages in advance of the sturdier body. The doctor, a bulky, perspiring man with a florid face framed by white hair, would rush, harried, from one room to another. With a few stock pleasantries, he'd raise her father's seat, swing a piece of equipment like a mask before his face and peer into his diseased eyes. Barking out his conclusions in acronyms to an assistant who typed his comments into a computer, the doctor would strap on a helmet with a light attached—much like, Maddy would think, what a spelunker might don before descending into a cave—and gaze through a scope into his patients' eyes. With the four of them crammed in the small room, the atmosphere seemed pressurized, claustrophobic. On visits when Dr. Giannetta determined that her father's condition had worsened, the afternoons would be even more prolonged by his needing to receive a shot directly in the affected eye.

"It's all right, I don't mind the needle." Albert patted, in anticipation perhaps, his eyes in which the pupils had begun to grow as large as the pupils of cartoon characters. "One has to be stoical. If I have to get a shot, then I shall. I'll think of Homer."

She looped her arm around him and whispered in his ear. "I don't expect anyone else here is thinking of Homer."

Sometimes he would have a different kind of scan that resulted in his urine turning bright tangerine. When that occurred, even a proper, circumspect man as Albert Victorine could hardly let such a remarkable occurrence pass without comment. He squeezed her hand on his shoulder. *"Vive memor leti; fugit hōra."*

"That's Homer?"

"Persius."

"And means . . ."

"Shame on you, Maddy. *Live mindful of death, the hour flees."* Albert glanced around the waiting room at the old men and women, more women than men, the remnants of his generation either stupefied by age or become garrulous, squawking at their adult children. "Except here."

She hugged him again. "I remember Mama's striped dress. It shimmered in the sunlight."

~ ~ ~

Today's appointment did end with an injection of Lucentis. As her father explored with his fingertips the black pirate's patch on his right eye, Maddy guided him across the glass bridge in the falling sunlight. She kept her hand on his arm. Stoical or not, a needle directly in one's eye would give pause to even the most stalwart of individuals. As the elevator doors began to close, two nurses came bundling in, chattering excitedly, their heads pressed together.

"What? *When?* I only came on."

"Now, *now*—I just heard it!"

"I thought he was out of the woods? What happened?"

"I don't know, organ failure, blood clot, I don't know! I'm going to find out. They called in practically the whole attending staff, but they couldn't do it, couldn't bring him back."

"God, I know them—*her,* his mother. The father doesn't live with them. She was all in a dither because she didn't think he was going to graduate, but then he pulled it off somehow, got the school's approval. He probably sweet-talked his teachers. He was quite a little operator apparently, a real heartbreaker with the girls. God, this is so *awful!"*

Driving to her father's today, Maddy had avoided the left-hand turn at the T&V. Had gone out of her way to wend a zigzag through Ganaego's old brick streets, and now, driving them home, her father dozing beside her, she did the same, plunging the car down one road after another, doing anything to bypass that turn. When she bumped the car at last up into his drive, Albert started awake.

"Here, already?"

"Dad?" She pictured the clothes strewn every which way, the glowing saucepot, an old man with diminishing sight scuffling through the rooms in ragged slippers. "I'm going to go in and pack a bag for you. I want you to stay with us for a night or two."

"Maddy, don't be such a—"

She put a hand on his sleeve. "You can make your famous buttermilk pancakes—Ethan'll love them. *Please,* for me?"

He folded his arms across his chest. "Oh, all right, if it makes you happy. I'll come in—I know what I want."

"Tell me, I'll get it for you. You know, I think it's coming time you're going to have to let me start doing more things for you?"

"Heady things, humble things?"

"Heady things, humble things, yes, Dad."

"One night."

"Two."

He was sound asleep when she slipped back into the car, an old pirate whose ship was entering troubled waters, and she was suddenly furious—this out of nowhere—with Dale, her ex-husband, who had missed unconscionable amounts of his son's childhood for his troubleshooting trips to far-flung regions of the country. Dale's circuits always took precedence over his family—until one day he came home to discover he no longer had a family. Now, he was missing Ethan's final days with them, these glorious, valedictory days of youth: a boy grown tall, who wore the most outlandish Lycra biking costumes and pedaled in dense, fast, synchronized packs of his fellow cyclists for hundred-mile stretches, who sprinted four-hundred meters in school-record time, whose name appeared above stories in the *Chronicle*—missing all that for a bunch of damn transistors.

A boy had just died.

A boy not all that different from their son, and she, however innocently, however unwittingly, had had a hand in it. Irritable—not only with Dale, but with herself, with the world—Maddy did not take a circuitous route home, but determinedly headed up Linden Street. If at rush hour the left into Linden was a trial, the left out of it onto Sutton Post Road was nearly impossible. She joined the string of left-turning automobiles and pickups creeping forward. Ahead, against the ruddy sky loomed the shoulder of the T&V. As the building drew nearer, its blocky shadow crept closer and closer until darkness fell across the car. What friends did Terry Boswell leave behind? Had he had brothers and sisters, aunts and uncles, grandmothers and grandfathers? Did he have a sweetheart? That abandoned mother, who longed to see her child graduate, where was she when his life ended? In the hospital, one prayed, and what was she doing right now? Actually, Maddy knew what Terry Boswell's mother was doing: You go home after the death. She knew that. It was what she and her father did after her mother died. Home to your familiar rooms, which no longer look familiar, and you call Butterworth's or Flipovitch's or Hoover's, or any of the score of mortuaries in Ganaego, and you sit in the gray silence of your bedroom and pretend that whoever you have loved and lost is in heaven and that your life will go on safely and securely—and, of course, neither of those things is true.

Her father groaned in his sleep, sighed.

As her turn approached, Maddy—imagining the body being transported through this same impatient Friday traffic to rest, as the police inspector prophesized should have happened, on a cold slab in a strange basement—looked over at Sutton Post Road, where her car had idled after the accident, blocking traffic and annoying the motorists behind her. She was required to look that way, but even so, had she wished not to look, she wouldn't have been able to keep her eyes from being drawn irresistibly that direction. Nothing was to be seen. But you would not expect to see anything, scrupulous as we are about tidying up our messes, removing anything that might cast a pall over our happy lives. But in the slanting sunlight Maddy did notice something, shards of glittering glass and chrome. From the boy's car? The truck? From some frightful amalgamation of the two as they attempted to occupy the same space at the same time? Tomorrow, she vowed, she was going to have two conversations. One with her father, a gentle but insistent conversation, and another with Dale, that one not so gentle: Things had to change, and they would. As she graduated to the head of the queue and anxiously scanned the unbroken stream of oncoming cars, Maddy saw more evidence: long smears of rubber down the pavement, where, she presumed, the tires of the boy's red car had been shoved sideways, against themselves. What stupendous force would it have taken to do that? Well, she knew that, too: She had been here, she had been part of it.

Seeing a break in the traffic, Maddy, catching her breath, took her left.

Tody Was a Seven

Summer 2003

"Shelly, are you going to take some time off? You must miss your brother terribly."

"Oh, I do miss him, but it's better to stay busy, don't you think?"

"Sure now? I wouldn't mind."

The plaid throw covering her client's palsied legs had slipped. On his gray skin gooseflesh rose, ridges of tiny pimples. It was a humid, close day, actually, but the summer's warmth mattered little in here, with the Plüddermanns' arctic air-conditioning. His sympathies, she understood, were far more fixed on his own approaching mortality than whatever sorrow she might be experiencing. And accordingly, when the old man, grateful to be spared the chore of mounting any more of a fraudulent protest, distractedly waved a skeletal hand, Shelly stole a glance at her watch and put forth her standard closing question.

"Ready, Mr. Plüddermann?"

She rolled him through the gloomy Victorian to the lavatory beneath the rear stairs. There, bantering his fussing with her teasing, she hoisted him under the arms and braced him. She was a tall woman, sturdy, strong. She yanked his boxer shorts to his knees and plopped him on his raised seat. His toenails curled over, they were ragged and yellow. He smelled. All the medicines he was prescribed—sometimes Mr. Plüddermann shat fluorescent green. But his feces, whatever hue they took on, were not her concern; she wasn't the visiting nurse.

Tody Was a Seven

Shelly returned to the frigid living room, to the chair she always occupied beside his study, a room upon which her own thoughts, just as distracted as his, were focused.

Two weeks ago she had stolen two hundred dollars from his desk. A stupid, impetuous thing, she could hardly say what madness had driven her. Anguished that she was jeopardizing a reputation she'd spent twenty-five years nurturing, she had, the following week, slipped back into his study while he labored on his toilet and restored the two hundred-dollar bills to the stack of identical bills in his desk. What worried her had not been Mr. Plüddermann. Even if he, however improbably, were to discover the missing money, the feeble old man whose family had owned the Hotel Himmellsbach had become too dependent on her to suspect her. It was the son, Alvy. Alvy Plüddermann was fully capable of knowing who had access to his father's desk and precisely how much loose cash his father imprudently kept there.

As she did. It was her business to be in people's houses. *Shelly Namarian—Your Personal Care Companion.* Besides assisting Mr. Plüddermann in the bathroom and rolling him in and out of his wheelchair shower, she fixed the old man his yogurt and toast and fetched him his check registry from the very same drawer in which those hundreds softly slept. For Mrs. Bartkiewicz, who was blind, she read the *Chronicle* aloud and the grisly letters from the niece serving in Iraq. For Mrs. Lindsey, not so old, she minded the twins while their mother drove to Stellwagen's to down whiskey sour after whiskey sour. Ever since her own ruinous, headstrong marriage had come apart twenty-five years ago with her seven months' pregnant and her bastard of a husband in bed with a bar tramp, she had made her own way, raised to maturity the child she birthed alone in Ganaego's surgery, fashioned for herself a respectable life.

So, of course, she was not going to throw all that away for two hundred dollars.

Shelly put the episode down to the shock of her brother's death. And it had been a shock, Tody's accident. A tragedy, people said. *Yes*, but what was a sixty-two-year-old man doing on a ladder, in the first place? God knows Tody, who'd been a daft moonchild all his life, remained one to the end, up there clinging to the clapboards of his house. But the thing of it was, and what kept gnawing at her, neither Alvy nor his father *had* noticed the missing money. They had seemed perfectly untroubled the entire week that she carried the two bills around in her purse. From her chair she could see the old man's ornate desk. Just a single note, something to slip Owen, provide her son with some mad money . . .

"Confound it, Shelly girl, where the goddamned hell are you? *Shelly!*"

She heard his howls and found him standing, more or less, clutching the wheelchair and tipping it so far that a wheel revolved in midair. He was ninety years old, his shorts were crabbed about his ankles, he was as fragile as a china doll. She grabbed a shoulder just he was about to go ass over teacups. "Why didn't you call me?"

"I've *been* calling you—for twenty fucking minutes!"

It was Friday, her last stop. Friday afternoons, by design, were hers. Sometimes she browsed the shop windows at the mall, sometimes she did chores. Today, she was looking forward to spending the afternoon with Owen. She had enlisted her son to help her clean out Tody's house. Owen was a busy fellow, it was hard to get on his calendar. Masking her irritation—she did *not* appreciate being sworn at—she restored whatever shred of dignity the old man retained, flushed without looking, wheeled him back to his living room. There, she waited impatiently for him to sign off on his yogurt cup and whole wheat toast.

"Do you want me to bring you your book?"

The old man, a bubble forming on his lips, beamed at his blueberries. "Please, dear."

She went into his study, slid back the top drawer of the desk. As her fingers found their way to his check registry, they grazed the stack of dozing hundreds, a handsome pile about the size of the Rueben sandwiches the Hotel Himmellsbach had once famously served in its café, and an image blossomed in her mind: herself, a ninety-year-old woman, twice her present age. She let a finger slip beneath a few of the notes, caressing them. Her brother had left her nothing. The bank would get his house. It was her savings that had buried him. Who, she despaired, is going to lift me off the commode when I'm ninety? Who's going to flush *my* green shit? *Who?*

She gathered three bills into her palm.

~ ~ ~

Her fingers were icy, she fumbled with her keys. Sitting in her car, furious with herself, she plotted how she might invent an excuse to get back inside and replace the bills. Then she felt the lump in her jeans pocket: The notes were wadded, crinkled. Even if she finagled her way inside, it would do no good: These hundreds could no longer lie anonymously alongside their mates in the elegant drawer that smelled of mentholated cough lozenges. Distraught, Shelly started her car and almost collided with a station wagon slipping into the drive— and her spirits reversed, instantly soared. The cleaning people! Four stout women bundled out from a car painted the color of a New York taxi. Three weeks ago they'd chipped a valuable gilded frame. Last spring they neglected to close a window and a grackle had fluttered from room to room, terrorizing the old man.

They were poor, they chattered like geese: She had nothing to worry about.

Relieved, she drove to Tody's and went directly up to her brother's bedroom. The foreclosure process would drag on for months, but she wanted to clear the house and *this,* what was stored in her brother's room, she wanted to deal with without delay. Her brother—half-brother—had been without a modicum of commonsense. A clerk in a yardage shop by day, Tody, by night, sailed under far more extravagant colors. Which was fine, his business was his business. It was not that she didn't love him, not that she was not grateful. When the mother they shared died and her father drank himself into dementia, Tody fought to keep her out of foster care. He cooked their dinners, combed her hair, quizzed her teachers on Parents' Night on his ward's progress. But Tody, who should have known better than anyone the fishbowls small towns are, was indiscreet—wildly, flagrantly indiscreet.

Ironically, his taste wasn't all that bad. Not tacky, not frou-frou. Much of what she was corralling from his closet and stuffing in garbage bags was charming: chiffon cocktail dresses, conservative British tweeds, summery puff-shoulder dresses, a blazer you could wear to your sorority homecoming dinner. Tody adored his *costumes,* as he called them. And, again, that was his life. But listening to the bells that old Father Opsatnick had set plangently tolling at the funeral, she had found herself taking issue, even after all these years, with her brother's fidelity to a store with wooden floors that had for forty years taken advantage of him and a lifestyle that placed the needs of the Lake Biddleford Players, a woebegone amateur thespian company, above his own. And none of it, the crossdressing least of all, had ever made sense to her.

Hearing Owen's rumbling pickup, she quickly emptied the dresser of her brother's collection of perfumed bras, panties, girdles, hose, garter belts. The ladies' scanties she really did prefer to bag herself. Was there a woman alive, other than a professional escort, who still wore garter belts? She hurried downstairs. Catching sight of her son through the window striding across the porch in his work boots, she was struck by what a comely creature she had brought into the world: six-feet-one, coal-black hair, laconic green eyes— no wonder he was busy! As a reward for his loyalty, he had been promised a home-cooked meal. Shelly yanked open the door before he could ring, taking him by surprise.

But the surprise was hers. "Mom"—Owen lightly fended her off—"can't stay, sorry, sorry. I got a chance to use a cottage for the weekend—gonna be great fishing."

She masked her disappointment. She had never clung to him, never tried to make him a mama's boy. Owen had been independent. He knocked about with his chums, he smoked, he drank—he was manly, she was proud of him. A week out of high school he'd already had a job. Changed the oil in her car, painted her kitchen, hooked up her new washer and dryer. But in girls Owen made terrible choices. She didn't have to follow the lazy swing of his arm toward his truck to guess the nature of its passenger. Last month she had stepped into his trailer and spooked a girl wearing one of his tee-shirts and nothing else. The girl, underage, squeaked, actually squeaked, covered her pubis, fled squeaking ever more urgently into the bedroom.

"Sure," she said. "I understand, of course."

The world thrusts the old aside. She didn't need Joseph Plüddermann and his shrunken, pustulated thighs to tell her that. Smelling fresh sex welling up from her son, Shelly pulled the three crumpled hundred-dollar bills from her pocket and shoved them down inside his shirt pocket, next to his cigarettes.

Fishing, she thought, *fishing my ass.*

~ ~ ~

It was better to stay busy: That part had not been a fabrication.

Tody's day clothes she kept separate. Those could go to the Mission. From her brother's room she moved on to her parents' old room. August heat gathered in the small frame house. As she worked, she tried not to obsess about the stolen money. But with evening's approach, she visualized Alvy pulling into the cobblestone drive in his Lincoln Town Car, stooping to pick up the paper and carrying it into his father. Would they talk about finances? Would Alvy be induced to go into his father's study and reach for the stack of hundreds?

She lifted the hair from her nape and shifted her work to the kitchen. Here there was much to do. She was not sentimental. Most things she threw out, filling one trash bag after another. But a few items she did linger over: a casserole, faded roses on its sides, the dish that her mother served watery scalloped potatoes in after her husband had drunk up their week's money; a Chinese tea set of her grandmother Iris's, its delicate porcelain infinitely crazed, that her Aunt Julie had kept until she herself had died; a cast-iron skillet that Tody had fried their baloney sandwiches in when he became her guardian. Eyeing the coffeemaker, which was relatively new, Shelly tucked it into a box, along with a set of ceramic mugs, thinking Owen might want them.

And when the bell sounded her first thought was, in fact, Owen: *He's come back!* Could she ask for the money? *Half?* This agreeable fantasy of her son's returning, remorseful for standing her up, lasted about as long as it took her to scramble down from her stool and cross through the house. Of course it wasn't Owen, and who it was provoked her even more. Just who, she thought, opening the door, do these people think they're fooling? On the stoop stood, smiling goofily, a tall overweight man in a maroon spaghetti strap dress with ruffles. His lipstick had been smeared on with a trowel; his breasts were crooked.

"You're looking for my brother," she said, cutting him off. "He's not here."

"Are you sure? It's the last—"

"Yes, I'm sure!"

Tody Was a Seven

He took the weight off a hip. She recognized the movement: His high heels were pinching his toes. "The last Friday of the month," he insisted, "Tody and I get together the last Friday of the month. We've been doing this for years, I can't imagine he'd go and forget now."

If he wanted female petulance, she could show him the real article. "You're obviously out of the loop. My brother died—in an accident—three weeks ago. He's *dead!*"

It was as if she had slapped him. All the artifice in his expression fell away. The fellow looked precisely as he was: a middle-aged man in a wig and frumpy frock. He started to cry. Shelly offered a tight apology. "I'm sorry, I guess that wasn't very tactful."

"My name's Mel." He mopped his nose with the back of his hand. "How did it happen?"

"An accident, I just said."

"But *how?*"

Unwilling to have an intimate conversation on the front stoop with a man whose sweat was caking his foundation powder, she stepped aside. "Would you like to come in?"

She meant into the hall, for a minute. But he paddled past her like a riverboat steamer right into the living room, and, as if he were perfectly at home, settled on the sofa. Biting her tongue, Shelly sat across from him and told him of Tody's death, her brother's obstinacy in declaring he could damn well paint his own house, the surprising number of mourners who came to the wake, the Biddleford Players who recited "Seven Ages of Man."

Mel daubed his eyes with a handkerchief. "I've been out of the country, China, I work for Wal-Mart. Such a gentle soul, I can't believe it. He'd tell me about crawling all over the stage sets, hanging from the lights or hanging the lights, whatever it is they do. We met at a Club Med. We both hated it. I fly in once a month from Chicago. I'm sorry, could I have a drink maybe?"

She wanted to get more done, but brought him what he requested, scotch neat. In the kitchen, shadows—shadows that Shelly recalled—lay across the counter, gauzing the corners, and she knew this stranger was right: How *do* you come to grips with the death of someone you have loved? Looking at the table on which her brother had once stoutheartedly helped her glop papier-mâché to fashion the world's ugliest replica of Canada's topography, Shelly fetched two mugs from her son's box and splashed out some scotch for herself, too, adding ice.

"These'll have to do," she said, handing him a mug. "I threw away the glasses." She softened her voice. "So, what do you do for Wal-Mart?"

Mel, scratching around in his purse, found his cigarettes, then, forgetting himself, crossed his legs—as a man would. Never were you going to be deceived: Maybe you weren't expected to be? Even so, it was disorienting. Shelly resisted the urge to peek under his dress. "Buyer," he said, batting away his smoke. "Constant travel, Asia mostly. Indonesia, China, Thailand, Vietnam now. Tody never talked about his family much."

For her, a big trip was Pittsburgh, twenty-five miles away. "Maybe he didn't talk about us because there wasn't much to say?"

"Don't be silly, I'm sure you miss him. He must have meant a great deal to you."

She considered that. "Someone else said that today. And I said I did miss him, but I didn't, not at that moment. I know that sounds awful." She was embarrassed for having volunteered that. "But I miss him now, this afternoon. I feel Tody in this old house. He was always more *Mom* to me than *Dad*. Would you, d'you want . . . his *costumes?"*

Mel shrugged a shoulder sorrowfully. "Tody was a seven."

Shelly giggled. "I know the feeling."

At some point she refilled their glasses and, at another point, brought the bottle with its two Scottish terriers on the label and set it between them. Once encouraged, Mel, who seemed to live a lonely life, enjoyed talking. She was not someone who drank very often and she felt the scotch. At the same time, though, the glow brought on by the alcohol helped her to imagine the sprawling factories he described, thousands of workers huddled over ratcheting sewing machines, the exotic dinners he ordered, things that looked as if they had just stopped wiggling. As he was telling her about a woman beside him on a train who was holding in her lap a plastic bag of eels swimming in water, a train whistle wailed from deep in the valley, and her spine tingled. Queried about her life, Shelly shyly told him about her clients, Mrs. Lindsey and Mr. Plüddermann in particular, trying to make her job, the business she had created, sound more glamorous than it was. She omitted Mr. Plüddermann's green poop and asked, to change the subject, "Where do you guys—ladies?—go?"

"When we go out?" Mel tossed his Jayne Mansfield curls. "There's places, you hafta know. And there's always lots of real ladies there, too, you know? Wanna come?"

"Now? Tonight?"

"Why not?"

Seeing her brother in his costumes had always been a little off-putting. At the thought of a whole roomful of such people, she shrank. "No, I don't think so, not tonight."

Before he left he asked to use the bathroom. He called it the *loo*. When he returned, they lingered awkwardly in the dimness of the living room. Shelly, suddenly seeing herself in handcuffs, blurted out, "I did something wrong today!" Before Mel had a chance to respond, she delivered herself of her confession. "I stole some money—from one of my clients. I got mad and I took it. Three hundred dollars. It was *stupid!*"

Mel looked baffled. "Are you in trouble?"

"I doubt they'll notice. If they do, they'll probably blame the cleaning crew."

"Kind of hard not to miss three hundred dollars? Maybe you should give it back?"

She pictured herself an old woman, counting the blueberries in a dish, fussing over her bowel movements. "I don't have it, Mel. I gave it to my son."

He scratched under a bra strap, frowning. "Cleaning people usually don't steal. I mean, I don't know anything about the company you're talking about, but those kinds of people are bonded generally. They know they're under suspicion. Maybe your son would give it back?"

"I shouldn't have said anything." She turned away, feeling even more foolish, then sat on the sofa because she was dizzy. "My son is a conceited, spoiled brat. That money's long spent—and not on his girl. Well, that's not quite accurate, sorry. Owen doesn't have girlfriends, Owen has convenient fucks—and he doesn't waste a dime on them. He's got himself a jim-dandy new fishing rod by now, I'm sure. And you're right about the housecleaners, I've known that all day."

She sensed him hovering, pondering her. He sat beside her, coming down heavily on the sofa, the huge cantaloupes of his knees poking from his dress, and kissed her on the lips. Her head whirled. Not so much from the kiss as from its unexpectedness. But she enjoyed it, being kissed, it had been a long time. She kissed him back. And that too was strange. She tasted his lipstick, felt its creaminess against her own lips, inhaled his perfume and his sweat. She sensed an ambiguity that thrilled her. She allowed him to ease her down. He unbuttoned her blouse and brushed his lips over the lace of her bra. Well, of course, she thought: *underwear.* He unfastened the hooks, freed her breasts, and suckled her nipples. Shifting her hips to accommodate his bulk alongside her, she unbuttoned her jeans and brought a leg over him, embracing him. They began slipping sideways. Flailing, Mel shoved the coffee table and its teetering bottle aside to make room for their slowly cascading bodies.

She moaned. "I always wanted to be a small girl."

"A seven?" he mumbled, bringing his cupped palm into her jeans.

What it would feel like, she wondered, to shimmy down a woman's stockings? Beneath his ruffles, she felt him hardening. "I couldn't tell you the last time I was a seven, Mel."

~ ~ ~

Some hours later, she stretched indolently beneath a blanket that had appeared as if by magic. And not only was the blanket the result of magic, so was, evidently, her reaccession to the sofa. Shelly gazed across the room to where a large man sat, skirt up to his lap, grunting over his garter stays. "You have to go?"

He looked up. "Early flight. Just time to get back to the hotel, grab my bags."

On the coffee table, beside a bottle whose cute dogs she now found vaguely nauseating, lay her blouse and jeans and underwear, neatly folded. The pile reminded her of her brother who did a laundry the day they buried their mother. "You'll come back—or not?"

Satisfied with the state of his unmentionables, Mel fluffed his dress to the edge of his knees. "Would you like me to?"

"I would. I want you to come back with more stories about eels and trains and monsoons. But I have a favor. In the kitchen, a box of tissues—bring them, please."

She had him sit on the coffee table. Raising herself, feeling her nakedness, reveling in it—her breasts still full and tender from being fondled—Shelly scrubbed off his lipstick, then reapplied it, sketching and filling in his lips rather than plastering them, delicately following their plump contours. His whiskers were black, thick. She shook her head. "How much face powder do you go through a week?"

"Last Friday of the month?"

She blotted the corners of his mouth and straightened a jug. "I'll be here, Mel."

~ ~ ~

She was a workhorse. Such was her fate. After the car's motor faded into the distance, Shelly rinsed out the two mugs and returned them to the cupboard, then started in on Tody's office. Here it was financial records she sought, important papers. Finding a cabinet drawer stuffed with his Biddleford Players scripts, she heaved them into a trash bag and combed through his desk. She didn't unearth anything useful, but did find something else: her entire school history as represented by her report cards and photographs. She had no idea Tody had saved these things. Shelly spread her pictures, her life, across the blotter, from gap-toothed first-grader through the high drama of the off-the-shoulder gown she had worn for her high school graduation portrait, and, surrounded by the ghosts of those who had passed away before her, wept for her brother, the first tears she had shed since his death.

A conventional guardian he had not been. She could have been the only kid in school whose lunch sack might contain sardines and leftover onion rings. When he was growing up, he had been taunted for his effeminacy. Fifteen years later—the remarkable persistence of a town's intolerance—she was taunted for his effeminacy, too. But a gentle, zany soul, he had watched over her and over his hapless thespians. He'd been Captain Hook, Prospero, the King one week and Anna the next, when, during midweek rehearsals, the real Anna toppled into the orchestra pit. In his adaptation of *Much Ado About Nothing,* he drove a car off the roof of the Biddleford lodge and sailed it down a track without brakes, a stunt that thirty years later, people—

shocked, scandalized, outraged—still nattered about. Shelly returned to the kitchen and emptied the coffeemaker and remaining mugs into a trash bag and carried the empty box back to the office. This morning she'd stop at the bank and request three crisp hundred-dollar bills. It would draw her account to a level dangerously low; in her future might appear some watery scalloped potatoes. But that was okay, that was all right. She lifted from their bag her brother's annotated scripts and stacked them in the box, then slipped her report cards and photos down alongside, where they would be safe.

He had been a hell of an Anna.

Velia Creaming Her Legs

Winter 1988

Max Fischman, in his nightgown, stood amid the wreckage of his store. Little cubes of glass gleamed at his slippered feet. Something like wings rustled in the darkness. A cold draft, menacing in its presence indoors, ruffled the black cushions now devoid of their gold bands and set the crepe bell hanging in the half-light swaying eerily. Old-fashioned, his wearing a nightgown, as old-fashioned as leaving in the windows overnight those gold rings, the watches with their jewel movements, the Seth Thomas travel clocks in their leather wallets, the cameras, the toasters, the electric mixers, instead of going to the trouble of bringing everything inside.

"Oy," he said. He had grown old and fat and this, tonight, would make him no younger and no skinnier. He had heard what he had heard. Overhead a dark shape flitted past: Was that a *bat?* "And where, I ask," he added, "is the cat—just when you need him?"

Max Fischman's cat, Mr. J. P. Morgan, was, in Ganaego, nearly as famous as his master. At least in the size department. Max, when he stepped up on Bunny Wiesenfeld's scales, weighed in at three hundred fifty pounds, a figure Max was not unproud of, even if Dr. Wiesenfeld clucked censoriously. J. P., who prowled the show windows of Fischman's Jewelry and Small Appliances, brushing his lush caramel fur against the chrome toasters and raising his topaz eyes over the crystal punchbowls to fix unsuspecting window shoppers in his burning gaze, weighed—when he settled on one of Max's Sunbeam bathroom scales to lick his paws—forty-two pounds, plus or minus, himself. A figure his master also took some pride in.

The phone began to jingle. Max shuffled over and interrupted his wife in mid-squeal. "It's all right, Velia, it's all right, sweetie."

"You shouldn't be down there alone."

"Sweetie, it's all right." Feeling cool fur against his bare shin, Max withdrew his previous complaint. "Mr. Morgan drove them off. You wanna call the police and toss down my pants? I'm up, I might as well stay up. Out the hole in my window I can sell cheese blintzes."

"Max, don't be a fool—they might come back."

"Velia, my heart," he explained to the woman who, so many decades ago, had cost him the love of his Brooklyn family, "thieves rarely deliver encores—no matter how swell their aim with the old brick is. Now, my pants, sweetie, please?"

When he switched on the fluorescent lights, he saw the blood. Smears on the jagged triangular shards still standing in the window frame, gouts on the shelves. The thief had worked fast, knowledgeably if not sure-fingeredly, scooping up the rings and watches and the two Nikons, bypassing the broaches, lunging for the gold chains. Not a finger? Forearm, an artery? It didn't matter: Captain Mackenzie of the Ganaego PD was not about to loose the bloodhounds. That carpenter, whose name he never remembered, he needed to call him, then Kapland's Glass Works. Sunday was Christmas. This was Wednesday—actually, Thursday, the cheerful chorus of Max's many clocks chimed three a.m.—the start of the biggest weekend of the year. How long would it take to fix his store? What would it cost? Ach, who knew?

"Maybe," Max suggested to his cat, "a passerby will poke his head in and make us an offer on the blender? It's practically a steal."

He found—inside the stairwell door, in a lovingly arranged pile—his wide drawers and even wider trousers, his white shirt and fuchsia bowtie, his vest and coat, his support stockings, his shoes and suspenders. On top, pressed and folded, lay a clean handkerchief. *Bless women,* Max thought, exhausting his nose into the handkerchief, then he fetched the broom and the dustpan and began cleaning up.

He was a tidy man, which was to a shopkeeper's credit, but he had no excuse. Break-ins in a doomed town—a town on the skids after its steelworks had closed—were common. Who was he so special to think he should be spared? Somebody wormed his way down the T&V ventilation shaft and left sooty fingerprints all over the hams; somebody swiped the day's meager gleanings from the wooden till Nelson's son still used in Gleason's English Shoes. The row bars—well, the row bars were shot up so regularly who could count? Frankly, he had no excuse, in the first place, to persist in this foolish notion to keep a store open—at his age, in such a town. When the phone rang again, Max leaned his broom against a full-size Santa cutout.

"Velia, please, my love, go back to sleep."

"With a big hole in your window? I'm calling Saul."

He saw the gathering creases beside the mouth, the accordion folds multiplying on his wife's cheeks, the shrunken breasts, the spotted hands—as he saw the shambling eighty-year-old walrus he'd become. Fate will blow you down, as it must. He worried about his wife, her erratic heartbeat, her balance on the stairs. He worried, especially, about the years-long depression that had, like a shroud, lowered over her. But when Max Fischman looked at his wife he still saw, as well, the small exquisite Italian girl with the darting eyes, the mischievous grin, the big, silly, simple laugh. They had laughed in bed: Was there any god in any heaven who had not envied them?

To laugh in bed, so long ago.

"Darling, please," he reasoned, "don't disturb the children. They have busy, important lives. What is the name of that man I can never remember—the carpenter one?"

"He put a nail right through the cupboard, Max."

"Anyone can make a mistake, sweetie. It was a long nail. But until someone erects a board over my window, I am going nowhere soon."

"William . . . William . . ."

"William Gallagher, thank you, sweetie. I will tell him to bring shorter nails. Now, go back to bed, please don't disturb the children."

"Why don't you call Peach?"

"Velia," Max, a man who seldom grumbled, grumbled, "let me assure you: The last person on the face of the earth I'm gonna call is Peach Litchfield. Go to bed, sweetie."

"It's because I'm a *shiksa,* isn't it?"

The calculus of lifetime marriage: He knew what she meant and it had nothing to do with ethnic slurs. "It's wrong for us to go on punishing ourselves. It was the will of God."

"It wasn't God, Max—it was politicians!"

About this, he knew enough not to quarrel. He chose the easier point to contest. "My love, by now you are more Jewish than I am: Go to bed."

"Why aren't the police here? What's keeping them, Max?"

"I don't *know,* pet. Perhaps they're busy stopping crime?"

"Well, if this is all the better job they can do of it, they ought to be ashamed of themselves."

Shouldn't we all? Max thought. Scrupulous to keep the grime off his clothes, he maneuvered in from the alley a smelly barrel and delicately deposited within the long scimitars of shattered glass. In the silent evening the sound of breaking glass was jarring, a sound no Jew could ignore. He searched for a brick or stone and decided the thief—and it had been a single individual, that he knew—had thoughtfully taken it with him. But Max Fischman too was a thoughtful man:

Before finishing, he saved aside a particularly bloody specimen of glass. The police would want a list of stolen goods. Settling in at his bench, J. P. Morgan curled beside him in a caramel ball under the gooseneck lamp, Max began his list.

It was, in fact, the officers' second question. The first was, "Did your alarm sound? We got no record of it at the station."

Two young men, one black, one white. They looked tired. Their shirts were soiled. The instruments of modern crime prevention dangling from their belts clanked. The equipment seemed to handicap them, make them ungainly, as though they might at any moment topple or be captured by a huge magnet. The lights of their cruiser sent blue orbs skittering across the merchandise. Max knew his size bothered people, especially figures of authority. Not only did he block their view of the horizon, he usually blocked their view of the sun. An uncomfortable question, but not unanticipated. "Parts I can't get anymore for the alarm. It's too old."

"It's *broke?*" the white policeman said. "You know what was taken, at least?"

"I do." Max's heart sometimes would send a ripple of pain through his chest. He patted his shirt, swallowed, held out his list. "Retail, four thousand four hundred dollars."

"You had that much hanging out in the street and no *alarm?*" The policeman clutched his belt with both hands, as if to brace himself. "Are you a friggin' numbskull, or what?" His partner scowled at him. "Sorry, sorry, but surely you understand you can't *do* that?"

How to tell people, how to describe it: the joy of seeing a shop window at night, snow falling perhaps, a display ablaze with color and light, watches and rings and bracelets and brass clocks whose swaying pendulums beneath crystal domes silently measure the span of our lives—these beautiful objects of civilization, things revered ever since human beings became aware of adornment. Gold bands one morning you slid across two knuckles and a lifetime later buried on that same hand, lockets your wife and sisters slipped around their necks and warmed with their flesh. Had it come to this—that he had to empty his displays every night so they resembled nothing so much as the dark, dingy windows of a thrift shop, three old shoes on a shelf? *Had it?*

It had. Max humbly accepted his scolding. *Yes,* he had a safe, and *yes,* he needed to start using it more. "It won't happen again," he promised the tired constables with dirty shirts.

"Any idea who done it? You didn't see them?"

A question he had not expected. Actually, he knew who had thieved him, knew the villain and the villain's squealing water pump. He had heard what he heard. A binding spindle, he supposed, automobiles didn't interest him. For the third child, the one who didn't live long enough to find a wife and raise a family, who perished far from home, Max said a silent prayer, then gazed over at Mr. Morgan, who was burring his whiskered cheek against the rim of the lamp shade.

"Oy," he said, "beats me."

~ ~ ~

By the time that he and Velia, wed by a maudlin, tipsy justice of the peace in Allentown, came to Ganaego, in the waning days of the Depression, Plan Thirteen on Eighth Hill had long been in decline. The Hotel Himmellsbach maintained a scandalous infamy, and, just down the street from Max and Velia's light-housekeeping rooms, the toyshop that Max loved, Dufresne's Miniature Train and Toy Repertorium, still smelled of machine oil and balsa and airplane dope. But white Ganaego, having decided that Plan Thirteen would be where the blacks moving up from the South to labor in the steelworks would live, poured from the hill in droves.

Seldom then did Max have occasion to come up here. It was

dangerous on the hill, and an old, waddling white man would be an easy mark. But a brick through your window? What choice does that leave you? He had closed his store at six and called up to Velia to tell her he was going out. He shook his head at the repugnant rectangle of blond wood that William Gallagher had nailed over his window as securely as if the man were hammering down the lid of a coffin and shrugged on his overcoat. He could find but one glove. Cruising Booker Street in his sixteen-year-old Buick, he took in the abandoned storefronts with their gray-dusted windows and buildings slid even further into dilapidation, many no more than burned-out carcasses. The closure of the steel plant had, to be sure, clobbered all of Ganaego—one more casualty in the hollowing out of America's industrial heartland—but Plan Thirteen it had torpedoed utterly.

Turning off Booker, he pulled to the curb before a building that had once housed Ganaego's only socialist trade journal. In the upper windows lights glowed. He discovered the outside door unwisely unlocked and, taking it slowly so as not to accelerate his heart, picked his way up the stairwell. He had been here before. He recalled the smell of gas from poorly ventilated heaters. Somewhere a baby burbled and a weatherman advised his viewers to exercise caution on slippery walks. Max paused before a door from which the aroma of cooking onions rose. His stomach growled longingly.

When no one responded to his polite knock, he knocked more sternly. That also going unheeded, he bellowed. "Sarah Jane—open the door!"

The door parted against its chain two inches. "What d'you want, Max?"

Even the slender slice of face brought back the whole face, the lovely, yellow-skinned girl his stockroom assistant and general handyman had brought into the store one night after closing and proudly introduced Max to. Hours they spent helping the girl in her agonies decide which of the modest rings Peach Litchfield could afford she would agree to display on her finger, a speck of a diamond. "Sarah Jane, you know why I'm here, so let's stop with the foolishness already. You don't want me to hand this over to the police."

She brought him into the steamy kitchen. A baby in a highchair played with his green vegetables; a young girl was absorbed in the news on television, the airliner that had been blown out of the sky over Scotland; a boy, in age somewhere between girl and baby, was navigating his fleet of metal trucks through the table legs. Sarah Jane was no longer the bashful, overwhelmed girl who had broken down into tears over a tiny diamond. Her face had hardened. Fate will blow you down. "He's a good man, Max." Her eyes met his. "Doesn't drink, doesn't carry on."

"I know that."

"He was never late, I don't think he was even ever sick."

Max had been fortunate in life. And not everyone is. The world had rewarded his cleverness and industry. When he and Velia took the plunge and leased a mouse-ridden storefront on Roosevelt Avenue, he'd bravely hung out his sign and world showed up. A deft fix-it man, he repaired watches and clocks and bracelets, but anything really, tube radios, windup toys, lamps, coffee mills, umbrellas. The single back room served as their sitting room, kitchen, bedroom; they had babies and diapers and lamb stews that stank up the shop—and still the world came. He was hot under the overcoat tonight. He felt sweat on his body, a sensation he disliked. For the boy who did not live long enough to change an infant's diaper he said silent Kaddish and agreed with the wife of Peach Litchfield. "It had nothing to do with his work habits, I never had anything but good words for Peach. Ganaego is dying, Sarah Jane, my business is dying."

She turned back to the stove, unmoved. "How is Velia?"

"The holidays, it's always worse around the holidays and it's worse this year, the stuff in the news. If he's not here, Sarah Jane, then where is he? This is not a trivial matter."

She turned off the flame under the skillet. "In the bedroom."

Peach sat on the bed, leaning against the headboard. He was watching a television on the dresser. Men in uniforms and helmets skated across a white rink, colliding brutally with each other. It was warm in here, too. One sleeve of Peach's shirt was rolled up, the right one; the other dangled to the wrist, unbuttoned. Through the flannel a slight bulge showed. *So, a forearm, after all,* Max thought, *he could've bled to death.*

"What's up, Max? Whaddya want?"

"Just what belongs to me."

"No idea what you're talking about. I heard about your window, sorry about that."

Peach Litchfield was a small man. The skin of his face was drawn tight against his cheekbones. His arms were sinewy, his hands prominent with veins. He had been a conscientious worker, Max's left-handed handyman, about that his wife was right. He'd once been a talented outfielder, as well, occasionally showing up for work in his uniforms. He played semiprofessional ball, mailed postcards from Rochester, Kansas City, Tulsa, San Diego. He was almost good enough to make a career of it. When Peach consented to abandon his hockey game on television and acknowledge him, Max said, "Maybe someone else has a car with a defective water pump, that could be. But I don't think anyone else has your blood. It's not each other we should be fighting, Peach. All I want is what belongs to me."

"Search the house, I don't got anything of yours."

His shoes pinched, his body stank, he was famished. But he was a tidy man, a scrupulous man: Max knew the ground he stood on. "All right, let's let it go at this: everything on my bench by ten a.m. tomorrow—or else I go to the police. And if you're fool enough to have fenced it already, I want twenty-two hundred dollars."

"That with your markup?"

More than two decades he had trusted this man. "I heard what I heard, Peach."

He noted as he came through the kitchen that the onions were happily sautéing again. Velia no longer cooked. A small loss lodged in the greater. Sarah Jane, back resolutely to him, spoke. "So, what is it, Max? What's he supposed to do?"

"I want my merchandise. Tomorrow, by ten."

Her shoulders sagged. "He'll be there. How much is your window going to be?"

Max recollected, out of nowhere, the little girl's name: Bonnie. She had three pigtails. "With the carpenter and the glazier, four hundred, maybe a bit less."

Turning, Sarah Jane strode up to him and, fumbling with a potholder, slid her engagement ring off her finger. She held it up. "Here—for your window."

Max took a step back. "I don't—"

"He can't find work, Max! There's no work in this town!" Frustrated, furious, Sarah Jane flung the potholder aside and thrust the diamond ring at him. "Take it, I don't want it!"

Not knowing what to do, embarrassed, feeling old and useless and vexed with these people, Max accepted the small ring in his big hand and buried his hand in his pocket.

~ ~ ~

Past glories: The store bedecked with the goyim's fairy-tale holiday, elves and flying reindeer, the fragrance of balsam from a live tree sold personally by the good Father Opsatnick, customers, boxes in arm, standing patiently—or not so patiently—in long queues; three children running crucial missions from stockroom to showroom; two, even one year *four,* sales associates, plus his stockroom assistant ferrying unwieldy bundles out to double-parked cars. You could watch the families streaming down the white wooden staircases from their Plans, payday money fattening their pockets. And him, in those blithe times? Plump and rosy in a jolly Santa cap covering an even-then bald pate, violet sapphire on a pinky that would bring a blush to a sultan's cheeks. And the merchant's wife? Dazzling: woven gold bracelets and glittering earrings and pearl necklaces, dresses like living creatures stirring at her knees, her slender ankles in stiletto heels that rasped across the tiles and across his heart. Roosevelt Avenue may have been but a small world forgotten in the greater world, but in holiday seasons it was, to Ganaegoans, a bejeweled and dulcet fantasy of gleaming lights and opulent evergreen swags swaying from telephone poles. All this the brooding proprietor recalls as he sits in his quiet store this damp morning, the twenty-third of December, all those years gone by. He had no bones to pick with anybody's deity. Broadminded he was, ecumenical he was, he *liked* Christmas.

He even liked Bing Crosby.

Traffic was desultory. He sold some decent kitchenware, a very nice pitcher, an electric razor, a Sheaffer fountain pen. He'd had the dream again last night. In this variant he had come racing out of his parents' Brooklyn tenement carrying his youngest child. The boy was feverish, sick. Panicked, Max raced down one street, then another. But the streets had changed, he became confused, and at some point, his heart pounding in torment, he'd lost the child: The boy vanished from his arms.

A few minutes after the municipal building's clock and his clocks chimed eleven, a worried Sarah Jane called. "Is he there, Max? Did he come?"

"It's a tomb." In his suit pocket rested a diminutive lump in a beige envelope. The stone needed to be removed from its dwarf setting and put into play. Inexpensive diamonds might be the only thing he could sell today. "Maybe the police will liven things up?"

"He got a call early and left. He'll be there, Max, I *promise.*"

Rain began falling, very cold, a degree or so from sleet, and Max recalled what the weatherman had cautioned last night. At eleven-thirty Maddy Schoolcraft, his sole remaining sales associate, stomped in. Coat dripping, she popped her umbrella to fling off the water. Deciding for the moment against removing Sarah Jane's diamond from its setting, Max ran the ring through a cycle in the ultrasonic, then buffed the stone, bringing a luster to its dainty facets, before returning the ring to his pocket. Saul, his oldest, the assistant district attorney who had turned forty-eight this year and announced he was feeling his age, promised to bring the family later, and Benjamin, the ophthalmologist, promised the same. Even if Max no longer required extra help, even if he didn't sell as much as a Presto Burger, the family would be together again as another winter solstice passed and the earth turned into its winter slumber. Not a whole family, no, never that again, but the store would ring with voices, Bing Crosby would croon about being home for the holidays, and J. P. Morgan would scrabble up to a tall perch and gaze down at the babbling crowds in leonine indifference. Max looked up at his old tin ceiling, looked, as it were, through his ceiling to the apartment above: Would Velia come down? Would she join them?

"Maddy?" Max slipped the girl her holiday bonus.

Newly betrothed, the young woman, coloring, tucked the cash into her bra. "I think it'll pick up, Max."

And indeed, toward late afternoon, with sleet now pattering the unbroken window and smearing one's vision of the colored bulbs glowing weakly over Roosevelt Avenue, Max, the blood of half a millennium of shopkeepers in his veins, felt the store's pulse quickening. The bell jangled merrily, the floor mats sopped underfoot, and the focus of shoppers shifted to more serious gifts, serious jewelry for fiancées and wives, serious cameras and electronics for the men, serious appliances for the house. Ben and family came spilling in, then Saul and his, all exclaiming over the horrendous Parkway traffic, the worst they'd ever seen, and one of the grandchildren sold—on her own—a seven-thousand-dollar pear ruby pendant necklace, a figure that made the girl, after the gentleman buyer had slipped into the night with his single tiny package no bigger than a child's teacup, press both her palms to her ears and gasp.

But no Velia, no Peach Litchfield.

It was when Max was waiting on William Gallagher, come to inspect his handiwork but tempted into considering the purchase of a pair of brass candelabras that had stood on the counter a dozen years unsold, that Maddy whispered, "Max, in the back? I told him he could just leave it, but he wants to talk to you."

Peach was standing beside what had been once his own desk. On the blotter sat a rain-spattered cardboard box. "Sorry I couldn't come sooner. I was offered work, I had to take it."

He was wearing a gray sweatshirt, stained and sodden, no hat, no coat. The dark planes of his face glistened like the brown-black handles of the burins on Max's bench. "That's good," Max said sincerely. "I'm happy to hear you've got work, Peach."

He shook off Max's enthusiasm. "Day work, loading crates. Twenty bucks. I'll buy the kids a pizza."

He'd just retailed a necklace for seven thousand dollars. A necklace that had cost him half that. But he'd had to undertake the risk of investing in the piece in the first place, of sinking that money in upfront, and he'd had the ongoing expenses of maintaining a store and reputation around the necklace worthy of its value, to justify the tag dangling from it. He paid taxes and worker's compensation. The world does not deal fairly with people. Fairness, even merit, has little

Velia Creaming Her Legs

to do with it. His youngest son had been torn in three by bullets. It wasn't merit that got Zeke born in 1947 and Peach Litchfield in 1950, and it wasn't fairness that placed both boys at the mercy of the local draft board in 1969. There was that year a lottery: Peach won, Zeke lost.

To his honor, the man had not just dumped the box and slunk off into the night. Max recalled Peach, home forever from his baseball wanderings, explaining in barely controlled pathos just how powerful the men in professional sports were, how fast the pitchers threw. He recalled that, *seeing* the loss of a boy's dreams registering in a man's face. But even so: Could you ever trust someone again who had picked your pocket? Well, maybe sometimes you have to risk it. "I have a proposition," Max said. "We're doing better than I thought we would. I could use some help tomorrow, and I'm going to need to put some money into this building this winter."

Peach would not meet his eyes. "Look, I'm sorry about your window, Max. It was a jackass move. But I brung all your stuff back, we don't need no handouts."

Max removed the envelope from his inside pocket and handed it to Peach. "Sarah Jane asked me to clean this for her. She should have it done more often. It's a very pretty stone. Not a handout. The chimney leaks and the rooms need a coat of paint to freshen them. And"—Max, a man who seldom grumbled, grumbled—"I need to install a new alarm."

~ ~ ~

From the vantage point of his height Max could oversee everything in his store, his merchandise, his customers, especially the shifty ones, his children and now their children. But where his eyes had always returned to was his wife. Velia's withdrawal from the life of the store had been the second greatest sorrow. Max tarried in the stockroom after Peach left. Mr. Morgan, annoyed with human beings, slept beneath the lamp. On his holidays J.P. got Sicilian sardines dressed in olive oil. Max caressed the animal's ear and rubbed his finger along his whiskered cheek. Why do cats like that so much? When you live a lifetime with someone you accumulate so many memories you almost need a college degree in accounting to keep them organized. But among the infinitude of memories that Max possessed, there was one he particularly treasured. It took place in this room, fifty years ago. Coming in from the shop through the curtain he surprised Velia fresh from their miniature corner tub in the hall bathroom. She lay on her back in bed, naked, applying lotion to her legs. In the ledger books of his memory, Max labeled this scene *Velia Creaming Her Legs*. First one leg lifted languidly into the air and creamed until it shone, then the other leg lifted and creamed, while the dark bush at the base of the woman's belly glistened with drops of bathwater . . .

He found her in the darkened living room, before the television. His heart sent him some small sharp pains. "Will you come down?" he asked softly. "The boys are here."

She ignored his question. "How is trade, Max?"

"Marsha sold a very dear piece."

"I'm happy for you."

"Everybody's asking about you?"

"Max, I'm not dressed."

"After we close? We can sit in the back. I'll order pizza for everybody."

"Why, Max, why?"

Her face was bathed in the lurid colors from the television. He worried when Velia went out, worried when she didn't. He thought the violence of their boy's death in Southeast Asia would tear them apart, rend their marriage, as the bullets had rent his son's body. Velia had pleaded with Zeke to flee to Canada, but Max had disapproved.

Velia Creaming Her Legs

It was an argument he had won and ever since rued winning. Zeke was more at home in the shop than the other boys. He might have someday joined his father here. Max crossed the room and kissed the top of his wife's head. "I don't know why, Velia."

"And now we're going to be *pals* with them? Make it all chummy so we can sell them Weed Eaters and toothpaste? All those lives, Max, stopped for no reason, for nothing, for someone to put wreathes on their graves and pretend to care so they can get elected. All those lives—just *stopped.*"

For this woman he had sold his soul. And if he had had a thousand lives and a thousand souls, he would have, for her, sold every last one of them. "I know, pet."

She leaned her head against his leg. "Do you want me to come down, Max?"

"I miss you, my love."

Dance of the Little Swans

"You got less this year. Even less than last year, ain't that so?"

Her father's eyes, enlarged behind his heavy lenses, were clouded. Their distortion and lack of depth gave his face a crazed, ravening appearance. "Daddy, please don't start."

"Two months behind in your rent, that's what I'm hearing."

Behind her, Julie heard her girls giggling, her tiny protégés, idle as children will be the minute left to their own devices. She knitted her hands in her lap. "Something you can always count on, the Old Boys' Grapevine. You get that piece of dirt from Dennis or Poppa Nelson?"

"Don't come asking from me. I don't got any money for this . . . *stuff.*"

Her father had developed cataracts because, for the four decades he had fed quarter-mile strips of steel—*skelp*—into the Welded Tube furnaces, Sam Namarian had refused to wear protective goggles. But the collision he'd had exiting Pascarelli's, the beer distributor, that had removed two inches from his tibia had not been his fault, and Julie, a dancer, appreciated, *felt,* what it would be like to lose your mobility. She had not been the daughter her parents wanted. She had scandalized them by running away to New York, then scandalized them again by returning and starting her studio. His accident had evened things out, more or less. "The faucet in the bathroom is dripping," she said. "If you want to help, you could fix that? Dennis won't."

"Don't got my tools."

"I didn't say this minute now. D'you want anything? There's coffee? Did Momma have a good time on her seniors' outing?"

"She fell, no thanks to you."

"How? You should've called?"

"Just bruises. Iris's got so many bruises you can't hardly tell 'em apart."

She hated the ugly way he used her mother to get at her. "You could probably tell them apart if you looked?"

"I'm the one who lifts her in and out of the tub, I don't need your lectures, little girl."

Through the long slits of the venetian blinds a dusky luminosity burned. You could hear, below, the splash of water: the men on this paper-dry October Saturday washing their trucks, the big chrome headlights and crimson fenders, the oversized black tires. In the two decades Julie Namar had lived in the apartment that her father had begrudgingly carpentered for her along one side of her studio loft, she had been neighbors with the firemen. They called their trucks *engines.* Sometimes they would turn the hose on each other, laughing like boys, like her brothers had once laughed in the backyard. But even *their* jobs—firemen, police—were in jeopardy now that the aging beast of the steelworks had begun to shutter departments and shed jobs. Dan Rather might report that the country was pulling out of its Reagan Recession, but the pulling wasn't happening here. Her father was right: She did have fewer pupils. Julie stood up. Someone had turned on the phonograph. Ballet, no doubt, was rapidly degenerating into the worst excesses of teenage theatrics. "It's a fresh pot? Sure?"

"You gonna marry that lawyer sheeny?"

Was that why he'd come? "Daddy, I don't need that kind of talk. My friends are none of your business—and no, I'm not going to marry him."

Sam shook off the lethargy that had settled over him. "It's the boy, not the old man."

So, *that's* why he had come. When she'd heard the distinctive tread on the rear stairs, strong left, shuffling right, the rhythm musicians call *long-short,* she had wondered whether there was anything specific in her father's visit—beyond the obvious pleasure he took in needling her. He'd slipped into the apartment and sat here in the shadows, strips of light from the blinds crossing his chest, door ajar just enough for him to stare at the nymphets in their tights. Ignoring his silent, predatory presence, she had concentrated on her class, taking her girls through their *demi-pliés,* their *eleves* and *releves,* their *battlements tendus,* pausing here or there to draw a latent curve from a child's buttery forearm, to release the tension from a damp nape. She hoped he might grow restless and leave, but when she had worn out those thinnest of hopes she drifted back to the apartment. Even though the cataracts that had hardened his eyes like cue balls probably kept him from seeing much beyond what his imagination could supply, *still,* the last thing she needed was some parent complaining that her ghoulish father had been ogling her child.

But she appreciated the warning. "Thank you, always good to know your enemy."

"He's gonna let you slide 'til the end of the month, then come down hard."

"Prick," she said softly.

~ ~ ~

For Julie's pupils it was the changes in season that were most fraught, particularly as summer's desultory cadences gave way to autumn's quickening. Because the studio was not air-conditioned, summer lessons were steeped in a comforting languor, a safe, drowsy feeling that time itself had thickened and never would there come a reckoning, a need to perform before the eyes of strangers and family, especially family. But all too soon the big steam radiators would begin to hiss and spit and the tall arched windows overlooking the fire station would mist from vapor produced by a dozen aspiring ballerinas of assorted sizes and races, bending and pirouetting. Even as the decline of the steelworks had begun to exact its toll on Julie's enrollment, those girls—rarely boys, and none this year—whose parents could afford the modest tuition attended to their exercises with an enveloping urgency. They erected their pasteboard palaces and muslin forests and rehearsed their entrances and, at the climax of exceptionally taxing passages, often burst into tears and fled into the dressing room, where, when Julie padded in, they poured out to her the burden of their troubled hearts.

That she was forty-five, well, that seemed impossible. Yet, for twenty-two years, ever since slinking home from New York like a whipped cat, you would have been able to find Julie Namar in her studio in the—ironically named—*New York Building* above Littlewood's Drugs and Prostheses. A fixture in the town's cultural life was her students' annual abridged *Swan Lake,* and thus Julie had by now passed through an entire generation of Ganaegoan baby swans, who, noses running, shins skinned, eyes glazed with fright, had on cue thrown their arms to the stormy heavens and fallen in little heaps across the stage, thrilled to be done with the whole thing. And marking the passage of their own unwinding lives, what greeted these now maternal swans when they again climbed the New York Building's creaking stairway to deposit their offspring? Same palm-stained wallpaper, same pieces by Tchaikovsky and Henry Mancini, same scents of rosin and sweat and canvas-clad feet, and always that same confident, ringing voice carrying out into the hall. *Julie:* long solid nose positioned high on a narrow face, dark hair drawn into a ponytail (a nowgraying lock loose at the temple), a tireless ribbon of energy in leotards and tunic coaching, coaxing, consoling: You would have thought the studio, that had lasted this long, would last forever.

"Fucking prick," she amended her epithet.

The Nelson real estate empire would not, for want of her rent, go to wrack and ruin. She would, she vowed, make the Nelsons whole. What distressed her was the decision of the new high school principal not to extend their annual invitation. When Mr. Lessard's secretary informed her they would not be scheduling her assembly, it had come as a blow. School programs were crucial: They furnished new pupils. The secretary, who'd always been, in Ganaego's crusty fashion, at least superficially friendly, was curt to the point of rudeness. "Schedule's tight," was all she had been prepared to offer. "Maybe next year."

"But we've always done my program?"

"We're very *tight.*" There was a rustle of papers. "Here, let me read you: *First,* we've got the State Police, their driver-carnage movie, then Thanksgiving and Christmas, then Chinese Ping-Pong masters—new this year, somebody on the school board is bugs about Ping-Pong—then Earth Day, that's also new. Mr. Lessard is very progressive. He thinks we have enough distractions. This isn't a variety show we're running, you know?"

"Can I talk to him?"

"Whatever for?"

"Please?"

A new principal with new ideas. This Monday morning, Julie chose the most conservative pleated skirt she owned, brushed the lint from her blazer, spat on a rag and cleaned her half-heels. Looking like the Avon Lady, she walked the length of Roosevelt Avenue and climbed the steep hill to the school. As she sat in the principal's waiting room, she remembered how, before school, she would race down the whitewashed staircases to Miss Herrick's ballet studio over the Goose Family Spa, then hurry to school, then return to Herrick's, trudging home finally then up the staircases in Ganaego's smoldering dusks, the flames of the steelworks shimmering through the trees.

School flew by, New York, alas, flew by, and now her studio? That, too?

Mr. Lessard, wearing a gag tie in the shape of a salmon, motioned without abandoning his reading toward a chair when she was allowed in. Julie sat on the edge of her seat, feeling, absurdly, like a student caught smoking. When Mr. Lessard looked up, she said, "I was—"

"Miss Namar," he interrupted, lowering his eyes again to his papers to confirm a final point, "we can't keep doing the same things just because we've always done them. Surely, you appreciate that? Does that sound progressive to you? Does that even sound intelligent?"

"But the—"

"Progressive! I asked you if that sounded *progressive?*" Mr. Lessard abandoned his papers and brought to rest on her his principal's grown-up gaze. "Permit me to save us both a great deal of time. Put me straight if I'm wrong, but aren't you about to say that you've done your program here for years and years? That you, in fact, have several of our girls and that this is a lovely way to showcase them? You will probably add that it costs us nothing and probably *not* add—although I wouldn't object if you did—that the programs usually provide you the good fortune of enticing a few new devotees your way. Are those, in a nutshell, your arguments?"

"Yes, but—"

"And those are wonderful arguments!" Like an official after somebody scores, Mr. Lessard threw up his arms. "But they are not *sufficient* arguments. This is a public institution with limited resources, and an activity that takes students out of their classes, that forces the teachers to patrol the aisles like prison guards, and that benefits only a very few—let us say, unusually inclined?—girls hardly sounds like sufficient justification. The Drama Club, I'm told, is hell-bent on staging a musical. Maybe"—Mr. Lessard shrugged helpfully—"there's some way you can lend your talents that way?

Assisting with the dance numbers?"

Dismissed as if she were a fractious tenth-grader, Julie stood up to leave. As she reached the door, the principal called after her. "To be candid," he said, as if this were the capstone of *his* argument, "I don't even think it's a prudent thing to encourage girls to take up—in the first place? It positively ruins the feet. You probably don't remember, but there used to be an old woman who hobbled up and down Roosevelt Avenue? Some sort of ex-ballet queen? She needed two canes, she clawed herself forward like a crab"—here Mr. Lessard stood up to demonstrate—"and she used to squawk—just *squawk*—about her feet."

"Most girls never go *en pointe!* And it's not only ballet!" Julie, frustrated, fists balled against her skirt, struggled to keep the whininess out of her voice. "We do modern dance, we do jazz, we do improvisation. I have a girl—she's from Vietnam, of all places— who's enthralled with tap. It's been *years* since I had someone seriously interested in tap."

"Well, anyway"—Mr. Lessard shook the tips of his fingers, as if he'd accidentally dipped them in the wrong pan—"I certainly wouldn't let *my* daughters do it."

"That was Miss Herrick."

"Who?"

"The old woman you're talking about! Marion Herrick—she had a studio in Ganaego for forty years. She was a remarkable teacher. She was revered! Several of—"

"Ms. Namar, this—"

"Let me finish!" Aware she was flinging everything away, but thinking of the four mites she was coaching in this year's Dance of the Little Swans—hands linked across their bodies, feet hopelessly entangled, how *hard* they were trying—Julie couldn't stop herself. "Several of her pupils went on to New York and danced in national companies, one danced in the Royal Ballet. Marion was an inspiration for thousands of girls—*and* a few boys. And she didn't go around *squawking* about her feet!"

Mr. Lessard, vexed by her impudence but perhaps caught up for another minute in sporting with this quite possibly unhinged woman, spoke up pertly. "By golly, I bet you're right! I bet she was squawking about the futility of trying to bring culture to the rabble? Us poor dumb acorn-crackers? Is *that* what all the squawking was about?"

What was the use? What Miss Herrick squawked at—and she did squawk—were girls who would not turn their legs from the hip, at indolence and indifference, at anything not fine and worthy. Julie shook her head and left.

~ ~ ~

Waiting for her outside her studio was Dana Cozma. It was as if the girl were crouched in the hall, waiting to pounce. Thin as a sliver of flint, salt-gray eyes recessed in their customary dark circles, the girl rushed toward Julie as she came up the steps.

"I can't come anymore!" she shouted. "I need a refund on my tuition!"

Dana was this year's Odette in *Swan Lake.* She had been last year's Odette and Odette the year before. Of the hundreds of girls Julie had mentored but a handful had possessed authentic gift—and Dana Cozma was one. Perhaps not for ballet, but for modern dance. Even at six, when her mother over the father's objections brought her to the studio, the child exhibited poise, balance, rhythm, and a preternatural, almost uncanny intensity, and now, ten years on, had gained exquisite control, being capable of metamorphosing in an instant from light to dark, from lissome to steely. More, the girl owned an even rarer lyric gift: She seemed instinctively to grasp that body could express story, could *be* story.

Julie took the girl, who was trembling through her wool jacket, by both shoulders. There was something wild and disorganized about her. "Dana, what's the matter?"

"I want a refund!"

"Are you all right?"

"It's not like I'm going to be using the lessons or anything."

Julie tried to tidy the girl's hair where it was slipping out from beneath her bandana. But Dana would not be solaced. Something *was* wrong. Home? Boyfriend? With teenagers you did not always know. "Why aren't you in school?"

"Julie, that's my money, I want it back!"

No, it was not. She wasn't a real school, she couldn't refer Dana Cozma to a registrar who would impersonally quote a policy manual. Neither was she a collection agency for those parents in arrears. All she did was teach children to absorb music's timeless rhythms and express those rhythms in their bodies' natural movements. Maybe in a better year, a flusher time, but this year? "Listen," she said, realizing that, oddly, Dana was using her first name, "I can't refund your money, I'm sorry. Come inside, you're shaking like a leaf."

The girl's eyes flashed, and she turned and clattered down the stairs.

~ ~ ~

Not only had she fallen behind in her rent, her utilities were past due and she was worrisomely deep into her credit at the Company Store. She owned nothing worth selling, nothing worth asking Max Fischman to take in pawn. Years ago she had advertised evening classes for adults, but of all Ganaego's lost souls, surely these were the most dolefully and irremediably lost. Her father, there to replace a broken pane, had pondered her hapless adults muttering *one-two-three-four, one-two-three-four* as they bumbled about colliding with each other like genial but preoccupied motorists, and remarked, "Skeletons at the feast—anybody in this godforsaken mess you can marry?"

Maybe she should have looked harder?

Julie changed out of her Avon Lady costume and went back downstairs. She crossed Roosevelt and climbed two familiar sets of staircases. Reaching Little Armenia, as it had come to be called, she circled behind her parents' house and peered into the gloom of the garage. Her father haunted flea markets and yard sales. He would bargain ruthlessly for stopped clocks, spattered hotplates, rheumatic vacuums full of someone else's dirt. Amid the boxes of *National Geographic*s wedged to the rafters, the narrow berth remaining for his car was vacant, thank goodness. She let herself into their side of the companyerected duplex that Sam and Iris Namarian, newly and precipitously married, had moved into forty-five years ago.

From upstairs the babble of television voices drifted down. Not wanting to startle her mother, Julie hollered first. Iris, grateful for the warning, had slithered her way up into a sitting position by the time Julie came in. Garish light from the television, the only source of illumination in the smoky, overheated room, flickered across the covers. Julie frowned at the screen. The picture was flipping vertically, then disintegrating into a dizzying herringbone pattern.

"When I heard you," her mother said, "I thought for sure it was your daddy."

"You expect him soon?"

"Who knows? He had two rummage sales—the Baptists and the Episcopalians!"

Julie turned down the volume of the television. "Why does he keep buying all this crap? It's some sort of pathology."

"If it brings him pleasure, honey, why should we complain?" Her mother patted the blankets, searching for her cigarettes. "Hungry? Sam got some good powdered donuts at the T&V."

"You fell, Daddy said?"

The old woman giggled. "Shame on him for telling. Heavens, I just slipped."

Julie helped her mother light her cigarette. "Momma, I need some money."

Iris instinctively reached toward a pressed glass relish dish on the bed table where, along with buttons, safety pins, and rubber bands, household change ended up. "No," Julie stopped her, "I mean, I need a *loan.*"

Her mother, in the unsettling way she had of searching for visual contact, swiveled her head. Sunk in a collapsed web of creases, her eyes, two tiny glistening wedges roved back and forth. A decade had passed since Iris could distinguish anything beyond shadows, but the habit of vision stubbornly persisted. When she returned from her seniors' outings, she unfailingly described exactly what she had seen. "You in trouble?"

"I'm just behind in some bills."

"How behind? How much money do you need?"

"I don't know . . . a thousand dollars, maybe a little more?"

Iris, frightened, pawed for Julie's hand. "Why don't you come back home, honey? Not a week goes by that Sam doesn't tell me about another mugging or stabbing. Roosevelt Avenue's no place for a girl to be living."

Julie looked at her mother's hands. It always came as a shock to see the cigarette burns on her fingers. Most of the sores were pink but sealed, but others, more recent, were a bright scarlet and seeped. The suggestion that she move back home would surface as her mother's answer to nearly every problem. It came as an expectation, sometimes just short of a demand. "It might take me a while to pay you back," Julie pushed on. "But I will, Momma, I promise."

"I think we should wait for your daddy and ask him."

Her mother had always been unusual, a little strange. But in recent years, especially after the death of Julie's brother, George, Iris had seemed increasingly lost in her darkening world. *Funny,* people in Ganaego would say. Julie recalled her father, forced to do the laundry when her mother was in the hospital, holding up a pair of Julie's sweat-stained leotards and scowling. He griped about the expense of her lessons, griped about having to go to recitals, griped about her dancing interfering with her helping around the house— never acknowledging that her brothers never lifted a finger. "It's no use asking Daddy, Momma."

Iris sucked on her cigarette. "Why so much?"

"You helped the boys with their down payments?"

"How could you've run up such big bills?"

Before Julie floated her four Little Swans: two black children, a Chinese girl, a tall Russian girl. She'd been a Little Swan. It was how Miss Herrick picked her out as someone with promise. "I have to heat the studio, Momma, I have to light it. I can't ask the girls to dance in a cold, dark hall."

"But it's a loan? The boys paid theirs back. Sam made sure of that—every nickel."

Maybe Tommy did. But Julie doubted that George, who drank himself to imbecilic psychosis, had. But all this was beside the point. "A loan, Momma. I'll get your checkbook."

Her mother flailed out for her wrist, squeezed it. "No, he'll find out. In my . . . *things.*" Shy suddenly, Iris pointed toward the dresser. "Inside a stocking, in the toe. But hurry!"

Losing one student was not in itself a calamity. But as she descended the stairs that zigzagged down Ganaego's hills, Julie tried to deny both the guilt produced by the thick fold of old bills in her pocket—*where did this money come from?*—and her disappointment in losing Dana Cozma. Teenagers were moody, given to histrionics. Dana might show up tomorrow as if nothing had happened. But that seemed unlikely, and the girl's quitting felt like a betrayal of the attention Julie had lavished on her, of the love she had showered on another woman's child.

~ ~ ~

No, she was not going to marry Harvey Silverstein. But recently she and the widowed attorney had settled into a routine: dinner at Stellwagen's, Mondays, Dutch treat. Julie tried to keep her problems to herself, but Harvey, who had a knack for reading people, guessed, "Bad day, eh?" Julie shrugged and said, "Tell me a story, Harvey." He had ordered them Hennesseys with their desserts and put a match to her cigarette and his cigar. "Something to lift the spirits of the petite bourgeoisie."

Harvey removed his big black-frame spectacles to rub his eyes, which always seemed oversized and bleary when they weren't confined behind thick glass, naked. "Family counseling, that's what I did today. Sicilian guy, old man, owns a lawn service that makes no money. Two sons, one shiftless, one good. The shiftless one, high as a kite, runs over his brother's foot with a mower, trims off the sap's toes. Old guy doesn't carry insurance. He cans the no-good son and refuses to pay for the good son's missing toes. The sons, now united in a common enemy, sue the old man. Good plan, except there's no money. So, I order everybody into the office—Mom, Pop, good son and his wife, worthless son, his wife, everybody's children—and spend the day playing Mother Theresa. Last thing I did was explain to a six-year-old why his daddy has to wear a funny looking shoe."

Julie brought her jacket up over her shoulders. "That's not a very happy story, Harvey. Or maybe, in your business, it is?"

He lay his fingers on her check. "Lemme pick this one up, okay?"

"Mr. Silverstein"—Julie retrieved her check—"you are in breach of contract."

Before her building, in the pool of light provided by Wesley

Littlewood's brilliantly spotlighted mannequins modeling incontinence underwear, she studied the attorney, shorter and only half a dozen years older but somehow—to use his words—a resident of a different ward and precinct. "Six months, I have maybe six months to pull off a miracle."

In the breast pocket of his suits Harvey always carried several glass tubes filled with an amber liquid. When he inclined his hawk-like nose toward the second floor, the liquid in the tubes sloshed soundlessly. "One of the union guys has a boy who's into dancing—creeps the guy out. I keep telling him, send the kid over to Namar's, let him dance. If nothing else, it'll make him a better linebacker. How many baby ballerinas ya got now?"

She'd had so few boys. One, her nephew, step-nephew, had possessed a quirky talent, a kind of spontaneity and verve, although more for singing and acting. He'd also had a proclivity for wearing women's clothes, a latency she had helped him liberate within himself and something for which her brother George never forgave her. She thought of her Little Swans who had collapsed last week in an amazing cat's cradle of arms and legs. "I don't know, Harvey, not enough."

"So, Monday?" he said, holding out his hand.

She shook his hand. "Monday."

Long ago Julie had relinquished any dreams of domesticity she might have once entertained. But surrendering her sexual life, which in a small town was expected of an unmarried woman to whom overprotective mommas and poppas entrusted their baby swans, had never been her intention. Five minutes later, as she finished blanking the venetian blinds in both studio and apartment, Julie unbuttoned her blouse and pulled down her jeans and met Harvey Silverstein as he tiptoed, shoes in hand, in the rear door.

She led him into the bedroom. She lifted from his nose the

heavy frames of his glasses, folded the stems back, set them on the end table. Eyes on his eyes, she rolled down his calf-length, formal stockings to uncover his feet. She unbuttoned his trousers and shirt, removed them, peeled his Marlin Brando undershirt over his grizzled head and tugged down his powder-blue shorts. Then she crawled across him and took between her lips one of his nipples and sucked it harshly, until he moaned and reached up. It was then, at his touch, it happened: Her skin tensed, she pulled back. After so many years of celibacy, such contact seemed unendurable: Every time she and Harvey Silverstein began making love, Julie felt she would bolt from bed. Harvey, patient, understanding, paused, and that, his pausing, tipped the balance. As his hands withdrew, Julie hungrily moved toward them. She allowed him to push her head to the bed, to shift behind, to massage her raised vulva with the cream he squeezed from the tube, using his hands on her deftly but impersonally, like a baker folding dough. But as her rhythms sharpened, the thread of her consciousness—worries about enrollment, a recital without her prize pupil—unwound and left her. Only dimly did she sense Harvey labor, not particularly agile any more, to his knees and wrap his arms around her waist; only dimly sense his pulling her, gasping, into him. He smelled of cigars and cognac, of courthouses and depositions—she didn't care. Into his belly she forced her buttocks, then came erect, her loosened hair falling in a shower across her shoulders, wanting to feel him inside her more explicitly. Behind her, the attorney's breathing coarsened, his smoker's throat gurgled with sputum, and, with the force of her developing climax sounding within her like the blows of a hammer, Julie fell forward, muffling with a pillow—or so she believed—her ringing cries.

~ ~ ~

In the silence of the night, as she extracted herself from Harvey's slumberous clench in search of a more comfortable position, she

Dance of the Little Swans

heard what she ought not: noises, coming from the studio. Julie pulled on her robe and slipped through her living room. Opening the door a crack, she saw that, although the studio was dark, from the front hall came a fuzz of light. Had she left her office light on? She might brush aside her mother's worries, but Ganaego *was* dangerous. Max Fischman had shown her his safe once: It sat immured like one of Harvey's unlucky mobsters in reinforced concrete. The smart thing to do was to call the police. But with Harvey here that would be awkward. She crept to the corner and peered around it. Her office light shone through the open door. She heard rustling papers. A moment later Dana Cozma, in peacoat and blue bandana, passed through her line of sight.

Tightening the sash of her robe, Julie strode up to the door. "What the—"

"A hundred and fifty dollars!" The girl waved her arm. "That's my money!"

Julie, torn between anger and a peculiar joy that shot through her at seeing the girl again, shifted into the room. "You want me to call the police? Is that what you want?"

"Julie, that's—"

"You're running away, I understand now, you're in trouble." Julie pointed at her chair. "Sit." She sat herself, on the wrong side of her own desk. How long had the girl been in the studio? Had she heard them? "How did you get in here?"

"The same way your dirty old men do. You should lock your door."

"Dana, you need to go home, your mother and—"

"I'm not going back there!"

One might think it a safe bet that parents who indulge their children with dance lessons were not likely to be abusive. But sometimes one would be wrong. Julie had at times speculated about the Cozma household. Mr. Cozma she had never met, but Dana's mother was depressive and unresponsive, and the girl showed up for class every once in a while with what could be suspicious bruises. Acquiescing to the probable truth of those suspicions, Julie said, "Then we're—"

Dana sprang from her chair. Julie cut her off before she reached the door. This time she was able to clutch the girl's arm. "Just settle down!" Dana was shorter than she, a smaller woman. Aware of her nakedness beneath her robe, Julie lay her cheek on the girl's head, then forced herself to pull back, to look directly into Dana's brilliant gray eyes. "I can return your unused tuition," she said carefully. "But I'm going to need to know what you're going to do, where you're going. Do you have relatives you'll be safe with?"

"Don't worry, I'll be fine."

"You're anything but. Have you thought this through? You haven't, have you?"

Dana turned aside. "The first bus to Pittsburgh leaves at a quarter to six. After that, I don't know—New York? I don't know, I just have to get out of here."

"Stay the night, all right? We can talk about—"

"I *can't,* Julie, he might guess that I'm here. Are you gonna give me my money, or not?"

"Sit," Julie ordered her again. "I'll be back."

In her bedroom long glimmering staves of light cast by the blinds lay across the bed and rug. Stealing in, Julie went down on her hands and knees to find her jeans beside the dresser, turning them several times in her hands to find the right pocket. Harvey's voice rasped across the room, startling her. "Don't give her money."

She found her mother's fold of bills. "For a senior citizen you have pretty good ears?"

"Blame it on your old man—shoddy building materials." Harvey

Dance of the Little Swans

thrashed softly on the bed. "She's underage, don't give her money. That's your lawyer speaking, and you should always listen to your lawyer. Call the police."

"Harvey, I'm not going to call the police on her."

"You don't know what it's like for a kid on the run."

Julie slid her mother's money into her robe pocket. "Actually, Harvey, I do."

She was afraid that Dana might have slipped away. But the girl sat where she had been told to sit, a small creature, wiry, taut, immeasurably talented, but tired, grim and dejected, slumped like any teenager would be who was in over her head. Light or no light, heat or no heat, without the girl the studio this winter was going to be cold and dark. "I still think you should stay here, at least until your bus comes. You're probably starved?"

Dana, eyes evasive, inwardly focused, shook her head. "I can't, I told you. He raped my sister, now he wants me. *And* he's good buddies with the cops."

Julie was not, until that moment, certain that she was going to go through with this. It was not the right thing to do, not in the child's best interests, nor in her own. But she pulled the money from her pocket anyway, realizing as she did, how this must appear to the desperate girl, this fat sandwich of cash. She cursed herself for not separating off in the bedroom a hundred and fifty dollars. Where *had* this money—so long sleeping in an old woman's stockings—come from? Her mother's life had taken a wrong turn early on. She'd gotten in trouble in Washington D.C., where she'd gone to work as a secretary against her parents' wishes, then come home in disgrace. Had Iris, over the decades, siphoned the money off in nickels and dimes? Played a winning number and kept her jackpot secret? Money held a mysterious power for Julie. Money had always been what other people had that she didn't. Her hands trembling, she counted off a hundred and fifty dollars, then decided to forgive the entire tuition and went on to count out two hundred, then counted out two hundred more and two hundred more after that. She thrust the entire six hundred dollars into the astonished girl's palms.

"Go!" she cried. "I know I'm going to read about you murdered in the paper tomorrow. You don't know where you're going, what you're going to do, nothing, *nothing!"*

Dana squeezed the money in her coat pocket and leaned up and kissed her on the cheek. For a lingering second Julie smelled the girl, her sweat, a trace of cologne, and registered against her skin the roughened lips. A real kiss, not a peck. Before she had a chance to reach out and embrace her, Dana fled, clattering for the second time today down the stairs and into the street. How long Julie sat there she wasn't sure. Footsteps, at some point, wakened her to herself. She turned to gaze up at Harvey Silverstein, dressed, tie knotted, test tubes neatly lined up in formation in his breast pocket. "I'm sorry, Harvey, I—"

"How much?"

"Six hundred. For me, it was the librarian, Sylvia Robb. There were nights I slept on Sylvia's sofa when it got too rough at home. It might've cost her her job, if anyone had found out. She only gave me two hundred when I told her I had to leave, but, you know"—Julie laughed forlornly—"with inflation . . ."

Harvey withdrew his billfold from his inside coat pocket. He slipped his fingers inside, flipped through it. He held out what she knew without needing to count were six one-hundred-dollar bills. She shook her shoulders, shrinking. "I'm not a whore, Harvey, not yet, at least. Put your money away."

He pondered the bills, then did what she requested. He leaned over and kissed her on the nape. "Monday then, Ms. Namar?"

She smiled up at him. "Monday, Mr. Silverstein. And you might as well leave by the front door tonight, what the hell."

~ ~ ~

Businesses in small towns rise and fall with a certain periodicity. A sudden death, a rash financial decision, perhaps nothing more than a years-long toll of exhaustion, but one day what has seemed like a permanent fixture presents to the world a bolted door, a drawn blind, a scribbled sign scotch-taped to a window. In small towns people will measure the unwinding of their lives with the appearance and disappearance of particular businesses. That night Julie Namar sat on the floor of her cavernous studio near a set of footprints that once, at her wit's end, she had painted on the tiles for her bumbling adult pupils. The slits in the blinds admitted a dim radiance. Outside, Wesley Littlewood's *Rx* sign hummed. Julie pulled her robe close to stay warm. Of all the ballets, most of all she loved *The Firebird*. And though she had never danced the ballet, there had been winter evenings, after her girls and their bright chatter had melted into Ganaego's smoky streets, when she would turn the blinds, put the album on, and follow Balanchine's choreography. The Firebird: Halfbird, halfwoman, crowned with enormous feathers, the stupendous creature overflows the stage with explosive leaps and dazzling turns *en pointe*. When she'd fetched up in Ganaego again, abandoning New York, she had promised herself she was only coming back to regroup, to get her bearings, to assuage her ravaged pride and replenish her bank account. She'd make another run at the city. But as autumn piled on autumn, she had come to believe that her life in Manhattan had been but a chimera. The minuscule fourth-floor walkup off Washington Square she shared with three roommates and a zillion cockroaches, the all-night conversations, the deafening subways propelling her to her nerve-wracking auditions—all those delirious moments she came to believe had been no more than the fantasies of a foolish, star-struck girl. Tonight, thinking of her mother, thinking of Dana Cozma, Julie realized she had sold herself short: What she'd lacked was not talent, but confidence. She could've gone back, waited tables, put up with the vermin . . .

But that time was long gone, and as Julie sat waiting for the sun to rise over Ganaego's knobby hills she accepted without bitterness that that New York dream was irretrievably lost. The morning light would soon outline the old brick streets that spiraled up to the Plans, would bring into relief the white wooden staircases as they plunged gracefully flight by long flight to the valley floor, would fire her venetian blinds from the top down in glowing filaments, and would, at last, rouse the bonny firemen sleeping in their narrow bunks. And while Julie waited for these familiar events to transpire, she made three decisions. *One,* she would bring the studio to an orderly close, at Christmas break. She would not allow herself to be publicly humiliated. The Little Swans, those sweet lambs, would dance their final dance, and, when the lights went down on Julie Namar's Dance Studio, she would satisfy her creditors, the Nelsons, the utility people, the Company Store, all of them. *Two,* she would find a job and support herself. Like Dana Cozma, she had entered life at sixteen: She would see it through, wherever it took her.

The third decision did not come so easily.

Years ago when she had come back to Ganaego, she would, on sleepless nights, embark on long walks. Ganaego had always been dangerous, but walking helped to preserve her sanity, so, throwing caution to the wind, she'd twist her ponytail under her collar, tug on one of her brothers' slouch hats, and sally forth. Invariably, she would end up at the Ashport Bridge, where she leaned over the railing to peer down into the dimly illuminated yards of the steelworks. She would watch the men operating the tiny orange forklifts whose electric motors purred and crackled and whose bells chimed over their drivers' heads. Sometimes, a window would burst into dazzling light, and within would be bulky silhouettes outlined against ruby flames moving purposefully about. What the men did there she did not fully understand. But whether she grasped the nature of their work, when the children of those unschooled laborers turned up in her studio, bashful and selfconscious, she had worked with them as raw material to be shaped into creatures of grace, the way the men worked in fire to transform ore into steel. She had never danced *The Firebird,* but she had played her hands—dancer, teacher, business owner—as best she could. Like the men whose jobs were being lost for reasons that had little to do with them, she had nothing for which she needed to be ashamed.

When Sam Namarian closed out his shifts in the Welded Tube and climbed the steps home to Little Armenia, the grime on his hands would be so deeply embedded in the whorls of his skin that the scratchy Lava soap her mother bought failed to cleanse it. His face would be gray, his eyes, bloodshot. His body stank. And that tonight was the third thing Julie decided: She would move back into her old bedroom and care for her mother, and, when her mother died, she would care for this man who was not her father but whom she had loved—tried to love—as a girl. Sometimes, when Sam came home he would discover in his pocket of his overalls a metal burr broken off the roughened beard of a glowing pipe. He would hold the jagged burr to the light as though it were a rare gem and award it to her. And so yes, this too, fully as stubborn and proud as the laborer who had given her his name to make her legitimate and cursed her for dropping its distinguishing ethnic ending, Julie Namar would stare into the furnace of her life, and she would satisfy those debts, as well.

Placido Lombardi's Funeral

Summer 1983

"Arthur, why do *we* have to buy him a suit? If the family can't provide one, Butterworth's will. That's what one pays for—their *service.*"

"Somehow that don't seem right."

"You know the proper form of the verb, Arthur, please use it."

"Com' on, dumpling, have a heart. He was only a kid."

To be annoyed by another's death was ungenerous. Pleasance Stubbs tightened her lips and inclined her head toward the window to catch what meager breeze streamed past the car. Death, she presumed, had come painlessly, like irresistible sleep, and, although she had little use for the Lombardi boy—an immature and ill-mannered 27-year-old—neither would she take pleasure in imagining a fellow creature's suffering. To be struck down on his last night, his final shift in the steelworks before his discharge, would be, for his family, a heartrending irony, and her sympathies did include his grieving parents: Placido's mother, rarely, apparently, out of her housecoat, and Placido's father, whom Pleasance saw in the yard that adjoined theirs, a dapper man in blousy white shirts and suspenders, meticulously snipping his hedges and puffing tiny black cigars. The young man, the Lombardi's lastborn, had shinnied down a pole into a basement under the tin mill, an area he had no authorization for entering—or so the *Chronicle* had reported—and was felled by lethal fumes. What was he doing down there? Up to no good, Pleasance warranted. The way the cheeky boy with a moustache so thin it looked as if it had been penciled in was forever loitering in their garage and regaling Arthur with some piece of tawdry self-promotion or—worse—urging on her gullible husband one of his get-rich-quick schemes.

"Besides," she went on, unable to leave her point uncompleted, "the outlandish way he dressed—I find it hard to believe he didn't own a single suit."

"Pleasance, it was only sixty dollars. Hey now, I got veal chops. They was on sale. Let's try to have us a good night tonight, how's that?"

A sallow-faced man with a round little tummy and a self-conscious snicker, Arthur had, stashed away in every niche in the garage, something special: calipers, clamps, hammers, jars of nuts, bolts, screws, springs. If Arthur discovered a board with a rusty nail in it, he saved not only the board, but also the nail, extracting it and filing it in the appropriate mayonnaise jar. "If we have to go to a funeral home," Pleasance pointed out, "it's hardly going to be a celebration. Let's go tomorrow? I'll be tired, but that's okay."

Arthur, who drove with the same due diligence he brought to every task, carefully steered his venerable Thunderbird Landau up the winding curves of Sutton Post Road Hill. On the roof, the Thunderbird's once-luxurious vinyl, now in tatters, ruffled in the wind. "Oh, stop being such a fussy pants. We won't stay long. All this bellyachin'—it's just because it's your birthday."

"My birthday has nothing to do with it. It's the heat. It's worn me down. God knows, I'm not the complaining type. You know that, Arthur."

The afternoon *was* warm, particularly because she'd had to wait in the car for Arthur to purchase the funerary suit and decide which motor oil would best soothe the indigestion he'd heard in the bowels of his beloved automobile. The thought that her spouse was spending more time in Gee Bee's choosing a motor oil than in choosing her gift, the Russell Stover cherry cordials he invariably bought, had also done little to improve her disposition. Any other year Arthur would have known she would not tolerate his woolgathering—and here lay, Pleasance knew, the real source of her malaise: She was wildly frustrated. Not to be engaged in doing at this point in the year what for thirty-three summers she had always done: drawing up lesson plans, clearing cupboards, restocking supplies, anticipating—oh, how she loved it!—that moment of shivery challenge that arises as the children, the first autumn morning, timidly crowd into the room.

Arthur, furloughed from the mill when he was fifty-one, eight years ago, had taken his dismissal as a providential gift, an invitation to consecrate himself to his hobbies. But as far as Pleasance was concerned even her present age, fifty-six, was too young to withdraw from life's rough and tumble, from the vocation to which she'd been called: civilizing nine-year-olds. In the first or second grades you might do as you pleased, but when you reached Mrs. Stubbs' class, you knew—or soon knew—you were to come to school with your hair combed, the gum removed from your mouth, and you were to sit up straight and pay attention. Whether it was all those years in heels that had brought about the arthritis or whether the condition was congenital and would have occurred anyway, it hardly mattered: Four years ago she'd undergone a difficult hip replacement; this past year the pain—in both hips—had been all but unendurable. Either retire, the orthopedic surgeon pronounced, or face not only a second operation on the right hip but an operation on the left, as well, and the very real threat of crippling. And so Pleasance had sat before Dr. Kovacs—a woman whom, as a child, she had cruelly belittled— struggling then and struggling still to come to grips with the bleak finality of that judgment.

"Look here, dumpling, I'm sorry." Arthur, who employed hand

Placido Lombardi's Funeral

signals as well as directional lights, executed a precise left turn across traffic. "You couldn't find a clerk in Gee Bee's if you was lying in an aisle bleedin' to death. You wait, the conglomerate shuts down the mill they're all gonna be singing a different tune."

"I thought the paper said they *weren't* going to shut it down."

"Not what I'm hearing."

Pleasance, annoyed with the never-ending rumors roiling Ganaego of the fate of the steelworks—now they were going to close it, now they weren't—shrugged it off. "Oh, well, it doesn't matter."

She had, in excruciating pain, battled through to year's conclusion, maintaining all the while how *thrilled* she was to be retiring. She vowed to her colleagues that she and Arthur would travel, yes, they would. They'd fix up the house. She would pitch in and help him in the yard. That dreadful water heater—beside the fence? that he refused to throw away? stuffing oozing from the ruptured seams?— that was first, that *had* to go! On her last day, inspired by the news that the United States was launching its first woman astronaut into space, Pleasance exclaimed that she intended to clear the clutter from their electric organ and sign herself up for lessons. As a girl, she declared, her voice ringing out across the faculty lounge, *I just adored music!* By now, however, after a long summer cooped up in their sweltering bungalow, frittering away her afternoons watching game shows on television, she had sunk into a self-pitying hopelessness.

At home, gingerly extricating herself from the Thunderbird's low seats, Pleasance pointedly ignored Arthur as he retrieved his packages. Stepping inside the house, though, she turned, unable to resist, to watch her husband—looking for all the world like the UPS man—marching up the Lombardis' walk, box in arms. He rapped on the door. A moment later, Mrs. Lombardi in her frowzy housecoat opened the door and indicated Arthur was to enter. He waggled his head and held out his box. Mr. Lombardi appeared and listened to

Arthur, his brow puckering. He shook his head, but Arthur insisted. At last, Mr. Lombardi accepted the box and solemnly presented it, in turn, to his wife, then threw his arms around Arthur.

That night, Pleasance, crabby and out of sorts, refused to eat the expensive chops Arthur had purchased at the T&V, refused to accept the rectangular gift he held out, refused even to attend Placido Lombardi's viewing. "You know perfectly well I have a big day tomorrow," she defended herself. "A peanut butter sandwich, that's what I'm going to make and that's what I'm going to have. I'm sorry for the family, but, personally, I don't care a fig."

Arthur, who, once he discovered aprons that were not frilly, had taken to wearing them when he cooked, made a face as he whacked the fat off a chop. But all he said was, "We can go tomorrow. And you're right, he had lots of flashy duds. But *shoot,* that won't do, not for your funeral, and you gotta know the old man's clothes woulda never fit him."

~ ~ ~

A secret so deep that even Arthur didn't know was Pleasance's phobia of driving. When had it begun? What had brought it about? She was not certain. All she knew was that she had come to dread even the short trip down the hill to Taft Elementary. Her eyes were fine; her reflexes sound. Even the convulsive pains in her pelvis did not, at least yet, impair her control of the pedals. As soon as she waked on a school day, however—and all the more if she heard rain pattering—tension would seize her, thicken her chest, and she'd be convinced this would be the day her brakes would fail. The solitary, albeit shameful, benefit that Pleasance did accrue from retiring then was her reprieve from driving. And so last week when her sister's youngest called—the boy, only in his sophomore year of college, but ambitious, already a wheeler-dealer—to announce he had for her the perfect freelance job, editing operating manuals for a company that manufactured earthmoving equipment, she was riven by contrary emotions. On the one hand, Nicky's offer was a chance to redeem what so far had been her very public failure of retirement. Opposing it was the fact that any job would likely require driving.

"Nicky, honey," she said, pressure gathering in her chest, "I'm more of a bookish kind of person? Goodness, I wouldn't know the first thing about construction machinery."

She imagined, behind his spectacles, the boy's enterprising eyes. "Aunt Pleasance, you know what a gerund is, right? Trust me, not an engineer in America knows what a gerund is. This is going to be a walk in the park for you. *Listen:* The technical people document the equipment in their Pidgin-English—okay?—then you slap in the periods and commas and—*boom!*—it's a wrap. But first, we gotta get you up here so my client can check you out. Their offices are in Carnegie, off the Parkway. Got a pencil? Write down these directions."

Of all her fears, negotiating the Parkway was the most implacable. Arthur volunteered to drive her and wait outside. But to accept his offer would swerve dangerously close to disclosing her secret, and Pleasance had gaily insisted that she'd enjoy the outing, maybe even take it as an opportunity to continue into Pittsburgh and do some shopping. Was there a back road route to Carnegie? But how would she match up another route with Nicky's directions? Recognizing the futility of that, she recopied her nephew's convoluted instructions, printing them on three-by-five index cards, a single direction on each. And then this morning her docile little Omni, which, all summer, had not budged so much as an inch, failed to start, and she was forced to contemplate driving Arthur's leviathan Thunderbird.

Arthur, lowering the hood of her car the way a surgeon might drape a sheet over a patient's head, repeated his offer. "Pleasance, I don't mind, I really don't?"

"Nonsense." She adjusted her pocketbook on her arm. "It's only

Carnegie, not the dark side of the moon."

Getting to the Parkway involved two treacherous lefts, a long serpentine hill down and another just as twisty back up, the airport and its monstrous jets shrieking across the road, and then the appalling Parkway and its maniacal drivers. *Lemmings!* Pleasance prided herself on being a model motorist. She kept out of everybody's way, moderated her speed to allow her fellow drivers room to make their entrances or departures, did not tailgate. But gone were the days when highway courtesy mattered. People zoomed up behind her and indignantly blared their horns; trucks thundered past, rocking even Arthur's heavy car in their turbulence; two men bent low across their motorcycles shot by like a vision of the Apocalypse. Ironically, it was a stray thought of Placido Lombardi—she once caught the horrid boy with a girl in their garage—that so preoccupied her, still capable of raising her ire, that she became bewitched by the inscrutable signs and flew off the Parkway at the wrong exit. Circling, trying to piece her way back, she ended up heading *north,* instead of south, and sailed off again. This time, once she had regained the Parkway, she no longer knew if her intended exit lay before or behind, and she rolled off again. Her disorientation now total, Pleasance found herself spinning out into the countryside, where, blissfully, the traffic became lighter. In a gluey daze she navigated Arthur's Thunderbird up one gentle rise after another, gliding down the backsides, her three-by-five cards flung across the seat and floor like so much colossal and useless confetti.

A little service station situated all by itself—a humble stucco building no larger than a cottage, with a red tile roof—attracted her eye, and it was into the station's side lot, beside a stack of lopsided tires, that Pleasance coasted to a halt. She switched off the Thunderbird's rumbling engine, pressed her fingers together before her lips, and wept. The heat of her body intensified her cologne. She felt distinctly unwell. Uncovering her watch, she stared at it in stupefaction: The trip, which Nicky had estimated at fifty minutes, had now burrowed deep into its second hour. The meeting with Nicky's client, of which she had also been intimidated, had long ago started without her and was going to conclude, whenever and however business meetings conclude, without her, as well.

Who was she trying to fool? She was not going to edit bulldozer manuals. Neither were she and Arthur going to travel. She was petrified of airplanes, trains, buses—anything that hurtled you through space. In her entire life there had been but a single location, besides the interior of her house, where she felt safe: her third-grade classroom at Taft Elementary. Huddled in Arthur's car, she remembered how mercilessly she had criticized, not the bullies and rowdy farm boys, whom she merely reprimanded and passed over, but the timorous ones, especially the poky, bashful girls. She would lecture her miniature captive audiences on their fears, ridiculing them for their terror of reciting aloud, of volunteering to go to the blackboard to work out a sum, of taking part in recess games—all the while knowing that she was every bit as much as they a coward.

"You hoo?" Someone—a mechanic with a curly black beard of Biblical proportions— tapped on her window. "Everything all right in there?"

The fellow had gobs of grease in his beard; more grease painted his nose. For once, however, Pleasance set aside her instinctive censure. She ran down her window. "Do you"—her voice sounded as weak as a child's—"have a phone?"

Her hips, frozen for two hours in the same position, were engulfed, the second she stepped out of the car, in a radiant burst of pain. Pleasance sagged, flailing for the flaps of vinyl on Arthur's roof. The mechanic grabbed her. "Hello!" he yelped. "You having a heart attack?"

"Just give me a second," she squeaked.

Riding the swells of pain, Pleasance, the mechanic's massive hand lodged in her armpit, wobbled into the station. While the fellow, summoned by his customers, clambered in and out his office, she concentrated on breathing deeply. Clinging to a series of successively sized radiator hoses, she managed to circumnavigate the room and reach the telephone. Their line rang and rang. She pictured the man who, three decades ago, had awkwardly proposed to her and whom she had accepted because she feared no one would ever have her, in his compulsively organized garage, under the glow of a lamp, magnifying goggles on, rewiring a window fan he'd discovered in the trash. She waited, pledging to the mechanic, who continued to frown dubiously at her, that she was feeling more and more chipper, then called again, and again, and again.

Shouldn't she just drive home? Pleasance peered through the advertisements on the gas station's windows at Arthur's car outside: *No,* the Thunderbird said, *no, no, no.* She rooted in her purse for her address book and called the only neighbors she knew well enough to ask a favor of.

"I'm sorry to bother you," she blurted out to Mr. Lombardi. "But it's an emergency. Could you go over to our garage and tell Arthur to come inside so I can call him?"

"Isa no problem," Mr. Lombardi said.

While she waited for him to return, Pleasance pressed the receiver against her ear, listening avidly to the voices burbling around the phone in the Lombardi household. It was not that she was eavesdropping so much as she was ravenously drinking in even this ephemeral connection with Anderson Township and home. Thus she was doubly crushed when Mr. Lombardi picked up the phone and said, "Sorry, he don't seem to be there."

"If he's not there, then where is he?"

The question appeared to perplex him. "Maybe," he asked instead, "I can be of help?"

"A person can stay in an auto parts store only so long. He's got to come home sooner or later." Pleasance collected her ravaged emotions. "Thank you for trying."

"No, wait." Mr. Lombardi implored. "What exactly isa your trouble?"

Pleasance poured out her story, omitting her Parkway misadventure and describing her predicament as car trouble, a funny noise. *I think it's a braking issue,* she confided. When Mr. Lombardi suggested he come for her, Pleasance—beginning to sniffle again, this time in shameless gratitude—only half-heartedly resisted. She read to him the service station's address from an invoice on the mechanic's desk and worked her way back, hose by hose, to her chair. She didn't know what model of car the Lombardis owned, only that it was an unusual lilac shade. She stared fixedly out the windows. Spotting at last a purple car heave into view, she shoved a twenty-dollar bill into the mechanic's grease-stained palm and lurched toward the door.

~ ~ ~

Pleasance had known that when the mechanic helped her into his station he had gotten grease on her. Under her arm were black stains. What she didn't know was that he had also left on the back of her blouse an imprint of an enormous hand. What had Mr. Lombardi thought? At home, she handed Arthur his keys, swallowed two Excedrins, retreated to bed. When he tiptoed in and asked if she was feeling up to the mortuary, she pulled the pillow over her head.

And actually, Mr. Lombardi had pretty much absolved them of that responsibility. Pleasance, floundering into his car, had apologized again for disturbing them and for not going to the funeral home last night. Mr. Lombardi readjusted the stogie the color of licorice clamped between his teeth and said, "Not necessary. If it wasa not for the family, I woulda buried him right away. Like the Jews. Come tomorrow if you like? Father Opsatnick will say a few meaningless words and we will give him back to the earth."

"It must have been a terrible shock?"

"Shock?" Mr. Lombardi steered with both hands, like a tugboat captain. "My dear Mrs. Stubbs, you must understand: Placido was the fruit of our old age. How you say—to our family an unexpected addition? I wasa against his working in the mill. I worked in the mill exactly one day. *This isa no place for a man to be,* I thought. And now the steel mill, it has taken my child, prematurely struck him down. I'ma never going to be the same again."

In the morning, lugging herself from bed to peek through the kitchen drapes, Pleasance saw Arthur's Thunderbird parked in the drive, like a lost hound that had found its way home. Her hips were less sore, but she still felt as though she had spent the night carrying boulders from one side of the yard to the other. On one of Arthur's passes through the kitchen she asked him whether he'd had a chance to examine her car.

"Oh, she's fine." He handed her—without comment—her three-by-five cards, neatly stacked and, doubtless, in order. "All she needed was a battery, but while I was—"

"Spare me the gory details, *please.*"

Fortifying herself with more Excedrin, Pleasance drove to Dr. Kovacs' office. The receptionist, vexed, adamant, pointed at the surgeon's packed appointment book. "A *minute,*" Pleasance pleaded. For the rare privilege of an unscheduled minute she waited an hour and a half, shifting uncomfortably in her chair reading and rereading the same *Cosmopolitan.* At least the long wait and an additional twenty-minute delay, once she was directed into an examining room, allowed her to fine-tune her proposition.

"What if," she proposed to the physician, "I teach sitting down?

Tina Longstreet used to plop herself in her chair after lunch and never stir again. She'd direct reading groups in the back of the room by waving her arms. I don't even *own* a pair of heels anymore, so that's no problem. And I can lose weight, this time I can, I promise."

In her brilliant white lab coat and blood-red lipstick, her platoon of assistants bustling in and out of the warren of examination rooms, the young physician, Aliz Kovacs, only in her early thirties, seemed far removed in time and position from the Hungarian immigrant child Pleasance recalled: the hollow-faced girl with crooked glasses who would, before school, linger close to the building, shrinking inside her thin cotton coat.

"Mrs. Stubbs," Aliz said, swiveling on her stool to face her, "you have degenerative hip disease. I showed you your X-rays. Your condition is not going to get any better, and, if you don't treat it with respect, it will get a whole lot worse. Listen to your body: You don't want another operation, most likely, two."

Pleasance buried her face in her hands, crying. She heard Aliz stand, pause, then sit again. On her sleeve she felt the weight of a hand. "Pleasance?" It was the first time Aliz had ever used her given name. "When my mother enrolled me in Taft, I don't believe I knew a dozen words of English. There was a morning—I'm sure you don't remember—you asked me what the date was, and I didn't even know that."

"I should've never criticized you like that, I'm so sorry, I—"

"No, no." Dr. Kovacs interrupted. "Don't apologize. I was mortified, I begged and begged you to tell me, and you refused. You told me to take responsibility for my life, to stop feeling sorry for myself. *Look around you, child,* you said, *you will find everything you need!* Do you remember that? I *did* look around—and there on the wall was a calendar. By the time I left your class, I had caught up to everyone else. You were—for what, thirty years?—a good teacher. Pleasance, look around you: You will find everything you need."

~ ~ ~

The day she carried her milk crates of files out of Taft, there had been about the abandonment of her room an air of unreality: This was not really happening, was it? And in fact only the following week—and twice thereafter—she'd had to return to the school to sign some paperwork. On that indisputably final time in the building she had lingered for a few minutes inside her cherished room. She looked, she smelled, she did all she could to savor what she had been obliged to surrender. This afternoon, dismissed by Dr. Kovacs but not wanting to go home, Pleasance drove by the school. Seeing Penelope's car, then Loretta's and Vera's, she guessed they were meeting, ostensibly to talk about the coming year, but to gab really, going on without her.

It was as if she were dead.

She had a mad impulse to slip inside and surprise them. But even as foolish a person as Pleasance knew herself to be, she understood how pathetic that would appear. She drove past Butterworth's Memorial Chapel and recalled what Mr. Lombardi had said. She swerved into the empty lot. As expected, the doors of the mortuary were locked. She rang the bell to the apartment above. On the stairs a scuffling of feet sounded, and Norbert Butterworth, thrice the size she remembered him, tie unfastened about his neck, swung open the door. At least today, she noted, his fly was zipped, that frequent absentmindedness being Bertie Butterworth's enduring contribution to the Taft teachers' lounge stock of humor.

"Interment service's at three, Mrs. Stubbs," he shyly explained.

Pleasance, aware that this was the last time she could play this card, said, "Bertie, I have a meeting at the school at three. Do you think it's possible for me to sneak in for just a minute? The Lombardis are neighbors of ours."

Although she still could not locate within her, as she stood over Placido's casket, a great deal of sympathy for the Lombardi boy, in the presence of death, its unfathomable silence, Pleasance felt chastened. The freak accident had not in any way disfigured him, and they had permitted Placido to sport into eternity his Clark Gable moustache and his gaudy rings and bracelets, even, she fancied, preserving in his expression a familiar impertinence. Whether it was due to some clever tucks on the part of the Butterworths or Arthur's shrewd guess, the Gee Bee's suit—a military-looking, navy blue—fit him very well. For himself, Arthur had never purchased a suit half so handsome. All in all, Placido Lombardi looked debonair, almost jaunty, probably not that different, she reflected, than his father had looked when he courted his sweetheart.

And that gave her pause.

Thirty years ago: What had Arthur looked like? What had she looked like? Oh, she knew, one did know, of course. One could produce photographs. But who *really* had those people been? How many times do you change until you are no longer yourself? The Lombardis had six children, she was pretty sure of that. The Stubbs had none, that she was sure about. She and Arthur had been spared then the unimaginable heartbreak of seeing one of their children prematurely struck down, as Mr. Lombardi had eloquently put it. But they had also been cheated of the joy of seeing their progeny, one by passionate one, brought into existence.

What they had had instead was her career, and now that was over.

What he could not possibly have taught her in life, the Lombardi boy was able to teach Pleasance in death. Indeed, she was a foolish person. She was, just as Placido Lombardi had been, a small-time fraud. Oh, she might offer up her years of service—and they might be accepted. She had not been a magnificent teacher, as Loretta Rodale had declared when she'd toasted Pleasance at her retirement dinner, but she had probably been, to use Aliz Kovacs' words, a good teacher. A career, however, was not enough, and a career ended was nothing. She recalled what Aliz had said, quoting her own words back to her, and she looked around at the funeral parlor, its lamps and sofas and chairs, the artificiality of a business trying to look like a home. She smelled the stale scent of flowers wilting in the heat and, for the first time in many years, she prayed to her God. Pleasance prayed that Placido Lombardi's soul might be granted everlasting peace, and she prayed, foolish, trifling, vain creature that she was, that she might be thankful for the gift she still possessed that had been cruelly taken from this young man on his very last day of work.

~ ~ ~

Pleasance today made one last stop. At the T&V, she bought a fourteen-pound ham, a can of Del Monte sliced pineapple, brown sugar, apple cider, dried mustard, whole cloves. Shooing Arthur out of the kitchen, she cooked the ham the way her mother had cooked her Easter hams, gashing the meat in a diamond pattern, studding it with the cloves and glazing it with the sugar, cider, and mustard. Later, she arranged the pineapple wheels around the baking shank, allowing them just sufficient time to caramelize. When in early evening the pan had cooled, she transferred the ham to a large platter, draped it with one of her fancy chintz tea towels, and carried it in her arms across the lawn to the Lombardis'. One of the grandchildren, a little girl in a smock with a pretty pattern of pleats, tugged open the door. Pleasance brought the platter down to the child's level, and her nose, like a rabbit's, wiggled inquisitively. Behind her, emerging from the noisy crowd, appeared her mother, one of the Lombardis' older children, whom Pleasance did not know very well.

"Sandra? What's that lady *got?*" The woman idly caressed her daughter's hair and smiled at Pleasance. "Would you like to come

Placido Lombardi's Funeral

in?"

"No, no." Pleasance passed over the heavy platter. "Tell your mother and father our thoughts are with them."

On her way home, Pleasance came to two resolutions. First, she *would* unbury their Hammond organ. Stacked on and around the old instrument were her sewing basket, Arthur's Parcheesi board, a pile of *Reader's Digest*s, who knows what else? All that had to go. What she had always loved were the hymns, *I Come to the Garden Alone, Blest Be the Tie That Binds, Give to the Winds Your Fears.* Dellmore George, their church organist, was in his eighties. She did adore music, that small scrap of her boasting had been veracious: Perhaps, with lessons and practice, there might be a way for her to contribute?

She would ask Maurice Begley, the choir director.

The second resolution Pleasance Stubbs came to on her short walk would likely cost her, she conceded, a day in bed. But it was a sacrifice worth making. Crouching behind the old water heater near the fence, she pushed, then pushed harder. When the fusty thing with its moldy beard of insulation failed to budge, she stopped to ponder: Had Arthur, so attached to his things, fastened it to the earth somehow? *My heavens,* she fretted, *is it growing here?* Pleasance stepped around the tank and clutched a pipe sticking from its top with both hands. Pulling with all her might, her hips flaring into an oratorio of pain, she succeeded at last in getting Arthur's rotting, prehistoric water heater to rise from its bed of yellowy weeds and begin rolling like a huge fat sausage down the hill toward the sidewalk.

It was, as they say, a start.

Ralphie's Clarinet

Autumn 1983

Mrs. Gleason she noticed. Dolores Gleason was hard not to notice. The blue bouffant through which shone the bony hemisphere of her scalp, the four-pronged aluminum cane she pumped with the precision of a drum major, the little bronchial explosions she periodically issued. But Audrey was so deeply embroiled with Mr. Del Greco, who had jumbled the figures in his passbook, that she didn't notice the *other* woman until she stepped out of Mrs. Gleason's shadow, appeared in front of the counter, and passed the note over.

An altogether pathetic sort of person, she was short and swarthy, furtive. Her face was crabbed and puckered. One eye, haloed in raw pink, roved sightlessly. Even though it was early in the season, she was wearing a winter coat, sun-bleached purple beneath the dirt. From the folds of the fabric seeped a piercing odor—perfume, sweat—no, no, something more astringent than that, something Audrey wasn't sure of and didn't care to identify.

But of this she was sure: The woman was *funny*.

Audrey, although new to her job, had had basic teller training, plus another half-day of in-service when they threw a tennis ball around and talked about their families. And if Mazi—steady, imperturbable Mazi Claprood, the flesh of her arms quaking like Jell-O but her fingers amazingly deft with the stacks of bills, a teller and nothing but a teller for thirty-one years—had been there, instead of having her crawl space treated for carpenter ants, there was no question: Audrey would have done the right thing. Definitely, if Mr. Hamm had been in his office (and it had been *he* who broke the first rule, leaving her here alone), she would have followed the instructions drilled into her. If there was an *incident,* she was to comply with the *perpetrator's* demands.

She knew that. She just didn't do it. "No," she said, pushing the note back across the counter. "We can't accept that kind of thing here."

The woman pointed at her note peevishly and pushed it forward again. The note was scrawled on a page torn from a tablet. Audrey had read it. She didn't need to read it again. Having gotten this far beyond the script, the vessels that fed her heart constricting, she looked the disturbed woman in her one sound eye and sent the note back a final time.

"*No,* I told you—that won't do." She forced herself to look over at Mrs. Gleason, who was rolling her shoulders like a prizefighter waiting for the bell to ring, and announce as authoritatively as she could, *"Next!"*

The perpetrator, caught between Audrey's implacability and the formidable presence of Mrs. Gleason, sidled up the counter, clutching her rejected note. Even then, with the bones in Audrey's hands giving forth strange little pangs and her skin dampening to such a degree that Mrs. Gleason's check adhered to her palm, she did not push the alarm. She recorded Mrs. Gleason's deposit and made direct eye contact with her next customer. The woman, at some point, drifted away—what else was she to do? But even when Mr. Hamm returned from the mall, concealing the tiny lavender shopping bag he carried, Audrey waited. It wasn't until Mazi settled in, mooshing her hemorrhoid pillow beneath her, that Audrey closed her window and walked back to Mr. Hamm's office to report that there had been an attempted robbery at his bank.

Mr. Hamm, recently promoted branch manager, was, as expected, aghast. "Audrey, she could have been carrying a weapon!"

It was Friday afternoon. Mr. and Mrs. Hamm's romantic sea cruise vacation started in forty-five minutes, plus or minus depending whether Audrey's and Mazi's teller drawers balanced, and, by God, they had known for months things had better well square on this particular Friday. Audrey recalled the nauseating odor lifting off the woman and, for the first time, permitted the icy fear that had been circling her heart to invade that organ.

What if she did have a gun?

"Oh, Audrey, look at the position you've put us in." Mr. Hamm rubbed his bald spot inquisitively, tenderly. "What're we supposed to do? Call the police, get the main office involved, draw up an incident report, put you on unpaid leave, draw up *that* report, and cancel my vacation—*or,* pretend this didn't happen and jeopardize my career?"

What Mr. Hamm had neglected to add but hung unspoken between them was that every one of those reports would have to include the fact that he had left her alone to buy lingerie for his wife. No one *ever* was to be left alone in the bank. "There wasn't a robbery," Audrey reminded him. "Just a feeble attempt."

"Makes no difference! That's why we have policies, rules, drills." Mr. Hamm warmed to his anger. "So we know what to do reflexively, automatically. D'you think we do all that for fun? To entertain ourselves? Tell me, Audrey, is this job something you really need?"

Audrey detested this tone, the sarcastic voice ignorant parents inflict upon their children. It had always struck her as strange that, despite Mr. Hamm's protestations when they threw the tennis ball of how he cherished his family, the photographs of his wife and daughters faced out, toward the customer's chair. She wouldn't have said anything, knowing his excitable temperament, but, by that same

Ralphie's Clarinet

training, she felt duty-bound to report the incident. Whether that was a mistake she didn't know, but she did know enough to let Mr. Hamm have out his exasperation.

"Maybe you don't need to work," he continued, "maybe you don't need this job? You're independently wealthy, is that it?"

They were *not* wealthy. In fact, ever since Ted had been furloughed from the steelworks, Audrey had become the family's sole breadwinner. Recently, he had taken up with two men from Plan Thirteen to peddle moldy potatoes by the side of the road. One of his partners appeared to be mentally unbalanced. The enterprise couldn't have been more humiliating. When her parents found out, they were appalled. *What's come over him?* her mother wanted to know. *Has he lost his marbles?*

A difficult year. Audrey took pride in the initiative she had shown by getting a job, her first real job. And at thirty-eight that had not been easy. But no one had warned her that the work world would be full of children parading around dressed as adults. "I *do* need this job, Mr. Hamm," she said when her boss's harangue seemed to have run its course. "I'm sorry, I'm very, very sorry."

Satisfied presumably, Mr. Hamm got up to close his door. "Does Mazi know?"

Audrey shook her head. "I didn't say anything."

"And no one else was in the bank?"

"Mrs. Gleason was here, and so was Mr. Del Greco."

Mr. Hamm threw up his hands. "Audrey, she could've done them harm! The Gleasons have been with the bank for *decades!* Dolores' father fitted me for my first pair of corrective arches. I didn't know there were other customers here! Oh, this is just a mess!"

"They didn't notice," Audrey hastened to reassure him. "Mrs. Gleason would've been quacking like a duck if she'd realized what was going on, you know her, and Mr. Del Greco, he's lucky to find his way to the counter. They didn't see anything."

Mr. Hamm smoothed his bald spot. "You're positive, absolutely positive? How could you not notice an attempted bank robbery? It defies reason."

"She was . . ."—Audrey searched for words—". . . like a street person, kind of foggy. I'm sure she looked like someone trying to cash a dodgy check or a money order without an ID. I said, no, we can't accept that, and went on to the next customer. Like you would, you know?"

Through the manager's office of the Crocker Farm branch of the Ganaego Savings & Loan, the heartache of Mr. Hamm's sigh fell softly, plaintively. "All right," he croaked, "we'll overlook this breach—*this* time. But I'm going to say this once, once and once only: If there's one more slip, the tiniest deviation from policy, you are going to be without a paycheck—you hear me?"

Along with her new job Audrey had inherited the task of doing the family's bills. If Mr. Hamm wanted, he could dismiss her on the spot. "I understand," she said.

~ ~ ~

If you were going to rob a bank, Audrey was thinking as she turned into the Oak Grove Music School, *would you wear a purple coat?*

This past week the weather had turned, and now, all day, a drizzle as sharp as needles had been falling. Rivulets sluiced down beneath the wipers of her car. Clearly, the woman last Friday had had mental problems. She was to be pitied, not taken seriously. But she had nearly cost Audrey her job, and that one was required to take seriously. Landing the teller position had been a stroke of luck. She—if not Ted—had realized this past year, as inconceivable as it once would have seemed, that the steelworks that had sustained and controlled their lives and the lives of their parents and grandparents was on the

Ralphie's Clarinet

verge of collapse. And now *had* collapsed, chaining its gates a month ago. Ted's discharge was permanent. He was never going to be called back. Why would he not face up to that? Nights, Audrey lay awake, gripped by foreboding. You could lose your house, your place in the community. She read about the foreclosures in the *Chronicle,* people crowding food pantries, pawing through dented cans of soup. You could be flung out in the snow!

Bronze oak leaves were strewn across the music school porch; one or two clung to the screen door, as though craving admittance. She was apprehensive about the conversation that awaited her, and, once inside, paused before the staircase to organize her thoughts. Upstairs, from the honeycomb of practice rooms came the now-familiar medley of squeaks, squawks, and aimless plinks. How atrocious it sounded, she thought fondly, but from all this off-key tootling and sour wheezing eventually came real music. And the thought that Ralphie, their youngest, might become a musician stirred her. Where had the notion to take up the clarinet come from? Not from them. Neither she nor Ted was musical. Ted claimed he got the idea from television. Wherever Ralphie discovered the inspiration, he deserved credit for trying. How many nine-year-olds could you name who had demonstrated this much ambition? Music was hard, harder than it looked. Perplexed but delighted, they bought him a clarinet with money they couldn't spare and enrolled him in this private music school because the public schools did not accept children into the music program until they were in the fourth grade. They fashioned a place for him in the rec room and sighed with parental pride when, from the basement, began rising—such tender, brave sounds!—tentative chirps, snorks, bleats.

And then, as suddenly as those precious notes began, they ceased.

He was only a child, Audrey chided herself. His interests

bloomed and faded overnight. One day he announced he was going to be a doctor, the next day a space ranger. Nonetheless, it wounded her. Both she and Ted admitted they had made mistakes with their firstborn, Teddy. Fifteen, not even sixteen, last spring Teddy had run off with the irresponsible Gromeka girl. For two weeks the house was plunged in crisis, then, dear God, he called from West Virginia. Ted brought the boy home, skin and bones, lice in his hair, ashamed and miserable for having been abandoned by his girl. With Ralphie they were determined to do better.

Steeling herself for a confrontation with the inevitable, she stood outside Mr. Weiner's room until Ralphie opened the door and slipped out, eyes lowered, lips quivering. In that moment Audrey felt her son's failure as poignantly as if it were her own. Impulsively, she hugged her child, her baby. Had their intense family focus made it even more difficult? Maybe they shouldn't have fixed the special place in the rec room?

"Why don't you go sit in the car." Audrey's eyes lingered on his strong little fingers clutching his clarinet case. "Mommy will be out in a few minutes."

She glanced up to see Mr. Weiner gazing down. Having seen his fill, apparently, the old man teetered back into his studio. Rocking on his thick-soled shoes, he lunged for the bookcase, then a chair. He rounded the piano and settled his weight on the bench, looking as if he were profoundly sorry he'd ever left that spot in the first place. Holding her pocketbook before her, Audrey followed him in. This rumpled old man, she thought, is a saint. He's devoted his whole life to teaching others, children mostly, to make music. She had sat in on Ralphie's first lessons. She marveled at how the old man's gnarled and spotted hands moved so sinuously over the ebony shaft of his clarinet, producing such exquisite sounds. She was humbled by his resolution, by the vast reach of a long life given over to a single pursuit. At the same time, though, she knew Mr. Weiner unnecessarily frightened Ralphie with his stern rebukes.

"It's too soon for the boy," Mr. Weiner declared. "He wants maturity."

"Maybe," Audrey ventured, "if we helped him a little more? There're kids here even younger than him."

"Bring him back in a year."

"Do you think . . ."—Audrey struggled to find a diplomatic way to phrase this—". . . he might do better with another teacher?"

"He wants maturity! He doesn't practice!" The old man thumped the piano with the flat of his hand. "You cannot learn unless you practice, practice, practice!"

"I'm sorry, I didn't mean—"

"Sometimes," Mr. Weiner said, breaking in to offer her some consolation, "the gift takes a while to manifest itself." Like a magician pulling an endless scarf from his sleeve, he tugged a long handkerchief from his pocket and blew his nose. "Be patient. People nowadays have no patience. Maybe the school will refund your unused tuition. About that, you will have to talk to the people in the office. *That's* what I have no patience for," he harrumphed, "people in offices."

On her way downstairs Audrey saw the woman from the bank. Lurid purple coat, hair sticking out from beneath a pillbox hat that had revolved off-center, she was tussling with a boy about Ralphie's age. The boy, straining to free himself, swore at her. She yanked on his arm, hissed, and, that moment, looked up. Before Audrey could avert her head, their eyes met, and there leapt between them a mutual recognition. Taking advantage of the woman's inattention, the boy pried himself free. He clattered past Audrey, escaping into a practice room. The woman dashed after him. Audrey could no longer see them, but heard somebody being hit. Forcing herself to step up to the door, she peered in. The boy was holding his arms over his head, while the woman struck at him with a large book.

"Stop it!" Audrey ordered her. "What's the matter with you?"

The woman turned on her. "None of your business!"

"This is a public place—if you want to discipline him, do it at home!"

For the second time now Audrey understood she had overstepped the bounds. She stared at the woman's sightless eye, wallowing in its radiant pink socket. "I don't know what the problem is," she continued. "If he's done something wrong, then he should be punished. But not by hitting him. And," she re-emphasized, having no idea why she felt so righteous about this, "not in *public.*"

"He stole my money."

The irony was almost too great to resist. "Well, he shouldn't be doing that." Audrey suppressed the compulsion to laugh. "That's wrong."

The woman seized the cuff of Audrey's jacket. "Don't think I don't know who you are. I can see right through this disguise, Eleanor."

The woman tossed the book on a harpsichord, producing within a small murmurous complaint. She shoved the boy past Audrey— that revolting smell—and out of the room. Audrey, once she was alone, her terrors given license, reached for the book, for no other reason than to give herself a task, to return it to the shelves, then began flipping through it. Her hands were cool and trembly; the bones issued those strange pangs. The book, for children, was a biography of Mozart, pastel drawings of a little boy sitting primly at a clavichord, poring over music scores. *What would anyone living now,* she thought irritably, *know about Mozart the boy?* Wasn't he the one with the horrid father? What preposterous things people write! Audrey jammed the book on a shelf, shook herself, and went into the school office. Behind the counter, extracting staples from a stack of

Ralphie's Clarinet

handouts, was Sara Kennedy.

"Did you hear that?"

"I hear a lot that I don't hear," Sara said, "if that's what you mean?"

"Who *is* that? She was hitting her son with a book."

Sara considered Audrey's question. "You don't mean the lovely Mrs. Zurlo, do you? All I can say is good riddance. We can only let them fall so far behind before we put our foot down." She nodded at a scratched clarinet case on the counter. "That, they haven't paid *any* rental fees on since last year, not a penny."

"She called me Eleanor. Why would she do that?"

Sara glanced at Audrey quizzically. "Are you okay?"

Audrey forced herself to smile. "I feel sorry for the boy."

"Well, that part *is* a shame. Jacob refuses to have anything to do with her, but he likes the boy, and he's pretty stingy with his praise."

Audrey recollected Ralphie alone outside. "I think I know the answer to my question," she said to hurry the conversation, "but is there any refund for unused lessons?"

"Only up until four weeks into the semester."

"Mr. Weiner said Ralphie isn't ready and that I should ask for a refund."

"God bless our artistes," Sara muttered. "There is *no* refund after four weeks, and Jacob knows that perfectly well. We can move Ralphie, if you want? Maurice has a few holes in his schedule. He's piano."

Audrey shook her head. "Mr. Weiner's probably right—he's not ready." She considered her next words, rejected the impulse, then voiced them anyway. "Could we transfer Ralphie's unused lessons to another boy?"

Sara set down, rather crossly, the clamp she was using. "Why is it," she complained, "that people can't do the simplest things? I specifically told Bunny she was *not* to staple these." Sara adopted an official tone. "School policy allows for tuition refunds up until four weeks into the semester, as I *said,* less the nonrefundable administrative fee, and, no, of course, tuitions can't be transferred. If we started doing that, we'd be nailing boards over our windows in a week."

"I know it's unusual, but how would that hurt the school?"

Sara reached for the ringing phone. "If your son's thinking of dropping out," she said acidly, "you're welcome to advertise his clarinet for sale on the bulletin board. That's why we recommend that parents rent their children's first instruments."

The following week Ralphie announced that for his school project he intended to construct a Van de Graaff generator. Neither Audrey nor Ted had ever heard of such a thing. When they discovered a Van de Graaff generator was a metal sphere as wide as a refrigerator that produced two-feet arcs of electricity, they put an immediate stop to those plans. Ted, recalling something from a high-school science class, suggested they use a lemon to generate a weak electrical current. Audrey, filled with visions of her son electrocuting himself, was still dubious, but Ted assured her it was perfectly safe, and he and Ralphie went shopping for a suitable lemon.

The Hamms were home. Except for a bumpy return flight that upset the maternal Hamm's sensitive tummy, the cruise evidently had been a spectacular success. By way of several sly remarks and what appeared to be an unlikely Caribbean swagger in Mr. Hamm's step across their tiny lobby, Audrey and Mazi were led to understand that aboard ship a certain marital rejuvenation had taken place. For that, the two coworkers, exchanging glances, were grateful: Bank life would be easier with the Hamms' felicity restored.

Later that morning, Mr. Hamm leaned over Audrey's shoulder. "Any more problems with that nutcake while I was away?"

"Haven't seen her," Audrey lied.

~ ~ ~

Their home was a pigsty, and Audrey wouldn't stand for it.

Bad enough that even with a full-time job she still had to shop and cook, was she expected to do the cleaning, too? Was this a hotel people checked in and out of? Were they waiting for the maid to show up with her mop? Ted, Jr., uncharacteristically out of bed early on a Saturday and sorry for it, was the first to catch her ire. "I want," Audrey demanded, "all the summer stuff, the lawn chairs, the table, the umbrella, everything, put away. Next, the windows need to be washed if anyone expects to see out of them and the storm windows slid down. When you're done with that, broom down the cobwebs in the basement. You might as well empty the dehumidifier and push it under the stairs, while you're at it."

The boy sulked. "Mom, I had plans."

"If you apply yourself, you can get everything done by noon. What're the chances that any of your buddies will be up before then? Besides, you're not going anywhere anyway—and you know this— until we've talked about your homework."

Ted, sleeping late—sleeping off too much wine, Audrey feared, noting the empty bottle in the kitchen beside the garbage—caught it next. Heaven knows, she was trying to be sympathetic. She understood that her husband's confidence in himself, despite his bluster, was fragile and, this year, had been all-but shattered. Twenty-three years of seniority, a responsible salaried position, technician in a metallurgical laboratory—gone in a flash. Son of a hopeless dipsomaniac, Ted had always taken pride in not following in his father's footsteps. Now, on top of everything else, he had begun to drink. Not like his dissipated father, not week-long binges; nevertheless, any overdrinking of his made her anxious.

This morning, however, she was without pity. "Either you rake the leaves, or I'm calling a service. Are you headed off to that potato stand today?"

Irritable before he'd had his coffee, Ted cupped his forehead in his hand to ease a headache. He was a lean, intense man with dark hair that ended in a sharp widow's peak. "Later," he grumbled. "And I was waiting until all the leaves were down."

"Well, don't I have good news for you," Audrey sang out brightly, "the last leaf just fell ten minutes ago!"

Hair cinched in a bandanna, Audrey started on the second floor with her rags and her Pledge. From time to time she glanced out to watch both the Teds in her life laboring below in the yard. Especially, she fretted over the younger one. She recalled clapping Teddy in her arms on the doorstep when Ted brought him home from West Virginia. So uncontrollably had she begun crying that she started to cough, whooping for air. She was convinced that she had lost him, that he had been assaulted, murdered, his bloody body thrown in a roadside ditch.

My child, she had mumbled, clutching him, *my child, my child . . .*

The boy was taller, more manly, suddenly handsome. Was that a good thing? Don't be silly—of course, it was. But Teddy had a propensity to skim the surface, and that concerned her. He appeared to be taking reasonably well to the special educational program at Our Lady of the Sacred Heart that she had enrolled him in over the bitter objections of Ted, but, even so, she agonized that by her forcing him into the program she had forfeited some essential portion of his trust. With Ted, he had long been sullen, resentful and uncommunicative. And now he was that way with her, too. It was as if he had gone underground. Anguished, she stole glances at him, showered by a luxuriant autumnal sunlight, fighting the umbrella, wrestling the chaise lounge into the garage, taking no pleasure in the tasks, no

Ralphie's Clarinet

pleasure in the day. Inside, he went at the windows just as bellicosely, yanking down the storm panes, ramming up the screens. She could hear him swearing under his breath, swearing steadily, savagely, the way a disgruntled middle-aged man swears.

On the windows he left great brown smears.

During one of her trips to the basement Audrey spotted Ralphie's clarinet on the floor and carried it upstairs. Ralphie's assignments had been to redd up his room, collect the scattered pieces of the space station model he was building, and clean the hamster's cage. When she checked on him, he had done nothing and was paging through a Harbor Freight catalog. Ralphie liked to cut out pictures of tools and appliances—chrome machines that polished shoes, jigsaws, soldering irons—that he felt he had to have. Beside him lay a sizable pile of clippings.

"We should make a decision on your clarinet," she said. He absolutely would need to clean the hamster's cage. "It shouldn't be left lying around."

About his failed endeavor Ralphie was still sensitive. It was the most public thing he had ever attempted. Moisture collected along the bottom rims of his eyes. Audrey reached out to him, drawing him in. "It's okay, darling," she murmured. "You gave it your best. We can just put it up. Maybe you'll want to try it again next year?"

He shook himself.

"Do you want me to take care of it?"

He nodded, his hair against her cheek.

When Ted, later that evening, fumbled with the bedside lamp, Audrey, who'd been pretending to be asleep, pretended to wake. Into the bedroom he brought the smell of whiskey. His hands, even his wrists, were brown with dirt from the potatoes. "We need," she said, "to keep sending out your resume." Her father had labored in the steelworks. Her grandparents were Lithuanian, peasants, people who worked the land. She wasn't embarrassed by a workman's rough hands. But her husband's darkened wrists provoked her ire. "We'll go through the paper tomorrow. I'll type the letters."

"I don't need your help going through the want-ads," he said. "I'll tell you right now what'll be there: three lab techs—all in hospitals—two more in clinics, two more after that in medical offices. I can show them how to test their steel for purity."

"What about the job-retraining program at the community college?"

"I–will–go–through–the–ads, okay?"

There are deceits in all marriages, places that harden over. But this—her husband's depression, no, his *unwillingness* to do anything about it—was intolerable. "I put the clarinet up," she said, changing the subject. "He's not using it."

"That's not my fault."

"I didn't say it was, Ted."

"He lost interest in it—little kids'll do that."

"But you were home, *here*," Audrey cried, unable to stop herself. "You could have encouraged him more. Kept him practicing. He *is* a little boy—you let him down!"

Foot snagged in his pajamas, Ted reeled about the room. "What the hell do I know about music?"

The day that had started so promising, the busy cleaning, the crisp sheets and fragrant towels, had turned to ashes. Ted squirmed in the covers for a few minutes, his back to her, then began to snore. Sometimes, when Audrey couldn't sleep, she would go downstairs and work the crossword puzzle. Sometimes, warm milk would help. Tonight, she went to the hall closet and lifted down the clarinet. In the darkness of the home she feared she might lose, she held the clarinet against her breast, then put it out on the kitchen counter to take back to the store Monday.

Ralphie's Clarinet

~ ~ ~

For two weeks now, the clarinet had been riding in the backseat of her car. The instrument was worth half of what they paid for it. The manager at Shea's had made that clear when they'd bought it. Even so, the sum wasn't insignificant. But what had kept Audrey from returning the clarinet was the memory of that other boy, arms arched above his head, while his mother rained down on him blow after blow. He was a short, sinewy little kid with pointy elbows. His hair was cut short on his perfectly round skull so that his head resembled a spherical bristly brush. He wore shorts and an ill-fitting sports jacket, although the jacket seemed wrong. *Was* it a sports jacket? No matter, what the scene revealed was abuse, not discipline, and, worse, suggested even more terrible things going on behind closed doors. That she could do little about, but she did have something she could give the family. But every time Audrey tried to concoct some indirect scheme of getting the clarinet into the boy's hands, she shrank before the peculiarity of the notion. Some days she talked to the clarinet. *What am I going to do with you? What would I think—let alone an unbalanced person— if a stranger knocked on my door and offered me a clarinet? And if they can't afford lessons, what use is an instrument anyway?*

What brought her decision to a head had nothing to do with the clarinet. At lunch today Audrey accidentally drove down a patch of Sutton Post Road she had been avoiding. Passing the ramshackle, homemade potato stand and seeing Ted standing behind a cart of rotting potatoes—like a hobo—filled her with rage. When she got back to the bank, she slammed through the cabinet in the breakroom in search of the telephone directory. Even for Ganaego, *Zurlo* was an unusual name. She had no trouble finding what she wanted. On Chestnut Lane in Rose Township resided the single Zurlo in the entire Ganaego Valley, George B. Zurlo.

The drive, as it turned out, was longer than expected. Chestnut

Lane, not as bucolic as its name implied, wound past a public dump and a basin where a swamp had risen and killed a stand of trees. The barkless trunks, some clothed in withered vines, stood rotting in slimy water. Long ago, when her father would take the family on meandering Sunday drives out into the country, they would sometimes come down into a hollow and see, spread before them, an entire hillside blighted by disemboweled cars, upside down iceboxes, moldering sofas and old school buses covered in brambles. Not a junkyard, not a business, as lamentable as that might be, but somebody's personal, lifelong desecration of the landscape. Amid these hodgepodges of scrap would often stand shabby, unfinished houses, weathered shells sheathed in peeling tarpaper. Such places threw Audrey into despondency: weedy yards, toddlers in undershirts and no diapers, the sense of hardscrabble lives lived out in anxiety and pathos. Tonight, as she drove deeper into the country, straining to read the names on the mailboxes, the smaller and meaner the houses became and the more her fortitude, like a rope under increasing stress, threatened to snap. Then, when she noodled around a bend and saw a sloping valley given over to piles of rotting lumber and rusty machines, she somehow knew that *this* would turn out to be—and indeed was—the home of the Zurlo family.

And at that moment her courage did indeed fail her.

What had seemed a praiseworthy undertaking now seemed inexplicable, even bizarre, a well-intentioned but dreadful mistake. But nobody ever promised that doing good would be easy, and Audrey, deciding that this clarinet was all she had to offer, and, that as such, she had no right not to offer it, squeezed the steering wheel and determinedly navigated her car down a rutted drive. If the boy's father pawned the instrument and drank up the money, so be it.

The next decision was whether to walk down to the garage, whose chimney sent up a tatter of gray smoke, and deal with Mr.

Ralphie's Clarinet

Zurlo, or knock on the door of the house and confront the boy's unstable mother. Audrey chose the former and made her way down the slope. The building, even from a distance, smelled of grease and corrosion. She could hear a radio, the banging of metal on metal, and voices, the voices of men, bellowing like steers. In her business suit and heels she felt vulnerable. She had brought her purse—rather than making a show of locking her car—and with that and the clarinet case to carry she felt burdened and uncomfortable.

"Hello!" she shouted. "Hello there!"

The voices paused, then resumed. *Should she shout again?* She did not want to go in there. Granted, what she had in mind was unusual, but it could be explained in a moment or two. She had her speech worked out. She had been practicing it the whole drive out.

"Hellooooo? Is anybody home?"

This time the voices ceased definitively, and a boy about Ted, Jr.'s age emerged, wiping his hands on a red rag no less greasy than his hands. He wore a T-shirt with the cuffs rolled up to show his muscles. On one arm was a tattoo. Audrey was outraged: What was a boy his age doing with a tattoo? He squinted at her as if he were nearsighted. "What you got in there, lady—a gun?"

"It's a clarinet," Audrey said, thrown off balance by the drift of his imagination. "Doesn't one of your brothers play a clarinet?"

And now, when the boy looked baffled, on the verge of hostility, it came to her that perhaps she had misheard Sara: It never occurred to her to question that. She took a step back. "Maybe I've made a mistake," she said. "I was looking for a boy whose mother is named Mrs. Zurlo, I think? He plays the clarinet. He goes—or used to go—to the music school in Oak Grove."

"You from that school? Whaddya want with us?"

From behind a truck out stepped a man dressed in pin-striped overalls browned by oil and grease. Not a big man, he had dark, sparse hair that fell across his forehead and failed to cover an ugly scab along his temple. Like the boy, he squinted. "We paid you what we owed you. We don't owe nothing more."

"I'm not from the school," Audrey said. "My son was a student there, too, but then he dropped out. He wasn't ready, you see? Mr. Weiner wants me to bring him back in a year, but, knowing Ralphie, I don't think he's going back." This had nothing to do with her speech. She struggled to find her way back to it, then gave up. "Here," she said, holding out the clarinet and feeling very stupid. "It's worth a hundred dollars at Shea's." She was *not* to tell them that. She had vowed to keep the price of the instrument out of the conversation. "I can't help with his lessons, but I can help with his instrument, see?"

The boy's father did not see, nor did he take the case. "We didn't ask for no clarinet."

"I know you didn't, it's just something your boy might use and our son doesn't want."

That sentence happened to be from her speech. Why it had picked this particular moment to come sailing back into her brain, Audrey had no idea.

"We don't need no charity."

"It's *not* charity, not exactly."

"I think it's stolen, Pop," the boy said.

"Shaddup." He turned on his son. "What're you hanging around here for? I need your help, I'll give you a holler." After the boy left— his shoulders, precisely as Teddy's would, expressing his towering disdain—Mr. Zurlo gazed at Audrey. "You should come inside and explain this. I ain't saying no, and I ain't saying yes. Come inside and we'll talk."

Audrey held out the clarinet case again. "Can't I just give it to you?"

"Look, you want to get back in your car and drive the hell off my property, that's fine with me!" Mr. Zurlo reached out before Audrey could react, not taking the clarinet but grabbing her wrist, not hard but firm. "You haven't even tol' me your name, you seem to know mine."

"Audrey," she said, frightened by his grasp. "Audrey Bachelor."

"Well, you come inside, Audrey," he said, releasing her. "We'll talk to Buster and his mother. I still don't get why you want to give us something that belongs to you."

The house was two-story, not blackened planks covered in tarpaper, but years and years had elapsed since those clapboards had seen paint. Mr. Zurlo went up a few steps and opened a side door for her. Audrey reluctantly stepped inside. She smelled the pungent odor she'd smelled before, then heard cats mewing and recognized its source: cat urine. Mr. Zurlo led her down a hallway and they emerged into one vast room, the entire first floor. Never had Audrey seen such a remarkable thing: a house without rooms. Down two sides stretched long clothing racks, like in a store, with everybody's clothes hanging in plain sight. Scattered here and there were card tables heaped with boxes of donuts and cupcakes, while other, more substantial, tables held those enormous cans of green beans and jars of mayonnaise you see in the back shelves of grocery stores. In a corner were several colossal crates of toilet paper, and lying over the few pieces of furniture in the center were sheets, blankets, and pillows, everything furry with animal hair.

Surely, Audrey thought, they don't sleep down here—*with the cats?*

She turned and close by, at her elbow, was the woman's face, shriveled and brown as a berry. "Motors," she said, pointing at her husband, "that's all he cares about. Ask him how many motors he's got? Go ahead, ask him: trucks, cars, tractors and lawnmowers—if it doesn't have a motor, he's not interested in it!"

"Audrey here," Mr. Zurlo said, "wants to give Buster a clarinet worth a hundret dollars, no strings attached." He turned to Audrey. "That's right, ain't it, no strings?"

Audrey nodded twice. "It's something we can't use and maybe your son can?"

From a chair Mr. Zurlo gathered up an armload of blankets, disturbing a cat nestled within. The creature, sluggish with sleep, tunneled out between his legs. Mr. Zurlo indicated Audrey was to sit there, then left the room. On her lap Audrey held both her purse and the clarinet. She had been too self-conscious to examine the chair before she sat. This was her good business suit. If anything happened to it, she'd die. Where had Mr. Zurlo gone? Mrs. Zurlo, not bothering to take up the blankets on the sofa, simply plopped down. With her one functioning eye she stared at Audrey. "You from that school?"

Had the woman forgotten her from the bank? She prayed so. "No, no, not at all. I mean my son was a student there for a little while, that's all."

"That old man's a bully, he pinched him!"

As opposed to battering him with a book? Mr. Weiner was strict with his pupils, but Audrey sincerely doubted that the old man would pinch someone's child. Not knowing quite what to say, however, all she managed to do was smile weirdly at the weird woman. Just then Mr. Zurlo reappeared, the boy herded before him. The child had an anxious look, as if he was convinced he was about to be charged with some wrongdoing. Mr. Zurlo urged him forward.

"You talk to Audrey about what she's fixing to do," he said. "As long as there's no strings, I don't give a hoot one way or the other."

The boy was wearing shorts and the sports jacket she recalled. The jacket, nearly as browned with dirt as his father's overalls, was too long for him. His hair was trimmed exactly as she remembered.

Ralphie's Clarinet

With his old-fashioned clothes, his pointy nose, his dark suspicious eyes and anxious furrows across his forehead, he seemed an unusual sort of child. Audrey held out the clarinet case, begging him to take it.

The boy accepted the instrument. His father slid a straight-back chair behind him, and he sat without looking. "Does it have a reed?"

Audrey nodded. "Everything should be there."

The boy lifted the clarinet free of its bed of crimson plush. "Is it a *good* reed?"

"I wouldn't know. I don't know much about them."

"It's not broken in, I can tell that."

Whether the boy meant the reed or the clarinet itself was unclear. Once he had the instrument assembled, he brought it to his lips, moistened the mouthpiece, and began to play. What piece he had chosen, Audrey couldn't say. And, to be honest, the sound did not move her, not like the honeyed tones Mr. Weiner drew from his clarinet. But it was music the Zurlo child was making, not bleats, not squawks. Notes took shape, tumbled over one another and filled the foul-smelling open space of the disorderly room as a flock of birds might. More than the music, however, it was the boy himself who captured Audrey's attention. *How dirty he was!* You'd need to soak him in a tub for three hours, and even then you might not get all the grime off. But boys were like that. Ralphie was no different. What was different about this child was the completeness of his self-absorption. Eyes closed, face scrunched, he bent his bristly head over the clarinet, his filthy fingers going determinedly at the keys. His thin bare legs bounced and the toes of his heavy shoes absently scuffed the floor. One of his socks, the elastic given out, slipped down his fleshless calf, loosely rimming his ankle. Watching him, his single-minded involvement in his playing, Audrey knew, even if she was murdered here on the spot, that she had done the right thing.

When he finished, she asked, "What *was* that?"

"A sonatina."

~ ~ ~

Audrey pulled into the T&V parking lot. She had decided to buy the family a treat, some Neapolitan ice cream. But what she really wanted was an excuse to sit in the dark for a moment with the doors locked. As she had stepped out of the Zurlos' house into the fresh air, Mrs. Zurlo, clapping her hands at a private joke, craned herself over the porch railing like a schoolgirl to whisper in Audrey's ear.

"With a hundred dollars you could buy yourself a pretty good gun, wouldn't you say?"

So spooked was Audrey that she took a wrong turn and drove back around the swamp, this time on the far side. The boles of the drowned trees, black and ghastly, glimmered in the moonlight. She heard ululating sounds, shrieks, howls. She was terrified she'd end up back at the Zurlos. But the road unexpectedly intersected the state route, and she pressed the accelerator, skidded on the crumbling macadam, and fled toward Ganaego.

She could still feel Mr. Zurlo's grip on her wrist. Tomorrow, she vowed, either Ted got himself cleaned up and enrolled in that job-retraining program at the community college—or he was moving out.

Invisible Weaving

Autumn 1983

Halloween, the day as dry as a biscuit, Nettie Bachelor stood on her porch scanning the street anxiously. She picked at the hem of her coat. This idea of going to Barrington was hers, and placing the call to the attorney and setting everything in motion, doing something so momentous without her younger son's knowledge, plunged her in regret. Going behind people's backs was not something she did. But she had come to understand that Ted had his own problems—losing his job, then hitting a rough patch with Audrey—and so, for better or worse, she had decided she couldn't sit on her hands waiting for everybody else to solve their problems before starting in on her own.

Time was short, and she had another son to worry about.

Shortly after the town clock struck noon, a large car pulled up before the row houses on Roosevelt Avenue. The sedan was cucumber-green with tinted windows. As the attorney stepped around the front of it, Nettie recognized him from their encounter last year, the night at the police station. And because of that night, she did not lodge her trust totally in him, yet she had overridden her suspicions and phoned his office in the union hall anyway. Her instincts told her that Harvey Silverstein was the fellow she needed. But here already, she was put on alert: The plan had been for him to remain in his car and toot his horn.

Clutching her pocketbook, she hollered as she started down the walk, "Coming!"

"Certainly." Stopped in his tracks, Harvey reversed himself and swung open the door of the car for her. That wasn't necessary, but she appreciated the gesture. He was short, hardly taller than she, not much thatch left on his top, big, black, square-framed glasses. "Mrs. Bachelor," he said with a small flourish, "you look like you're dressed for a drive in the country."

He smelled like cigars and so did his swanky car. That helped. Went a good ways to confirming her hunch: Men who smell like cigars know how to arrange things. They write contracts that get signed and can tell you who you need to speak to in city hall. They also tip better, her husband Gunther had maintained, a man who went to his grave smelling like a Dutch Masters panatela. It was her German Club Ladies Auxiliary dress. She'd had to nip in the waist.

"Just so we understand the ground we're standing on," she said, sitting upright, pocketbook in her lap, "I don't need a Cadillac to drive to the Goose Family Spa, if you know what I mean? Nothing fancy."

"We shall dispense with any and all trappings." Harvey smiled widely and rolled the big car into traffic. "No lawyerly jargon, no gold seals. If you don't mind, I suggest we take the back roads, the old way to Barrington? I actually think it's faster than the freeway."

"That's how Hugo came when he visited. Course he couldn't take that tiny scooter on the big roads anyway. Trucks would have blown him away like a bit of dandelion fluff."

"Your brother drove a scooter?"

"Oh, I don't know what it was—some kind of toy motorcycle. Sounded like a hornet. You'd hear the pennywhistle of its motor long before you saw it. Set your teeth on edge. He'd buzz it all the way up to Ganaego and consent to sit long enough to have a glass of iced tea, then he'd buzz it back home. Sometimes he'd stop first at Stahrenberger's for a box of chocolates for Rags. You can't get better chocolates than Stahrenberger's—anywhere."

"That's true," Harvey agreed.

"When my brother put his helmet on, all you'd see was his big French nose poking out. Are you, by chance, a wine drinker, Mr. Silverstein?"

"My lady friend and I have been known to enjoy a glass at dinner, yes."

She took that in, and, as they fell under the spell of Western Pennsylvania's golden autumnal countryside, she glanced at a rundown house they were passing. A woman was pinning her wash on a rope draped the length of the porch. She seemed tired and rundown herself. How many times had that poor woman laundered her husband's drawers, her children's frocks and britches, her own slips gone sheer with age? "Remind me," Nettie said, "to fix you up with some of Hugo's wine. If your friend doesn't take a shine to it, you can use it to strip your furniture."

"I remember your brother's shop, Mrs. Bachelor. It sat across from the courthouse, did it not? I have the distinct memory of an indomitable sort of man, despite his short stature, standing in a white jacket beside a barber pole, arms folded across his chest. I take it you remained close?"

Sticking up from the breast pocket of the attorney's suit were three glass tubes that perplexed her. The tubes were filled with a brown liquid that silently splashed with the motion of the car. She had taken to Harvey Silverstein's raffish smile even back in the police station where it was clear that her son Ted had enlisted the lawyer in a plot that threatened her older boy. *Shoot,* the only crime that Rags had committed was to show up at a vegetable market he'd worked at for twenty-five cents an hour for forty years to help move the turnips. But let bygones be bygones, the Tambellinis had withdrawn their complaint, and, when this fall she decided she required the services of a lawyer, she recalled that reckless smile of Harvey Silverstein's and his vest. Gunther wore vests, at least the years he tended the big bar at the Briggs Hotel.

"The day Hugo retired," she said, "he bought that fool scooter. He was seventy-two. He had more—you'll see—camping gear than Savage's Hardware. He bragged he had slept under the stars in every state of the union. A lot of tramps could make that same claim, I told him. He was my big brother, even though he wasn't very big like you say, he nursed our father and then our mother when I couldn't and kept their graves neat, and so, yes, I am bereaved."

"No other brothers or sisters?"

"Just the two of us." She thought of the mortician who, for reasons known but to him, elected to dress Hugo with a white scarf instead of a necktie at the throat. "Mr. Silverstein, I have a question for you: Do you think the steelworks are going to reopen?"

"I don't have any inside dope, but I doubt it."

The mill had been dark for nearly three months now, an enormous silent hulk along the river. Nettie thought of her son Ted, his certainty that the conglomerate would change its mind and reopen the works. "I don't think so, either," she said.

"Ganaego's in for a serious tumble, I fear."

Nettie folded her hands on her pocketbook. "Hugo's old house has been shut up so long even the ghosts must be stir crazy by now. I should've done this a long time ago."

"Hard to let go sometimes." The attorney concentrated on his driving. "I held on to my wife's things for years and years."

She took that in, too. Life, Antoinette Bachelor had long ago decided, could be sliced like a rhubarb tart into three generous pieces: *Then, Now,* and *Coming.* Things worked better if you kept them separate: your memories; the day's passing tribulations; tomorrow's worries. But like it or not, *Coming*—like Father Opsatnick swinging his smoldering thurible—had sailed into *Now,* and Nettie settled herself in the deep cushions of the attorney's luxurious automobile in the full and fateful knowledge that she had no choice but to go through with this double-dealing.

~ ~ ~

If Pennsylvania were a pool table, then Barrington, fifty miles southwest of Ganaego, would have been a corner pocket. Hugo's house perched on the high side of one of the town's tree-lined streets, just beyond the business district. Nettie directed Harvey Silverstein to turn upward into the alley behind Hugo's and park there. Then they took the cement staircases that stepped down the backyard's three steep terraces. Nettie gave Harvey the key and he worked it in the tarnished brass lock until the mechanism yielded. Inside, the wood floors, long asleep beneath a nap of dust, creaked under their advancing tread. Wisps of spider gossamer dangled from the light fixtures. A moth rose from the folds of a dusty curtain and flapped woozily off. Nettie stood in the living room without taking off her coat.

"We are survived by our things." She appealed to the lawyer. "What do you *do* with people's belongings? Gunther used to say, just throw me out with the trash when I die. And there were times, lemme tell you, when I wasn't in the mood to wait until he expired. As much as I loved my brother, I can't honestly say there's a single thing of his I pine for."

"I have an associate who specializes in liquidations." Harvey was examining the books stacked about, by the Morris chair, on the tables, in the window seat. Beside the fireplace a glass-front bookcase was double-stacked with still more books. "Liquidations of the deceased and the divorced—I don't know which is more sorrowful. With your permission, I will call him. Mrs. Bachelor, may I point out that the books in this bookcase, all travel books if I don't miss my guess, are organized by geography and, within those geographical groupings, alphabetically by author? Did you have any difficulty probating the will?"

"A fellow down here took care of all that for me. And everything, as you say, was very well organized. Hugo's will was dated May 1, 1939."

"I'm not surprised."

Nettie, brushing the dust from a lamp shade, sneezed, then fell to coughing hoarsely. She tugged her hanky from inside her sleeve to cover her mouth. "I'm going to get a glass of water," she managed to eke out. "Would you like one?"

"Why don't you sit? I'll get it."

She waved him off. "I know where everything is."

"I'd advise you to run the water in the tap for a while first."

Nettie watched the attorney slide open a drawer and rustle through the papers within. Before your doctor and your lawyer you are naked: She prayed that her instincts had not betrayed her. "Barrington always had sweeter water than Ganaego," she remarked. "Couldn't tell you why."

"Springs, probably. Ganaego pumps from the river."

"Well, that would explain it."

You could crack a rib coughing. Collecting herself, Nettie lingered a moment in the kitchen, reintroducing herself to a diagonal of sunlight falling across the table in a fuzzy slant she recalled as if it were a dear friend. She grew up washing and drying dishes in this room, rolling out pastry, plucking pinfeathers from chickens. When she looked around, she saw and didn't see the deep double sink propped up by slender porcelain legs, the icebox, short with rounded shoulders, and the red and white checked linoleum across the counters, scorched with ring marks from red-hot pots set down carelessly half a century ago. As water from the spigot ran rust-red as a fox's tail, she idly opened the icebox, pulled a long face, then

Invisible Weaving

brought down two glasses from an oilcloth-covered shelf. Even long shut up, the kitchen still smelled like a kitchen. She could tell you where to find the fruit-patterned platter they used to carry the Easter lamb into the dining room; could, even with her eyes closed, reach down the proper spices for her mother's sweet and savory pies; could in a jiffy polish the delicate etched goblets with the gold rims in the china closet and pour out, for her father, drams of his Armagnac, and for her mother, her crème de cassis. The windows over the sink looked out on the terraced backyard: She thought of picnic tables beneath snowy white cloths, of music rising from the brass horn of a Victrola and warbling through a grape arbor. The day before she knew she was pregnant—knew it with the violence only a sixteen-year-old girl raised in a Roman Catholic family could know such a monstrous fact—she had helped her mother squeeze brilliant violet grape juice from a cone of butter muslin suspended from the ceiling. A few dead plants in small pots lined the windowsill.

"My mother was a gardener," she said, returning with her water. "Out of respect for her, Hugo kept her flowers flourishing. But it was the vegetables he raised on a plot of land he owned in the country that he loved. Beans, squash, tomatoes, garlic, onions, eggplant—a man serious about his eating, my brother. He treasured his Sunday supper, his wine, his pipe. He was a gifted cook, even better than my mother, which is going something."

Harvey had collected the mail that lay scattered under the slot in the front door. "I take it," he said, separating advertising circulars from letters, "we'll want to sell that, too, the country plot?"

"Everything, Mr. Silverstein."

Upstairs, the attorney marveled at the black wool suits they found hanging in Hugo's closet. "These are actually quite handsome." He ran his fingers approvingly along a crease. "And they appear to be identical. Isn't that interesting?"

"Gunther used to slander Hugo that he was the only person in North America who went camping in a three-piece suit. Would you . . ."—she agonized—"like them? They're kind of old fogeyish?"

"Rest assured," Harvey said, smiling, "we will locate a good home for these sturdy suits."

"I'll show you something—how those suits were made."

Nettie led the attorney down the hall, passing without comment the bedroom with sloping ceilings that once had been hers, and into a room converted into a workroom. She pointed at a very large sewing machine. "My father's, he worked at Vacherweill's all his life. He was their bespoke tailor. Papa would take a torn pocket or a frayed crease and do invisible weaving that really *was* invisible. Judges, politicians, big-time businessmen from Pittsburgh would order shirts from him. When he retired, he bought his old machine from Mr. Vacherweill and went on working. People brought their sons to the house to have Papa hand-sew them their first grown-up suits—for their confirmations, graduations, marriages. I had this dream of him someday making a suit for Gunther. Anyway"—Nettie waved a hand at the complicated sewing machine, its pulleys stitched with cobwebs—"you'll need two gorillas to haul that thing away."

Against the wall stood a tall desk. The top was amber-colored, while the cabinet below with its many small drawers was stained dark. "That's a watchmaker's bench," Harvey said. "Were any of your people jewelers?"

Nettie shook her head. "No idea where that came from. Hugo's camping buddy fixed watches—maybe that's where he got it?"

"Would you mind if I had a look through it?"

Harvey rifled through the drawers. Each held something unique: screw, bolts, washers, nails, tacks. Some held stationery supplies, also organized in categories, others held papers, receipts. Nettie thought of her jumbled china closet drawer—how it would scandalize her brother. The attorney surfaced with a checkbook, a ledger, and a tiny key. He rocked back on his heels, hand cupping his chin. Behind the square rims of his glasses his eyes swam hugely. He led them back into Hugo's bedroom, peered under the bed, then opened the closet and bent down to search under the black suits and into the far corners. Beside the dresser was a wooden chair. He dragged it over and stood on it to see deep into the top shelf. He struggled for a moment, then stepped down, a small strongbox in his arms.

"Pay dirt."

He set the box on the carpet and opened it with the key. Inside were papers, envelopes, manila folders. He flipped through the papers, nodding. "The moment I walked into this house, Mrs. Bachelor, I said to myself, 'Here is a lifelong bachelor, a man of civilization and rigor. We shall find everything we need, in perfect order.' And so we have." He held up the papers. "Copy of the deed, I assume the original is in your possession, copy of the will you probated, social security card, birth certificate, death certificates of your parents, these look like securities, his license to barber, warranties for his camping equipment, even the title of his Vespa, which, if I don't miss my bet, we will find in the garage in spotless condition. To be sure, there's nothing we absolutely need here. The counsel you previously retained has done most of the heavy lifting, but, if you have any concerns at all, Mrs. Bachelor, permit me to allay them: We will have no trouble in converting your brother's holdings into cash, precisely as you wish."

They climbed to the attic, where Hugo stored his camping equipment, in categories, on shelf after shelf, then Nettie, downstairs again, led the attorney through the back hall to the cellar door. She pointed out the rectangle on the wall where the family's original telephone had been. "I was the first person Hugo called when he had it installed. Then he scolded me for keeping him on the line and running up his bill. I do believe Hugo was more French than my parents."

She stepped sideways down the steps, clutching the rail with both hands. The mildew in the dank cellar set her to coughing, and she covered her mouth with her handkerchief. She pointed at a door, rounded on top and made of slats. Harvey, with some difficulty, pried it open. Inside stood racks of bottles sheathed in gray dust and densely ribboned in cobwebs. "Hugo claimed the spiders were his friends." Nettie balled her hanky in her fist to conceal it from the attorney. "Go on, take a few—more if you want?"

Gingerly, Harvey withdrew three bottles at random, making a point not to let them touch his suit. The bottles were unlabeled except for strips of tape around the necks on which the year of vintage had been printed. Upstairs, Nettie insisted on washing the bottles in the sink, then wrapped them in tea towels she found in a drawer her hand reached into instinctively. She slipped the gloved bottles into a grocery bag and presented them to him.

"Here's mud in your eye."

"We called it Pisano Red." The glass tubes in the attorney's pocket chimed merrily with his laughter. "On our street it was the Spinazolas. Thank you, I shall decant a bottle tonight."

"Just don't sue me if it gives you beriberi."

The attorney set the bag on the table. "Mrs. Bachelor, we need to talk."

Nettie sniffed at the scent of mothballs that seemed to permeate the closed-up house, worse today, she supposed, because of the afternoon's warmth. She remembered she needed to buy candy for the trick-or-treaters this evening, a holiday her boy Rags never quite fathomed: Why were you giving away the candy in the basket in the hall?

"Yes," she agreed, "we do."

~ ~ ~

"My mother used my formal name. She was the only one who

called me *Antoinette*. She didn't bear me a grudge the way Papa did, but she remained disappointed in me all her life, maybe because she *had* loved me so much? I was her princess and I disgraced her. And so, even though Papa died soon after I left—he was fourteen years older than Mama—our visits, Gunther and me and the baby, were few and far between. Hugo would have us down for Sunday picnics occasionally. And those, when they came, were dilly days, Mr. Silverstein."

They had decided to talk where they were, in the kitchen. They sat across from each other as the afternoon sunlight crept away from the windows. "There's a picnic table," Harvey said, "on the top terrace—we came past it?"

She respected men who noticed things. Most men didn't. "First thing, when we showed up—I'm thinking of when Gunther was driving the Studebaker he bought for thirty-five dollars, only one door worked—Hugo would take Gunther down to his shop and clip his hair. He'd slick down the thistle of his cowlick with pomade and dust his shoulders with talcum. While they were gone, I'd spread one of Mama's tablecloths across the table under the arbor and set it with her plate and crystal, and when they came back spiffed up and smelling like a couple of New Jersey swells we'd ferry up platters of Hugo's beef Bourguignon, his bouillabaisse, his coq au vin. And oh yes, we knew those dishes, Mr. Silverstein, my family knew those dishes."

She met the attorney's eyes squarely. There was no good reason to tell him these things, but, if he was going to help her dispose of her family's property, it was important that he see it as she recollected it, in its glory: The table ladened with food, the grapes hanging fat and perfumed from the trellises, Hugo's stories of mobsters and molls and politicians who confided in their little barber a tad more than was prudent. As the skies over Barrington colored, deepening from rose to caramel to plum, Hugo and Gunther would smuggle the Victrola out of the living room without waking her mother, and they'd have a candle-lit party swinging the baby around. Possessed even then of no more than a fringe of hair, the Jimmy Durante schnoz, Hugo, jabbering like a Marseilles street vendor, would rush into the garden and return, his arms burdened with the double peonies their mother raised, the tall gladioluses like unfurling scarves, the dahlias, the irises, and she—dizzy with wine, dizzy with love, dizzy with her new maternity that made her breasts warm and heavy with milk, this before she knew her baby was destined not to be like other babies—would plunge her head into those fragile blooms and drink the scent of life. You die *into* this world, Gunther had taught her, and, lying in the arms of that lovely, mixed-up man, she knew, despite the cabbagey odor he was known to bring with him to bed, about that Gunther was right.

But time was short. "What more do you need from me, Mr. Silverstein?"

The attorney removed his glasses and rubbed his eyes, then continued the motion, rubbing the loose skin of his scalp. He returned his big glasses to his nose. "Let me ask you some questions, if I may? It will help me in formulating a suitable strategy. On the surface it looks like all this will amalgamate into a respectable nest egg. I haven't much sense of housing values in Barrington, other than they've likely held up better than Ganaego's, but that is easily ascertained. The bank account appears depleted, and I will need to chat with the other lawyer to see if there are any loose ends, medical bills, utilities, property taxes, or liens we need to satisfy. Are there any other assets I should know about?"

"Just my own house. I don't suppose that's worth very much."

"I'm assuming Ganaego housing is going to decline sharply. With the mill's closure, I don't see how it can help but fall fast and hard."

"My Christmas Club," she brightened, "I forgot about that."

The attorney studied the grocery bag holding Hugo's wine, then moved it a few inches. "Please help me now while I do some thinking out loud? Just converting everything to cash is not going to be enough, do you agree with that? In fact, carrying the project through to that point but no further might actually prove unwise?"

Nettie understood where he was headed. "I know what you mean."

"Am I also correct in assuming that, while we're at it, we're going to need to draw up a will?"

Nettie nodded at that, too.

"Here's what I suggest," Harvey said. "A trust—and it needn't be fancy. A will for your assets, a trust for Hugo's—separate documents, separate purposes. Does that sound like a good start?"

"A good start," she agreed.

Harvey moved the bag another inch. "There are many kinds of trusts, we needn't go into that at the moment. But please help me out now: Am I also correct in thinking that, as far as any trust we design goes, its sole purpose is to provide for your elder son and"— he stopped to frown severely at the bag and move it back to where it had been—"it needs to be irrevocable? Do you know what I mean by that?"

Nettie looked at the ancient sink. She saw Hugo in a long, old-fashioned waiter's apron, cuffs of his starched white shirt folded back, wrists disappearing in suds. "My brother," she said, "was known to shop the grocery store for things that came in interesting bottles. He closed up his shop once to fly off to Louisiana to talk with a man about a woodpecker. You understand, Mr. Silverstein, my brother wasn't like other men? I was never sure whether he liked camping so much as he and his camping friend appreciated the privacy they found in the wilderness. I've not done fairly with my boys, I know I haven't. Ted bore more growing up than he should have. He was a seed in the wrong garden. I don't approve of what we're talking about here, I want you to know that, Mr. Silverstein. But if what you mean by *irrevocable* is that it can't be changed by anyone for any reason, then that's what I want."

"Until the death of your elder son?"

"Until he joins his mother and father, yes."

The attorney tapped the cork tops of his glass tubes with his fingertips. "You're not wearying of my questions, are you?"

Until this minute she hadn't been sure she would go through with this: It *wasn't* right, *wasn't* fair. What had been right were her instincts: Whatever mysterious potion was sloshing around in those glass tubes in his pocket, Harvey Silverstein was the man for the job. He was someone you could trust to get things done. "Fire away, I'm all ears."

Harvey smiled widely. "I don't believe that. But I need to ask two more questions. Will you need help finding a suitable situation for Rags—so it's in place when the time comes?"

"You don't know how much I've agonized over that."

"I'll start making some calls."

"You said two questions?"

Harvey shifted his grocery bag one last time. "And we need do all this quickly: Is that correct?"

"That's correct."

"Very quickly?"

"Very."

~ ~ ~

Making an excuse that he would go off to buy gas for the car and smoke a cigar, the attorney left Nettie alone in her brother's house for half an hour. She didn't need that much time, goodbyes were best when they were short. But she did wander through the dusty rooms, seeing Hugo and her parents, their friends and cousins and neighbors, holidays, birthdays, weddings, and funerals. She knew where in the attic the boxes of Christmas ornaments were stored, first cupboard beneath the eaves. She could tell you where the warm comforters could be found when snow filled the heavens over tiny Barrington and lay across the backyard terraces transforming them into tiers of a wedding cake. She thought about going upstairs and spending a few minutes in her bedroom and decided against that. Instead, she picked up a glass paperweight and studied the kaleidoscopic swirl of colors beneath the shimmering hemisphere of glass. Her mother's, a gift from her father on some anniversary long lost to memory. About to slip the paperweight into her coat pocket, she changed her mind about that too and set the paperweight back down where it had been.

Candy, Nettie Bachelor thought, can't forget to buy candy for the ghosts and tiny princesses tonight.

Mrs. Kattlove's Clerk

Summer 1971

"What are we to make of this, Mr. Wolding—this *stunt* you've pulled?"

"Ah, you know journalists, they sensationalize everything."

She was new, this woman. Their former caseworker, with whom he had established a working relationship, would have given him her Almira Gulch face, then accepted the story for what it was, a piece of zany stage business, and gone on to ask about his ward's grades. Not Virginia Poorman. She ran her finger—searching for something—down the front page of the *Chronicle*. "There was no motor in it? No motor? Were there, dear God, *brakes?*"

His experience with Family Court had taught Tody Wolding a few things, don't explain, don't argue. Risking the suspension of his rules, he said, "Sure, sure, we got a mechanical genius, Harold Robinson, literally born in a gas station. Harold was our Officer Dogberry. It was enclosed in a track, you see? Like a big chute? We didn't need a motor, it was a stage prop, that's all, a mock car, a giant soapbox derby."

The curls of Mrs. Poorman's white hair were as stiff as cup hooks. She shook them in a tidy passion of disapproval. "Sailing down from the roof? Mr. Wolding, you're thirty years old—have you no commonsense?"

"We thought it all through."

"Thought *what* through? You could've killed yourself."

"Nah, there wasn't any—"

"As well as"—Mrs. Poorman cut him off—"the actress fool enough to be in that car with you—and I don't care a hang if it was a *mock* car, whatever that means. For pity's sake, it says here you nearly ended up in the lake? What were you thinking?"

He was a small man. The air-conditioner, gurgling on its phlegm in the window, chilled him through his light shirt. He chided himself: He should've worn a suit and tie. Costumes were important. So was contrition, even mock contrition. *Don't argue.* "You're right, one hundred percent." Tody Wolding gave it his actor's best. "Super dumb move."

Finding no summons within herself to respond to his remorse, Mrs. Poorman fell to her papers, comforting herself in their bureaucratic blandness and predictability. In the heavy silence, Tody studied the floor. Strands of gluey hair wound around the base of the desk legs; fumes of stale cologne rose in the air like turpentine. The soulless government office brought back the smear of afternoons that he and Shelly, his half-sister, had sat on their hands waiting in judges' chambers. But the thing was, speaking in his own defense, it had *not* been a dumb move, Harold Robinson's motorless DeSoto. The forsaken vehicle, a convertible coupe from the 1940s, wrested from a soupy pasture and redolent of cows and crows, had been inspired, the climax of a climactic year. Reaching the limits of what he and his half-sister could endure, Tody succeeded in having his stepfather declared incompetent, removed from the house, and institutionalized. It had not been pleasant: George Namarian had not gone gently into that good night. And on Shelly it had fallen hard. With the illness and death of their mother and George's descent into alcoholic psychosis, Shelly, entering her teenage years, could not have escaped feeling that she was witnessing her life—*all* life—unraveling at the seams. Even though Tody had for a decade essentially functioned as her parents, he was not her mom, not her dad. Confronted, however, with the dissolution of their household, they fell into a prickly partnership and formed an ersatz family, as Tody—unmarried, an effeminate man who clerked in a yardage shop, someone subject to small-town innuendo—strived to gain the court's reluctant confidence. And from that precarious victory, as if released from an evil spell, he had decided out of the blue to persuade his ragtag troupe of amateur thespians, the Lake Biddleford Players, to undertake the challenge of a Shakespearean play.

That was madness.

The weed-entwined hulk of the DeSoto, once somebody's rolling boudoir, made a huge sucking *smuuuuch!* as Harold's tow truck hoisted it from the mire. They had to be insane. Ask anyone in community theater: the complexity of Shakespeare's Elizabethan grammar; the length of the speeches to commit to memory; the size of the cast required; the suspension of disbelief you are calling upon an unschooled audience to exhibit—*Who's that man behind the tree? Why can't they see him?* Oh, it was audacious, it was demented, it was glorious.

But not if it destroyed their lives.

Virginia Poorman, satisfied with the disposition of her documents—perused, sniffed at, stacked—returned to him her troubled gaze. "Mr. Wolding, you know our only purpose here is to safeguard Shelly? She's undergone what appear to be some rather traumatic experiences for a young girl, I know you must recognize that?"

That actually sounded sincere. "That's true," he admitted. "She has."

"I'm going to visit tomorrow, and I'm going to ask that we have a good frank talk. And I want Shelly there, too, I want to hear from her. She's old enough to be part of this conversation. Two should we say? You own a fabric shop, is that what I read here?"

"No, no, I just clerk in one—Kattlove's. Would it be easier if we came here?"

Ignoring him, her confusion persisting, the woman let her eyes drop again to the *Chronicle*. "Some things I still don't grasp? This chute business? It extended—is that it?—all the way through the audience?"

The paper that lay before her was replete with apocalyptic reports of anti-war riots, chemicals and bombs falling in jungles, politicians at each other's throats—and their caseworker was obsessed with a chute. "Well, no, not exactly."

"Then how far exactly—to use your word—*did* it extend?"

He forced himself not to squirm like a schoolboy caught in a prank. "To the bottom."

"The bottom of *what?*"

"The lodge, in front of the verandah."

"So, you were, in essence then, by the time you reached the audience"—Virginia Poorman's eyes on him, reflecting her dawning comprehension of the scene her imagination was gradually painting in, grew round with disbelief—*"free-wheeling,* if that's the proper expression?"

"Well, yeah, I guess you could say that."

"You drove a car straight *through* a seated audience?"

"But see, we thought of that? We had ropes everywhere and we made the center aisle plenty wide since we were staging the play outside and had tons of room, so it wasn't—"

Mrs. Poorman's hardened curls quivered. Breaking in on him as if he were no more than an errant schoolboy, she cried out, "Let me ask you a question—*two* questions, pardon me! *One,* was your sister in that audience? And *two,* did you think of *her* safety, Mr. Wolding, *ever?"*

~ ~ ~

Honestly, it had never crossed his mind.

On the drive back to Ganaego, Tody had time to ponder the caseworker's questions. Where *had* Shelly been? Terribly self-conscious, she'd never had much commerce with his Lake Players. She came only the first night and helped the run crew. But when the play ended, she was no longer backstage. What Virginia Poorman didn't know, and Tody Wolding fervently prayed she never had occasion to discover, was that the instant the DeSoto hit the chute Harold's brakes collapsed beneath his foot. With Ortensia Costello—Beatrice to his Benedick—no longer acting beside him but throwing her arms up and screaming, it was a stomach-churning shot down and a wiggly bowl through the astonished audience. The Ganaego *Bee,* the weekly freebie, had the previous week run a story about the old car on the lodge roof, an advertising gimmick—including building the chute to get the car up there—for which they had obtained permission. And the unauthorized swoop down the chute fortunately escaped the town's censure—the first swoop did, not the second. It was the *Chronicle*, the town's dour paterfamilias, that tut-tutted them down its long vinegary nose in the story that had outraged Virginia Poorman. But it worked. That was what was so tremendous about it—*it worked!* Between the first and second weeks the Lake Players printed extra tickets, rented another truckload of folding chairs from Tonnesdatter's, and, after decades of plying their art in obscurity, entered the public mind, entered it in a big way, you might say.

Had Shelly been out front? Where else could she have been?

Home, Tody wended a path through scattered piles of unwashed laundry. Upstairs lay more piles; in the cellar more. Dirty dishes teetered in the sink; black sugar speckled the sills; cobwebs rounded the corners of the rooms. The single toilet in the house was toxic; the beds were unmade. Facing months of undone housework, he phoned

Mrs. Kattlove's Clerk

Mrs. Kattlove and begged his boss for the rest of the afternoon and tomorrow off, then manfully tied himself into an apron and began. Shelly was at work, her first real job. She helped prepare lunches at a nearby nursing home. If she would not help him clean—and, given the frostiness of current relations, he doubted she would—at least she might redd up her room, stuff things in drawers, wash her face, make herself presentable.

When she came home, they quarreled. "I'm not missing work." Shelly worshipped money. Moreover, she appeared to be good at earning it—a talent Tody assumed must run in the Namarian bloodline. Certainly didn't in the Woldings'. "You got us into this, Tody, you get us out."

A big girl, big frame, big hips. She took after her bruiser of a father, George, his dark lank hair, his meat-cleaver nose. Already, she was taller than Tody. But she was thirteen, on the cusp of fourteen: She had too many zits, not enough friends. George, to Tody's knowledge, had never abused her sexually, but he had with a belt. Respecting her feelings, he said, modulating his voice, "Shelly, you don't show tomorrow, we're food for the fishes."

"I didn't get my name in the paper."

"I know you didn't, babe, but we gotta deal with the consequences. Trust me, this new caseworker smells blood. We need to look like one big happy family."

She slammed her bedroom door; the little house rocked, something that happened often these days. Tody, stymied, transferred an armload of dripping clothes to the dryer, reloaded the washer as if it were a revolver, attacked the kitchen. He tried to imagine the inside of his sister's head: He visualized a nuclear power plant control panel with all the needles on the dials bouncing in the red zone.

At dinnertime she showed in the kitchen. "I'm going out."

Half-girl, half-woman: She had swept her hair back into a

ponytail, sprayed herself with a perfume from the G. C. Murphy that smelled—to his nose—like Mr. Clean. "Would you mind," he asked cautiously, "if I tidied up your room a little?"

She slammed the refrigerator door. "Keep the fuck out of my room!"

He tried not to overreact. "We're not going to have a door left on its hinges," he joked. "I'm making a meatloaf. Why don't I make some Gooseberry Fool for dessert? You like that."

"Why don't you just marry this Costello whore?"

"Shelly, I'm not going to even answer that."

"Dress her in one of your *frocks*, stick one of your plastic diamonds on her finger. You gonna tell the caseworker about your Saturday nights? I'm sure she'd just *looove* to hear about those."

"How about a meatloaf sandwich before you go out?"

"It's too hot for meatloaf."

Well, about that she was right. Fanning himself with the newspaper, Tody sweated his way through a plate of greasy meat and potatoes. With each laundry cycle requiring an hour or so, he calculated he might finish by tomorrow afternoon. He might have time to mop the kitchen floor, to run the vacuum, to straighten up his disorderly study. As for washing the windows, for mowing the grass, for proposing to Ortensia Costello and marrying her, there would be no time. In the feverish weeks of his editing *Much Ado About Nothing* into a script that the Lake Players had even a snowball's chance to master, bringing the setting into the 1940s, the manic months of rehearsals periodically derailed by Officer Dogberry's morose benders, there had nevertheless been time for his simultaneous affairs with Ortensia and Harold, time for extracting petrified condoms from the moldering upholstery of a blasted car, time on Saturday nights for slipping into hose and a pretty number and driving to a certain unlicensed speakeasy, time for anything and everything—except

Shelly. Maybe it hadn't been so glorious, after all?

Maybe it had been nothing more than tawdry?

~ ~ ~

You couldn't, from Plan Ten, see the steelworks. But you always knew it was down there, all nine long miles of it lying against the river like a grimy lover. Across the night skies the open hearths sent up strobes like summer heat lightning, the tube mills clanged and jangled, pillowcases hanging in the backyard to dry came inside streaked with soot, and a taste of chemicals lay everlastingly on your tongue. He worked a year and a half in the mill, shoveling glowing chunks of slag in the slag dump, a brutally hard job in a place that seemed to have little to offer but brutally hard jobs. One side of him flinched from the searing heat; the other side froze from the wind that rose from the river like a god from the underworld. He lost twenty pounds he didn't have to spare, received a suspension for getting caught stoned, witnessed a man lose a hand to a train's coupling. Bolted to the wall beside his locker had been a sign: *Please Do Not Spit on the Floor.*

Indeed.

One morning, rather than punching in, he appeared in Lillian Kattlove's office on the mezzanine of her yardage shop and entreated the tightfisted old crone to give him his high-school job clerking back. And that's what people had come to call him: *Mrs. Kattlove's clerk.* At one-thirty this morning, switching off the emphysemic vacuum, Tody listened to a neighbor's Good Humor truck noodling its way home, the peal of the bell through Plan Ten's crooked brick streets sounding like a town crier announcing the end of another long and useless summer day.

But no Shelly.

Two-fifteen, she breezed in, passing him as though he were the cleaning lady, tee shirt outside her jeans, reeking of tobacco. When she said, "So when's the big wedding?" Tody, about to round on her, bit his tongue. "Babe," he said, "please stop with this business about Ortensia. I'm not the marrying type. I'll pay you double what the nursing home's going to pay you tomorrow, I need you to be here."

"Tody, I *can't*—people are depending on me."

And I'm not? he wanted to snap, then realized, chagrinned, that she was sincere. "And you're doing swell, but maybe the golden-agers can get along without you for a day?"

She turned her back on him. "I'll think about it."

"She's coming at two. Her name's Virginia Poorman."

"Why would I care what her name is?"

Somewhere just shy of three-thirty, Tody swallowed two vials of cough medicine and crawled into bed. Harold Robinson had magic pills that would knock you flat in ten minutes. But Wes Littlewood's personally compounded cherry elixir put you under, you only needed patience. Sometimes when he couldn't sleep, he would pull back his roles. He had a lockbox memory: Willie Loman, Brick Pollit, Major-General Stanley, Captain Hook. Some nights, he would block out a play his company could never conceivably mount. Tonight, Tody thought about his sister. Living with him could not be easy. He'd always been the odd duck, the scrawny little boy who had been shunned, taunted, chased and beaten. And Shelly caught—*still* caught—some of that bigotry. Maybe she would be better off in a foster home? Wafting up through the house came the exotic—exotic for them—scent of Clorox. Once, he mixed chlorine and ammonia and nearly asphyxiated the family. The firemen in their big black helmets delivered him a stern scolding. Under his breath, one hissed, *Damn fairy!* The last thing tonight that Tody Wolding takes cognizance of is the patter of drops on the roof, a summer rain. Maybe next year they could do *Singin' in the Rain*?

Wouldn't that be a hoot?

He slept through the alarm and would have slept until noon had not the crash of the front door brought him off his pillow: Shelly leaving, blowing him off, blowing them off. It had been Harold Robinson, who, because he lubed cars alongside teenagers, reminded him of what he had forgotten, the exacting rules of the teenage world: *You hurt me, I get to hurt you, and, if I can't, I get to hurt someone else—which might be me.* Tody, alone in the kitchen, considered the socks and underpants lying before the cellar door like commuters waiting for the next train. If Shelly wanted to break up the family, there was nothing he could do to hinder her. He shaved and went to early mass, as he often did. While sleepy Father Opsatnick wiggled a finger in the canal of his ear, removed it, and studied it inquisitively as he mumbled *Praybrethrenthatmysacrificeandyoursbe acceptabletoGod,thealmightyFather,* Shelly Namarian's legally appointed guardian appealed to the minor—but, no doubt, one hot-ticket—deity who watched over crossdressers.

Whichever that one was.

~ ~ ~

"Tody, you gotta come to my grand-opening party. Looky here!"

Exiting St. Ursula's, he'd made a decision. And he granted the point that for these occasions you were expected to have chocolates from Stahrenberger's and little boxes from Fischman's—except there was no time for props. Before he could lose his nerve, Tody had driven straight to Ortensia's. But just as he was to embark on a speech that—actor or no actor—he had immense difficulty envisioning himself delivering, Ortensia thrust in his face one of her new business cards. She was in her real estate agent costume, suit and heels, dangly earrings. "We're gonna have Cold Duck and cupcakes and we're gonna cut the ribbon and make toasts and things—just like on TV. The *Bee*'s sending a reporter. So, you're gonna come, right?"

"Sure, sure. When's your debut?"

"Next week!" Ortensia preferred shrieking to talking. "You know Aziz's Pizzas? It's right between that and Gromeka Plumbing. I already got four clients and a girl willing to throw in with me. Everybody's been lying low until I got things squared away. God, I haven't slept a wink since I signed the lease."

Ortensia and he had met taking dance lessons at his step-Aunt Julie's studio. In high school they co-starred in *Our Town*. She had invited him to her wedding, a short-lived union that barely lasted past her baby's christening, and accepted their long-term on-again, off-again affair for what it was, a tension release. But this business side of Ortensia's, Tody never grokked. He exclaimed over her calling card, searching for an opening.

"Every penny I got I've sunk into this," she ran on. "You think someone in Oak Grove is gonna trust their Taj Mahal to a girl working out of the front seat of her car? You gotta have desks, butts in seats, maps on the walls, paperclips." Stopping for breath, Ortensia peered at him. "Why aren't you at work? Lillian's gonna have your head. What's up?"

It was his cue. But he could not mouth the words. Desperate, however, not to lose the opportunity, he decided on an oblique approach. "I was thinking, why don't we do a musical? Something big, lush, with an orchestra?"

They were about the same height. Ortensia pecked him on the cheek. "Tody, you came all the way rushing over here to tell me that? You're turning me into Old Lady Wendy to your Peter Pan. How's this, I'll help? But you can't count on me anymore, my diva days are over."

He felt like a fool, like a peculiar little boy with peculiar little dreams. He might someday be Hamlet or Stanley Kowalski or even Macbeth Thane of Cawdor. But Ward Cleaver, no, never. "Oak Grove? You really aiming that high?"

Ortensia's face shone; she gripped his wrist. "Tody, they're painting my name on the window today—we're going live. I'm tired of working my ass off so someone else can get rich. I want it all, every last bit."

The pity of it was that Shelly, despite her sarcasm, liked Ortensia. He hugged her. "Break a leg, babe."

~ ~ ~

When Virginia Poorman came striding up the walk, attaché case at her side, Tody met her at the door and told her directly. "My sister's not here, I'm sorry. She works in a nursing home and felt she shouldn't take the time off."

The caseworker's snowy curls registered her displeasure. "Mr. Wolding, I've come all the way from Sutton. It's a very warm day. I would like to get out of this sun—*if* you don't object?"

He had thought of stopping at the nursing home and beseeching his sister one last time. But Shelly had—as Virginia Poorman herself had pointed out—a voice in this matter, even more than he: Maybe this was her way of saying what she could not say aloud? He had long assured her that, if she wanted a start in a new family—and, given their family, who wouldn't?—he'd support her in that decision.

So, the world had called his bluff, all right, so it had.

In the silence of the freshly vacuumed living room the brass clasps of Virginia Poorman's briefcase snapped open like pistol shots. Beneath the case, her knees looked—loomed—like skulls. What he hadn't known, and only now felt within himself, was how much he would miss his sister. He wasn't her father, not even close, but in some ways he truly had been her mom.

"I'm sorry," he said again.

Mrs. Poorman closed her briefcase and leveled her gaze to meet his. "The ultimate disposition won't be up to me, you understand? All I'm going to do is gather whatever pertinent information is required and write a report."

"I'll help in any way I can."

She condescended to bestow upon him a smug little smile. "Mr. Wolding, you mustn't take it personally. I can't tell you how many people go into this thing with blinders on. They have no conception of the challenges involved. It's easy to get overwhelmed by childrearing."

He had a stiff-upper-lip face he used in British dramas. Tody put on his doughty Colonel Nicholson mask. "Would you like something to drink? I have iced tea?"

"That won't be necessary. I won't be here that long."

"Sure? No trouble?"

Before she had a chance to decline a second time, the front door banged open and Shelly stamped in. She looked like the tomboy she'd been as a girl, hair loosened in a wild nimbus from her ponytail, face bathed in sweat. She stretched out her big hand to the startled caseworker. "You must be Mrs. Poorman? How do you *do?* I'm *so* sorry I'm late! One of our most beloved patients had a stroke in the cafeteria! Tody"—she turned to him her earnest red face—"where are your manners? Mrs. Poorman, let me get you something to drink?"

"Oh, I'm fine, dear, you—"

"Don't be silly! How about iced tea? Sugar? Lemon? Oh, this house is such a *disgrace!* I apologize, you'll have to forgive us— we've both been *sooooooo* busy!"

Last week, across Kattlove's long deal table Tody had unrolled an expensive bolt of Thibaut fabric. He measured, cut, and rerolled the seven yards his customer had requested into a heavy tube and toted it on his shoulder to the front. After he had rung up the sale, the woman accused him of misleading her as to the price. He had not: About money he was exceedingly diligent. If carpenters measure twice and cut once, yardage clerks lock down agreement long before they reach for the shears. Mrs. Kattlove, disturbed from her afternoon nap, descended her mezzanine like a peevish czarina and sided with her customer, which she felt an obligation to do, and publicly reprimanded him, which she did not need to do. He wasn't going to marry Ortensia Costello or anyone else, and he wasn't going to troll the alleys looking for castaway men like Harold Robinson. Shelly was as close as he would come to having a daughter, and, even if they emerged victors in this particular skirmish with Family Court, soon she would be leaving him behind. He was going to spend his life in a musty shop, Mrs. Kattlove's clerk, and die a biddy bachelor, someone who cooked hot meals in summer and fanned himself with a rolled-up newspaper. As he listened to Shelly laying it on thick—as thick, as Harold Robinson might say, as mustard on pastrami—the artistic director of Ganaego's stouthearted if hapless theater company nodded approvingly.

"I say *therrrre,*" Tody said to his half-sister, "it's just beastly hot today, isn't it?'

A Question of
the Minister's Wife

Summer 1993

Maybe it was Pleasance Stubbs, whose control of the Lowrey's pedalboard was erratic, maybe it was Figgy's heartfelt but adenoidal tenor—something, some blue note, set the hounds across the ravine baying as if possessed. The howls of the animals only added to the evening's oppression. An urn of wilting flowers—white irises, white gladioluses, and white chrysanthemums studded with blood-red roses the size of an infant's fists—gave off in the saturating humidity of the sanctuary a sickening fragrance. A more empowered choir director, Maurice Begley lamented, would be able to hire a decent organist and dismiss from among his singers the well-intentioned but congenitally tone-deaf. But with the dwindling fellowship of Ganaego's First Congregational numbering, even on a holiday Sunday, under seventy-five, Maurice's resources were limited.

Grimly, he suspended choir practice to crank in the windows.

"We'll perish." Teddie Livingston fanned herself with her music. "You close all those windows, Maurice, sure as shooting we're goners."

"The Methodists installed central air," Judy Van Horst said.

"It's cooler in the basement," Figgy suggested, and they all craned their heads to peer at him: possibly the most hapless singer they'd ever heard.

"There're spiders down there"—Teddie spoke for the group—
"that are bigger than even *you,* Figgy. Maurice, these orphaned
flowers are giving me a piercing headache."

Which faith was it that came to church and just sat silently?
What a blessed notion. Maurice watched Figgy Larkspur bury his
scarlet face in his music. Decades ago, Figgy had lost his right arm
to the elbow in the Tin Mill's scrap baller. Beneath his shirt, made
translucent with perspiration, hairs swirled in vivid patterns across
his sagging abdomen. Maurice understood that he should go to the
poor man's rescue, but with the penned dogs' clamor subsiding to a
discordant murmur, Maurice, anxious to conclude practice for what
he had set himself to do later, pressed on. The six-part "Precious Lord,
Take My Hand" he had meticulously arranged was, as he feared,
beyond his group's modest capabilities.

"Why don't you drop down and sing with Mabel and Bridget?"
he asked Teddie. "Norm, you and Dwight move up to baritone. And
Figgy, you're doing fine, but if you can't make a note, please drop
out. Ready, Pleasance?"

~ ~ ~

For someone like Maurice Begley a church was as much a place
of work as a place of worship. Since his earliest years in children's
choir—moving back row-by-row as his silvery soprano moved down
the keyboard, coming to rest on the second *G* below middle *C*—he
had been involved with liturgical music. After practice, hurrying
back into the darkened chapel to fetch the music he had forgotten, he
suffered a moment of doubt: Had the church come to represent to him
no more than a series of wearisome obligations? A tall but ponderous
man, trouser cuffs bunched over his shoes, not a hundred hairs left
spanning his domed skull, Maurice wondered if his faith had worn
too thin for his own good.

He had befriended the minister's lonely wife and inadvertently led them to stray over the line—or, to *appear* to stray. Nothing untoward had happened. On that he was adamant: Paulette was an honorable woman, he an honorable man. They were not having an affair. For goodness' sakes, he was fifty-eight, nineteen years the woman's senior. But their Friday afternoon music lessons had come to make Maurice uncomfortable. Tongues were wagging, and he had resolved tonight, on the pretext of dropping off the choir's Sunday selections to the minister, whom he knew would not be home, to have a word with Paulette. Dawdling in the chapel, mired in indecision, he removed a mum from the urn. In the gloom the corolla—grossly oversized, profusely petaled—gleamed as though illuminated from within. Teddie Livingston had been right to kvetch. If the Sawyers, after Minnie's memorial service, didn't want the flowers, they should have disposed of them. He should stuff them in the trash. But sensing his resolution weakening, Maurice laid the desiccating bloom alongside the urn and left.

~ ~ ~

"It's just better."

They were sitting at the kitchen table in the parsonage. He was careful to keep his face bathed in light so she could see his lips. That Paulette Schumacher had never fit comfortably into First Congregational was no secret. She was sharp with people, scathing in her criticism, and so Maurice fretted: Would she cause a scene? This was not an easy thing to put into words. But he had rejected the more expedient route, to plead, dishonestly, that he was simply too busy.

He repeated the words he had rehearsed. "Better for you, better for the church."

Paulette's face, especially her eyes, held her customary look of precarious anxiety as she strained to decipher his words. It was an altogether extraordinary expression—naked in its lack of guise, ferocious in its focus. Talking with the minister's deaf wife, church people were heard to demur, could be a trial. Her eyes would clamp on you and *not* release you. And should you, under her assault, glance aside, she was capable of seizing your two shoulders and turning you in her direction. But perhaps because he had taken her by surprise, Paulette was uncharacteristically docile.

"Maybe I could come to your school, Maurice? It would be like I was taking regular lessons? How could people gossip then?"

"Idle tongues, you know they will." The kitchen smelled of apples and cinnamon. Paulette, discovering Maurice's fondness for sweets, would always prepare something for their lessons. He guessed, despite the heat wave, that she had for tomorrow baked a pie. "Especially when it's a question of the minister's wife."

"Are we allowed to *talk?* Or is that against the rules, too?"

"Of course we can talk. And I can find you another music teacher, if you want?"

She rejected that idea. As they stood at the door, Paulette, childlike, lay her head on his chest. Occasionally, they would touch, and their shoulders, when they sat on the piano bench together, would brush. But never had they lingered in such an intimate way. "I'm sorry, Maurice," she said. "I upset you, I upset everybody."

He recalled how off-put he had been when he first met the minister's wife, hearing her voice, her malformed pronunciation. For someone who all his life had been ravished by the beauty of the human instrument, enduring Paulette's tortured attempts to shape words she had never heard had been agonizing. Her voice was loud, hollow, *lusterless,* the way only a voice without tone can be. What had gone wrong in her marriage? Never had Maurice understood people very well. His own wife, a brittle marriage that fell apart twenty-five years ago: Had he ever understood Adele? But *this* woman, imprisoned within a silence he could scarcely bring himself to contemplate, Maurice understood least of all. Was it, in fact, her impenetrable isolation that drew his sympathy? It didn't matter, no one believed a deaf woman was taking music lessons. It wasn't creditable. And thus gossip was rife, and gossip, as everyone knows, is pernicious. Longingly, Maurice drank in the forbidden scent of Paulette's hair, then turned and lumbered down the porch steps.

~ ~ ~

Ten years it had been since the Search Committee had lured the young Richard Schumacher—along with his wife and two daughters, the younger of whom had been, like her mother, born deaf—from the backwoods of Ohio to Ganaego. But it was not until last summer, at the church picnic at Lake Biddleford, finding themselves assigned by the picnic coordinator Ted Bachelor to man the iced-tea station, that Maurice and Paulette were provided an opportunity to venture beyond polite conversation. Of that afternoon *his* memories were limned by a squeaking pump handle, the splash of cold spring water on the bare feet of the children and their delicate-as-china squeals; by the inexhaustible mimicry of a catbird perched on a limb above; by the thwack of the softball and the cries of the players. But for Paulette existence held no aural dimension. Poplar leaves spangled in the sun soundlessly; trains possessed no far-off, sonorous whistles; lightning split the heavens and storms pelted the windowpanes with a silent menace. They talked about their children: Paulette's older daughter, away at college, and her younger daughter, fifteen that summer and a troubled and troubling girl, whom in desperation they'd enrolled in a specialized boarding school; and about Maurice's daughter, Trisha, who had separated from another husband and trailed home with three shell-shocked children, each the product of a different alliance.

But it was music, ironically, that fused their friendship.

"My father had an old wooden radio. Big round dial." Paulette formed her fingers into a large circle. "On Saturdays he listened to the opera. I would sit in his lap and *smell* the radio and I would look at the numbers on the dial, and I would think that music must be made up of numbers and that when I went to school I would learn how to hear it. I was so sure that music was just like arithmetic."

He was entranced by her pronunciation of his name, *Mau-wice,* and moved by her story. "The fact is," he agreed, "one *does* have to learn how to hear music. And you have to learn how to count it, too. There are *lots* of numbers in music. Just because you can hear doesn't mean you can *hear* music."

"Could a person without hearing ever hear music?"

"Beethoven!" Maurice sang out passionately. "Beethoven sawed the legs off his pianos so he could *hear* the music through the vibrations on the floor. We forget: He wrote the Ninth without being able to hear a note of it. The night he premiered it, he had his back to the audience and didn't hear them applauding. Someone had to turn him around. His eyes welled with tears."

Had he overstepped? But no, Paulette clutched his hand. "In the parsonage—there's a piano. Would you play for me so I could hear it? Like Beethoven?"

And so he'd begun playing for this impulsive woman. Friday afternoons, he'd leave the Oak Grove Music School and drive to the parsonage. They would discuss what he had selected, a Clementi sonatina, a Chopin nocturne, a Brahms intermezzo, then, as he played, she would spread her arms across the top of the piano and lay the side of her head flat to the wood. With the dark tresses of her hair scattered to either side, she'd close her eyes in intense concentration. Periodically, he would stop to explicate the harmonic structure of a passage he had negotiated, laboring to translate the oscillations she felt traveling through the Chickering's ninety-year-old frame into music theory. The exercise, ironically, rekindled his own sense of music's physicality: the shudder that would cascade through her when he brought his hands down on Beethoven's thunderous chords that would, in turn, cascade through him. This, then, became something else he could offer the church: music lessons with the minister's wife to break up her solitary weeks. And they *were* lessons. But it was not Paulette Schumacher's musical education Maurice was thinking about as he sat in his car in the church lot tonight. His carefully rehearsed speech had deceived only him, and now even him it failed to deceive. What he was thinking about was Paulette's hair spread ravishingly across the piano and the soft slump of her body a few minutes ago against him. While he sat here, the hunting dogs started up again. An infirm and blind black man owned the wretched beasts. Maurice had seen him waving a stick over their pen like an Old Testament prophet. But at least the crazed hounds offered this consolation: Their howls covered up his sobs.

~ ~ ~

His self-pity was swiftly punctured. At home, wobbling toward him on her small rubbery legs, a diminutive welcoming committee, came his youngest grandchild. What was she doing up at this hour? He scooped the baby into his arms, kissed her on the cleanest spot he could locate on her bare chest, and carried her into the living room, where he found Trisha's other two, Megan and Randal, sharing a bag of Oreos. The cookies, like errant tires, had rolled every which way. In the kitchen, Franco-American raviolis, having escaped their skillet, were glued to the stovetop like tiny pillows, and both peanut butter and jam jars were impaled by butcher knives.

"Where," he asked the oldest, Megan, as calmly as possible, "is your mother?"

"Gone."

"I can see that, honey, but gone *where?*"

It was too late for baths. His daughter's children, jaded beyond their years, saw through adult contrivance, especially eleven-year-old Megan, who pragmatically suggested that, under the circumstances, face washing and teeth brushing would be sufficient. While she roused Randal, her mopey but philosophic younger brother, Maurice changed the baby's diaper. Later, as Maurice sat on the side of Megan's bed, she rested her solemn eyes on his. "She's with the Jaguar man," she said, answering him in her own good time. "He loves his Jaguar more than he loves us."

Maurice kissed his—already-wounded-by-life—granddaughter. He saw no reason to prevaricate. "He loves his Jaguar more than he loves you, yes—or her, for that matter."

"They left precisely at four, Maurice. The kitchen clock is six minutes slow."

It was one of their ongoing gags. "I'll be six minutes late for my own funeral."

She giggled forlornly. "Better six minutes late than six minutes early."

Five hours unattended. While his daughter smoked a joint with a second-rate architect who did lavish more genuine affection on his vintage sports car than he did on his own progeny and certainly would on somebody else's *and* while he suffered his droll little crisis of faith over the estranged wife of a cleric, the house could have been enveloped in flames, the baby could have choked on a paperclip, Randal could have slashed himself smearing peanut butter on his brittle toast. The evening was moist and airless. Maurice could not sleep. At one point he thought he heard his daughter and padded heavily over to the window. It was only the teenage boy next door, returning home from work in his Kentucky Fried Chicken uniform, but Maurice lingered there in his pajama bottoms anyway, sweat trickling down the swell of his belly. He listened to the chorus of insect life that riddled the stillness of the night and gave it depth. Something he long wondered: Was his memory of the summer night Adele left with another man and he was required to tell a seven-

A Question of the Minister's Wife   151

year-old that her mother had abandoned her as painful as Trisha's memory? Within him Adele's image had faded. The wound had been absorbed the way a tree gradually enfolds the face of a sawn-off limb. His memory of *telling* Trisha, however, remained vivid: the evening's heat and primrose scent, the drumming of crickets, the confused, weeping girl he held in his arms. That memory, possessing an unwonted persistence, had taken on a life of its own, tempering and coloring everything that had come afterward.

~ ~ ~

The memory had also the insidious effect of undermining any criticism he might make of his daughter. As Maurice could readily see coming downstairs in the morning, Trisha—halter top knotted behind her neck, makeup cakey—had been out all night. Phone wedged under her chin, she served breakfast and issued commands to her tumultuous brood.

Maurice ducked under the phone cord. "Do you have any idea how long they were alone?"

Trisha returned Randal's pilfered Hawaiian Punch and made a throat-cutting gesture to Megan. "Shelly," she said to her phone companion, "lemme call you back."

"They were also," Maurice added, "filthy and unfed."

"I'm sorry!" Trisha refused him eye contact. "I forgot it was choir night. It won't happen again. As a reward for being such good little goobers, we're going swimming."

"Patricia, we—"

"Everybody up!" she shouted. "Grandpa thinks we stink! Up, up and away to the bathroom! God forbid we should pollute the lake!"

Maurice washed the dishes and chiseled encrusted raviolis from the range. Gathering his things for school, he realized that last night, when he had dashed back into the chapel for his music and a hymnal, he'd remembered the first, not the second. Which meant, this

152   *A Question of the Minister's Wife*

morning, an extra stop. Parking before the church, he encountered Richard Schumacher coming down the steps.

"Maurice!" Under an arm Richard had trapped an enormous stack of manila files. "The very person I was thinking about. Paulette tells me you have to terminate her lessons? Look here, my good man, could we offer to pay you a small stipend, would that alter your thinking?"

Like his wife, Richard Schumacher was an odd bird. Not the sort of ecclesiastical figure you might expect in a working-class community. Scholarly to the point of pedantic, the minister, after days sequestered in his study furiously writing, brought forth dry, complicated sermons that did little but baffle his congregation. The nominal obligations of the ministry—comforting the sick, visiting the homebound, just making *small talk*—appeared to subject him to a morbid self-consciousness. Whatever gossip was circulating First Congregational, its minister—contemptuous of any form of scandalmongering—would be the last to hear.

"Well, I feel bad, too," Maurice equivocated.

Richard put on his synthetic empathy face. "Maurice, one does not need to be a clairvoyant to see that this is a heavy burden on you."

"It's not a burden, Reverend."

"I still think if we paid you it'd be more like a regular thing?"

"You absolutely cannot pay me!"

Richard shifted his files. "Is there not an hour *somewhere* in your schedule for Paulette? I ask this, not as your pastor, but as a personal favor? She lives for your lessons, Maurice. It's made a difference, especially, as you know, with all the trouble we've suffered with Jessica?"

Once, helping Paulette grasp the concept of chord structure, he had placed three fingers on her arm and used the pressure of his fingertips to illustrate the tones of triad inversions. Later, after the lesson, his desolation had been bottomless. For him it was no less true: He too lived for their Friday lessons. "Why don't you tell her I'll come by today after all," Maurice said weakly. "Maybe we can figure something out?"

The minister brightened. "Maurice, what an *ace* of a fellow you are! Now look, I'm off to my coffee klatch, the monthly meeting of the Council of Ministers, and since I'm archivist"—Richard hefted his voluminous files—"I, for one, had better be on time! Why not tell Paulette your blessed news yourself? She's in the fellowship room."

As he cut through the chapel, Maurice frowned at the memorial flowers. The white petals had turned a cachectic salmon color and were decomposing in heaps on the polished table. Hastily formulated, his thinking was this: Were not Paulette and he adults? Could they not establish the boundaries for their friendship? She had offered to come to the school. In the recital hall was a concert grand. While the hall would provide a degree of privacy, it was, indisputably, a public space. Would that not mollify the church magpies? Turning into the fellowship room, which had been set up for a luncheon, he saw Paulette unrolling rolls of white paper down the folding tables. He watched her smoothing the paper with her palms: Even in the smallest task she undertook she was possessed of a riveting absorption. Unless she saw you coming, it was impossible not to startle her, and, indeed, when Paulette glanced up, she jumped.

"I was talking to Richard," Maurice rushed into his speech. "Outside? He thinks we should continue our lessons. I think so, too."

She frowned. "What's Richard got to do with this?"

"I was too rash." Maurice was sensible that in his nervousness he was exaggerating the motions of his lips—something that irritated her. "There's no reason, if we approach this maturely, that we shouldn't be able to establish some clear-cut boundaries, don't you agree?"

"Has he left? Richard? Is there anybody else here? You know I can't know that, Maurice?"

"I don't think so."

Paulette, satisfied, clenched her hands. "I'm leaving him, I'm leaving Ganaego. I don't want to live with him and I don't want to live in this godawful town anymore."

Maurice, spooked by her announcement, looked away. He started to respond, only to recollect he was required to face her. "Are you sure?"

"Yes, I'm sure!"

"But Richard, your marriage vows?"

"Mau-wice"—her deformed voice echoed harshly in the room of empty tables—"my personal life is none of your business."

Provoked, she turned aside. He went around her and clasped her shoulders. Anyone else would have refused to look at him, but, given the implacability of her deafness, Paulette had no choice but to stare up at him. Her eyes shone with tears. "God," he said, "what have I done? You're really going to do this, aren't you?"

"Yes!"

"Where're you going to go?"

"Maurice, this has nothing to do with you."

"Where?"

She tried to pull away. "I don't know! My sister's, I guess."

"Where's that?"

Paulette switched her head. "It doesn't matter."

"Where does she live, your sister?"

"Nebraska, somewhere outside Omaha, I forget the suburb."

"How do you intend to get there?"

"I took a bus there once, Maurice, I don't know?"

"How're you going to get to the station—you can't call a taxi! How're you going to call your sister when you *do* get there?" He tried to kiss her, but Paulette averted her head. "Listen to me," he said, pulling back so she could see what he was about to say. "When do you want to go? Today? Do you want to go today?"

"You don't know what you're talking about."

"Do you want to go *today?*"

Paulette nodded her head bleakly, and he bent to kiss her. This time she permitted him. Her lips were warm, full, soft. They tasted of salt, from her tears. "Three o'clock"—he leaned back so she could see the lips that had kissed hers—"I'm going to come at three o'clock, our regular time, and I'm going to drive you to your sister's. And on the way I'm going to teach you how to hear music."

~ ~ ~

Madness! As hurried to his car, the old man's hounds began bellowing. *Who cares?* He yanked open the car door. *Howl your fool heads off!* He had so much to do: pack, arrange to take Monday and Tuesday off—maybe he should take the whole week?—talk to Trisha, stop at the bank, buy toothpaste. Once back home, he recalled that Trisha had taken the kids swimming. He wrote her a loving letter, fatherly and wise, unburdening himself to his only child, and propped it against the ketchup bottle on the table. If nothing else, Trish would appreciate a respite from his meddling—*forever?* The thought brought Maurice up short. He knew where he and Paulette were going, more or less. But *how* were they to travel? Friends? More than friends? Fretful, he phoned Sara Kennedy and asked her to cancel his Friday, Monday, and Tuesday lessons, and patch him through to the director.

"He won't be in until two, Maurice."

"Put me in his schedule punctually for two then."

Sara had a nose for trouble. "Is something wrong?"

"I'm running a little late today."

"If you have to cancel three days' worth of lessons," Sara snapped, "I'd say that's pretty late. You know who's going to have to call everybody, don't you?"

A Question of the Minister's Wife

He rummaged in their crematorium of an attic for his suitcase, an ancient Pullman, cracking his skull on a rafter, only to face the vexing problem of deciding what to pack for the parameters of a trip which remained undefined. But as anxious as the practical details were making him, it was not, in the end, practical concerns that held sway. To have missed love was to have missed a great deal. He'd always known that. But what he had not known until today was that to deny love to someone else was, in its own way, equally damning.

When, shortly before two, he strode into the music school, Sara regarded him apologetically. "Maurice, you should've told me!" He looked at her in perplexity. "That your grandson's been hurt?" When Maurice's bewilderment only increased, Sara guessed. "So, you *don't* know?" Her voice, as though she might be considering rescinding her apology, took on a more matter-of-fact tone. "Anyway, your granddaughter called. She said, 'Tell Maurice precisely this: He is not to worry, everything is fine. Randal has shattered his wrist, and they could use Maurice's assistance at the hospital.' "

Maurice had time for one stray, fond thought, that is, Megan's current rage for the word *precise*, then he was hurtling down Sutton Post Road. In the emergency room lobby, he discovered the girl— poor creature—still in her damp swimsuit, the baby fussing in her lap. She looked like a miniature, overwhelmed mother. He relieved her of the infant and listened to her report.

"They've been wheeling him around like a box of bananas."

"And how's the patient holding up, during his transport?"

"His usual bubbly self."

"Stoical is he?"

"What's that mean?"

Megan, to his dismay, appeared to have in her not an ounce of music, although he cherished hopes for Randal, who would lean against him when he practiced. Regardless of that, however, Maurice adored this child. *"Resigned to fate, calm before calamity."*

Megan considered that. "I think he's a jerk, frankly."

"Megan, he's your brother."

"Half-brother, Maurice. And maybe half of him is stoical, but it's the other half I'm worried about. How clumsy do you have to be to trip over a yellow lawn chair?"

Maurice had no recourse but to shift the baby back. "I won't be long," he promised, glancing at his watch. "I'm just going to cheer up the unstoical half of him. Why don't I give your mother money for pizza? Would that help assuage your anguish?"

He had taught her that phrase. "I have sand in my suit." Megan made a surprisingly adult face. *"Nothing* is going to assuage my anguish."

Between Paulette and his daughter were but a few years: Paulette, thirty-nine, Trisha thirty-two. But in intelligence, maturity, fineness of spirit, the differences were telling. Maurice had been tempted to interrogate Megan on her mother's role in Randal's accident. Had she been zonked out on her towel? Flirting with the lifeguard? He discovered his daughter and grandson in an alcove within. Trisha had been provided a physician's lab coat for protection against the air-conditioning and, doubtless, to cover her miniscule bikini. Randal sat huddled beside a bowl of ice water. Beneath the shimmering surface of the liquid lay the boy's wrist and hand, the flesh swollen, empurpled.

"No lectures," Trisha warned. "If you can take Megan and the baby and drop them at Shelly's, I'd appreciate it. There's some sort of Indian doctor here. She says she can set the wrist herself or they can take him to Pittsburgh to see a specialist. I want her to do it. Once she gets around to it, we'll be able to come home, too."

Randal, subject of this conversation, grimaced in pain. "Why is she recommending a specialist?" Maurice asked. "Is it that severe?"

"Dad, let's do what I want for once, all right?"

"If the doctor herself is suggesting a specialist, I think we need to listen."

"It's a broken bone. Little boys break bones all the time."

Maurice was outraged. "That is the most *idiotic* thing I have ever heard! If the bone isn't set correctly, the wrist may never be right."

"So he won't be forced to practice the piano?"

Incensed she'd use her son's injury to bring up, even in an indirect way, his futile attempts to inculcate music within her, Maurice completely lost his temper. "So he won't be able to throw a baseball, wield a scalpel, work on a computer—that's his right hand! Patricia, for God's sake, girl, it's high time to grow up!"

"Who are you to talk?" She grabbed an urn of tongue depressors and slammed it down. "Someone having an affair with a minister's wife? If you don't want to help, go away!"

Maurice blushed violently. His daughter's voice had carried the length of the emergency room. But it wasn't the strangers, it was his grandson: old enough to understand enough of this. "I am *not* having an affair."

Trisha, making a face not unlike the one her daughter had just made, said, "I don't care."

"Well, I do. I care very much what you say around the children."

"Dad, I can't afford a specialist."

"Surely your insurance will—"

"I don't have insurance!"

"How could you not have insurance?"

"Because I can't afford it! Why do you think I'm fucking some jerk with a Jaguar?"

Maurice heard, far away, the peal of a siren. Unlike most sirens, whose sound usually reaches a climax and diminishes, this one would only get louder and louder. Peculiar how the aural world permeates our lives, providing it dimension and solemnity? To someone who could not hear, how flat and shiny the world must appear. "I didn't know that," he said. "About your not having insurance, I mean."

"Chuck let it lapse. Like everything."

Maurice looked at Randal: About the boy's eyes was a pallor that claimed his heart. "Trish, please, let me pay for it?"

"You're sure? It's going to cost you an arm and a leg?" She laughed hollowly at her meager joke. "The doctor said they could take him in an ambulance. I've talked to Shelly—you can drop the kids. I'll follow the ambulance."

Maurice visualized, in the trunk of his car, his overstuffed Pullman, its leather as dry as lizard skin. How pathetic were the things he had packed: a madras sports jacket that no longer buttoned properly around the middle; a tie with an opossum he thought Paulette might find amusing; underwear with holes. What was he going to do? Compose symphonies while she sat beaming at him? He thought of his note propped against the ketchup, its Song of Solomon paeans to love, and of Pastor Richard Schumacher and his no less pathetic bundle of files, their pages filled with twaddle. How small their lives seemed. "I didn't know you knew," he said, "about Paulette?"

Trisha shivered inside the lab coat. "It was a guess—the way you talk about her."

Maurice kissed Randal on the head and gave his daughter an awkward embrace. "Why don't you ride up with him in the ambulance? I'll take care of Megan and the baby and come along straightaway. I can help with the paperwork."

~ ~ ~

Rather than going on to Shelly Namarian's first, the sensible thing to do, Maurice swerved down Linden Street and parked before the parsonage. It was a few minutes after three. He appealed to Megan. "Just a minute." The girl, cradling the soiled infant, seemed on the verge of tears. "Here, sweetheart," he added, "give me the child."

Maurice Begley possessed sufficient self-knowledge to understand that he had spent the better part of his life in what amounted to a state of eternal irresolution. Irresolution lay across his eyes like a gauze. This afternoon, climbing the parsonage steps, he became aware that his habitual faintheartedness, his endless shrinking before life's challenges had, this morning, spontaneously lifted, and was now, in all probability, about to close back down. He stepped over to the window and peered in. Paulette was sitting in the front parlor, turned toward the small light that illuminated when the doorbell was pressed. Maurice clandestinely studied her. Despite the day's warmth, she wore a heavy black dress and a long-sleeved white blouse. Under the brim of a large black hat her hair shone. Beside her stood a hard-sided suitcase, the color of coral. Her legs were crossed at the ankles, and her calves glistened with a sensuous luster. On her lap lay a yellow book: his Schirmer edition of the Beethoven piano sonatas. About the circumstances under which they were to travel, Maurice was now confident that he had his answer.

Having no faith in anything he was about to say, he rang the bell. Paulette's look of joy was, when she saw him balancing a baby on his hip, replaced with astonishment. Maurice slipped inside. "My grandson's been gravely injured," he said, plunging into an extemporized speech. "A shattered wrist, they don't know how bad it is, but it's serious enough that they're referring him to a specialist." The words were tumbling too fast from his lips for her to follow, but he would not stop until he had it all out. "Trisha's on her way with him to Pittsburgh, in the ambulance, and I have to go, too. Paulette, I'm sorry, I'm very, very sorry!"

He understood, guiltily, that his bringing the baby along had not been done without a certain element of guile: Who could resist a man with an infant? What he had not counted on was, in the stuffy warmth of the house, the powerful odor of a soiled diaper. Paulette sniffed, switching her head. "Maurice, you promised me?"

Under the prosecution of her unblinking gaze he felt the deeper truth forcing its passage out of his mouth. "Paulette, this isn't right. Have you and Richard tried counseling? Maybe if—"

"You promised me, Maurice!" She turned away, furious. Beside her the telephone sat on a small side table. She snatched it up and thrust the instrument at him. "Order me a cab!"

Maurice shrank back. "I think you should talk to a—"

"If you won't help, then get out!" Paulette, flinging the phone aside, shot her arms across the baby and seized Maurice's shirt under his chin. Her voice was so distorted that for a fraction of a second Maurice, shielding the child's head, was uncertain of her meaning. She began striking at him with her fists, shoving him and the infant with all her frenzied passion across the threshold. "Take your filthy baby and get *ouuuuut!*"

Death in the 5 and 10

Spring 2002

It was in the same instant that the Fire Chief's aging sedan beetled past the windows of Pitzele's Pharmacy that Darlene smelled smoke. Acrid, stinging, the unmistakable fingerprint of noxious odors that ensues from the combustion of horsehair plaster and varnished timbers, shingles and linoleum. In a town with numerous decrepit and abandoned buildings people took a lively interest in smoke. Darlene certainly did. The simultaneity of these two events, in fact, the Chief's red car, which she recognized from his visits to the library, and the eye-watering fumes, served to throw her off her decision-making.

Nevertheless, she pressed forward, concentrating on three options she had narrowed her shopping to: the herbal bath soaps and salts, which felt too spinsterish; the hairdryer, which felt too practical, even though Fanny needed one, her existing dryer being bandaged with adhesive tape like an accident victim; and the tortoiseshell comb and brush set, which fit her budget, would be a cinch to wrap, and gave her, imagining Fanny's lustrous auburn hair, a certain illicit thrill. And for that reason alone, fretful lest a present of hers provide occasion for the least embarrassment, Darlene Paczkowski, assistant head librarian, returned the comb and brush set to the shelf and selected the hairdryer.

Remington. A good brand, right?

By now, the street was pandemonium. Pitzele's clerk, a young black woman, agonized over her register, then, rattled, stabbed the wrong key. "Sugar!" She swatted the machine, and Darlene had the impression, had she not been here—Pitzele's sole customer—the girl would have been drawn out the door to the fire as if on an invisible tether. A hook and ladder truck, bristling with pickaxes, muscled through the knotted traffic, and, in the back, a door slammed. Walt Pitzele, Jr.—his skin looking, for a man who had to be in his eighth decade, unnaturally glowy (from the application of his own products?)—appeared above, on the pharmacy department platform.

"Old G. C. Murphy's." He leaned through dual displays of hearing-aid batteries. "Just heard it on my scanner."

An abandoned structure, so that was a relief. But as Darlene, shopping bag in hand, headed up Roosevelt Avenue—away from the fire, deliberately—she found herself dissatisfied with her purchase. It was March, a flinty March offering few signs of spring, and that didn't help, either. Snow, yesterday's snow, the same grainy pellets that had clattered across the roofs the day before, was being uplifted a second time, only dirtier now, and sweeping the pavement like sandpaper. The Remington people, didn't they manufacture guns, too? The question asked, summoned not an answer, but an image: her father, shotgun brandished aloft, long-legging it across the barnyard to rescue his gobbling turkeys from some predator, four- or two-legged. For years as a child Darlene had believed that she carried on her person the odor of turkey manure. Were there two corporations with the same name? She could look it up in their Dun & Bradstreet, but it didn't matter. An inept gift, not what you would buy for a professional friend.

Oh, Fanny was more than that, but *still . . .*

The careworn avenue, luckless-looking even on a good day with its squat buildings and pinched clapboard houses, was truly in disarray. Men and boys rushed wild-eyed past her through the brown haze; drivers, thwarted, sounded their horns in umbrage, while an ambulance wormed through the congestion, its klaxon, expressive of the emergency personnel's own exasperation, emitting intermittent, ear-piercing squawks. As Darlene reached the library steps, the salmon and white medical van pulled abreast and squawked again, before disappearing into smoky chaos.

Why an ambulance?

The G. C. Murphy building, the town's beloved 5 and 10, had lain forsaken a decade, sheets of warping plywood over the broken windows, out-of-date campaign posters over the plywood, graffiti over the peeling posters. The apartments above? *Tenants?* No, not possible. She distinctly recollected seeing pigeons flying in and out of the upper-level windows. *So long ago,* Darlene thought, yielding to a memory of her mother: how they had loved coming into town and, after her mother had finished paying her bills, betaking themselves to the G. C. Murphy. Darlene recalled her agonies in Murphy's aisles trying to decide upon which bauble she was going to lavish her fifty cents allowance. *Ladies for lunch!* her sweet mother sang as they drove into Ganaego in the family's rattling Chevy station wagon. Well, bless her mother with her pets and pet words like *betake*, and the memory, as long ago as it was and as fond as it was, failed to allay Darlene's misgivings. The hairdryer would have to go back to Walt Pitzele's shelves.

All that shopping had been for naught.

~ ~ ~

The afternoon, off to an unpromising start, only got worse. Darlene's tiny wedge of an office, whose sovereignty normally brought her a guilty pleasure, offered little solace. She stared through her casement window at the patio behind the library: three cement benches laden with crusty, blackened snow; behind them, the tall retaining wall that held back the tumescent advance of Second Hill. And now the tarry smoke, infiltrating, first, the lobby, then the reading rooms, wreathing the bronze head of Fredrick Booth III, founder of the steel mill. The fire was all people talked about. *Inferno,* they called it, parroting the clichéd language of television newscasts. It even beat out the Afghanistan War. But when Mr. Tattershaw sidled up to the counter and announced, "Squatters, there was squatters in there! They just carried a body out!"—that, for Darlene, did it. The old man's voice, despite his efforts to keep it couched in the appropriate tragic register, rose triumphantly.

"I seen it, a little boy! Burned to a crisp—a little boy!"

To escape, Darlene retreated into the recesses of the old library. This was where she had worked for twenty-five years, the only place she had worked. She had been awed by the library when her mother brought her here as a child—and she still was. Endowed by Frederick Booth's daughter, Ganaego's library had always been in this hardscrabble mill town an inspiring sight. Designed in Italian Renaissance style, limestone block now darkened with mill soot, marble walls, travertine floors, brass fittings, and, best of all, as far as Darlene was concerned, stacks closed to the public. In college, when she had interned here, she and her fellow interns flitted through the glass-floored archives bearing slips of paper with patrons' requests. When business slackened, they were assigned the tedious task of reading the shelves, that is, checking call letters to ensure the holdings were in order. How they dreaded that chore! And now she searched the job out, assigned it to herself. The papery smell of the old volumes, the silence, the sensation of being immersed in the prodigious product of human intellect: here it didn't matter how attractive you were, how popular you were, how powerful your political connections. She had been a smart girl, a smart girl who grew up on a turkey farm, a smart girl with a gentle mother who'd passed away too soon and an ignorant father, for whom she now made a home—a smart girl who had dreamed the wrong dreams, met the wrong men, placed her bets on the wrong horses. Deep in her stacks, Darlene Paczkowski, forty-three-years old and in nearly unremitting despair, could be alone, lost to the world.

~ ~ ~

By four p.m., she was in the gloomy 900s, the basement: geography and history. Drainage water seeped in here. Mustard-yellow streaks oozed down the ancient foundations, and mice, generation after generation, happily fashioned their homes between, sometimes within, the tomes of Mesopotamian history that a Romanian brakeman had lovingly collected over his lifetime and whose children, when he died, had foisted off on the library. This was where Darlene had come to brood the day the World Trade Towers fell, and it was where she sat now on a low stool when Chip tracked her down.

"Gracious, I've been looking for you for *all* day!" The young director, prone to hyperbole, waved a sheaf of papers. "I have no idea what we're going to do about this compressor stuff."

"We need to follow the contractor's lead, Chip." Her boss would never understand, nor care to understand, the technical details, so Darlene omitted them. "If we don't, we'll just end up five years from now begging for another one."

"It's not what the town engineer recommends."

"If Dennis Nelson has set foot in this building—in his entire life—more than four times, I'll eat my hat. He's thinking of the municipal building, Chip. That's a much newer structure. Billy's right on this. I've been *up* there, on the roof? This leaky old vessel needs a bigger unit."

"When were you up on the roof?"

"That isn't important."

"Yes, it is." When the Board finally got around to filling Mrs. Robb's position, it had been Chip, ten years her junior, who, with the long reach of his family's political pull, beat Darlene out of the directorship. "Tell me: When were *you* ever up on the roof?"

Would they really squander fifteen minutes on this? Documenting the times when, during any given downpour in the late 1970s, she and Mrs. Robb had climbed the scary rung ladder and swept off with their brooms the reservoir of water that would pool up there, this before Mrs. Robb finally wheedled a new roof from the borough council? Or, in the 1980s, when maddening leaks began developing in that new roof and she—for those wonderful few years, acting director—and Mr. Harrington, their custodian, would rush around with flapping sheets of plastic? Or last week, when Billy Clauston said flatly he wasn't sufficiently interested in their business to install an inadequate compressor and took her up there and showed her?

What was the use? "I'm going up toward Kensington, tomorrow," Darlene said, adopting a less confrontational tack. "To visit some friends? Billy works Saturdays. I could stop at Clauston's. Maybe if I get him to give me the facts and we write a proposal, we could go to the council—like Mrs. Robb did—and make a case for the more expensive unit? How's that?"

"Times are different now."

Darlene gazed at the sulfurous blotches on the bulging walls. She longed to tell Chip of Mrs. Robb, an old woman, skirts tied to the top of her shriveled thighs, shoving a broomful of dirty water across a sagging roof, and, half an hour later, in that same dress, lecturing on Mozart's Vienna to a room of rapt patrons.

"Shouldn't we at least *try?*"

"These friends—they going to fix you up?" Chip bestowed on her his impish grin, the catch-me-if-you-can-look he employed when he stepped over the line. "Just curious?"

Darlene flushed. Boss or not, as a fundamentalist Christian who supposedly had a direct line to God, he had no such right to make personal remarks. But Chip did and would, and it seemed one more thing not worth fighting over. "Hey," she called out to his receding back, "she's a librarian! We're writing a paper for *The Library Quarterly*!"

Last one out this evening, setting the alarm, Darlene tried not to think of the fire. But outside, the smell was far more pungent, and, with every inhalation of that lingering smoke that carried within its breast the ashes of some unfortunate child, Darlene's loathing of her own life rose to meet it. Despite her arguments to reassure herself concerning the hairdryer, she knew it was a dreadful gift. Pitzele's stayed open until six-thirty. She should take it back. But to return the dryer would be to admit how superficial a person she was, so, no, even though the last thing she needed was a new hairdryer, she had no intention of returning it. Where she was going was home, to fix Friday dinner for her querulous father. Later, after she had washed the dishes and put through a load of laundry, she'd go upstairs to wash the smell of smoke from her hair and to lie in the darkness of her room, alone in her desolation.

~ ~ ~

Ladies for lunch!

Darlene wakes thinking of the G. C. Murphy parakeets. The birds fill her room: parakeets with sky-blue breasts and speckled wings; parakeets the color of ripe bananas; parakeets a muted, glaucous green. Yakkers—you could hear them all over the store. The aquariums, their unworldly sapphire-blue, bubbling reservoirs: goldfish, guppies, silver dollars. *Angelfish!* Angelfish with their elegant fins like enormous eyelashes. Hamsters—or gerbils, what's the difference?—those cages always smelled cheesy. Buttons, spools of thread! Rows of different weights and hues of thread. Potholders and aluminum saucepans, lipsticks and fingernail polish, rouge and mascara. Socks. Fruit of the Loom underwear for her father, cotton panties for herself, hose for her mother. Her sweet mother. In their hats and white cotton gloves they would not deign to sit at the counter. But to be seated at a table, you were required to stand in line. Smells of tuna fish and eggy mayonnaise, chili con carne and franks tumbling on their rollers, chicken noodle soup, tomato soup, coffee and cigarette smoke, the cloying miasma of a dozen different perfumes. Plates clattering, silverware clanging, waitresses shouting, infants fussing, laughter arising like chimes—and *that,* this dark Saturday morning Darlene dallies in bed, pauses her: the laughter of adults. In their house that didn't happen. The floors—how could you forget the G. C. Murphy floors? Unpainted planks oiled and oiled until the grained wood shone as darkly as blackstrap molasses. No one could make a grilled cheese that could hold a candle to a G. C. Murphy grilled cheese. Two-penny nails, three-penny nails, lampshades, girdles, jigsaw puzzles, three-colored ribbon taffy.

The first book she ever bought, *Heidi,* she bought at the G. C. Murphy . . .

Saturdays her father liked his *bigos.* Her mother's recipe, the trick was to start the day before. Last night, while the pork roasted, Darlene sautéed sausage and ham, then layered bacon, sauerkraut, tomatoes, and apples in her mother's cast iron Dutch oven, sprinkled it with caraway and allspice and peppercorns, set it to cook. This morning, while she made breakfast, she diced the cooled meat and combined everything. The stew could simmer all day. As she worked, she went on fretting over the hairdryer. Her thinking had begun to turn around: Though an inept gift, you could not claim the dryer was an unthoughtful gift, and so, before coming downstairs, she had wrapped it and attached a card. But try as she might to settle this in her heart, the decision would not settle.

And now Poppa, waking up on the wrong side of bed. "Damn fool thing!" He slammed the toaster against the backsplash.

"Sorry." Darlene rushed over. "Here, let me get it."

Churlish by nature, on her Fanny and Dominic weekends, which occurred, at most, two or three times a year, he was worse. He rasped his palm against his whiskered cheek, pleased with himself in a vexed sort of way. He had not been mean to her or to her mother, didn't drink, didn't carry on. Put food on the table and a roof over their heads, the same roof he fell off hammering down his own shingles at an age when most men were hard-pressed to summon the energy to cross the room and change channels on their TVs. But he never loved them, either.

"So, when you gonna be back?"

"Sunday afternoon, Poppa."

"Snow." With his fingers he pushed the scrambled eggs dangling from his lips into the cavern of his mouth and lunged for the bacon. "Gonna find yourself nose-down in a ditch."

It was she who insisted, after his accident, that he come and live with her. In her there existed, just as fiercely as it had existed in her mother, a *I-will-do-the-right-thing-no-matter-what* stubbornness. "I'll be careful, Poppa."

He unfurled the *Chronicle,* checked the weather, snorted smugly. When he shoved the paper aside to shake the ketchup with both hands, a photograph of a child slid into view. *I seen it*—the shrill cry of Mr. Tattershaw's echoed in her mind as it had in the library—*a little boy!* Darlene didn't need to read the caption. Derek Driscoll: ears like open car doors and two Robin Goodfellow dimples that, had he lived, would have guaranteed him no end of girl trouble. Child of a too-young mother who read your lips to understand you and whose breath, Saturday morning when she dropped her son at Darlene's story hour, reeked of alcohol. Put off by the smell of the cooking meat, Darlene snatched up her suitcase and her gift and fled the house.

~ ~ ~

"Where were his parents?" she asked Chip. She removed her

boots from the plastic bag she'd used to carry them inside in and stationed them beneath her coat. "Were they in there, too?"

Chip was delighted to fill her in. "No, no. Momma Bear—she's twenty-four—she took a powder, evidently some weeks ago, while Papa Bear—he's thirty-nine—was otherwise occupied yesterday getting bombed. *Rafferty's?*—that's the last place he was seen. Some row bar, I'm sure you've never heard of it."

Ganaego's row bars. The steel mill could, and did, collapse, bringing about a massive depression that the valley continued to wallow in. But Ganaego's row bars soldiered on decade after decade, and actually she knew Rafferty's, had frequented it, briefly, eighteen years ago when a man—a cad—she had invited to live with her (*that* lasted three weeks) tended bar there. But that wee bit of personal history she saw no reason to share with the Evangelical Assembly of God's Head Deacon. For Chip to be in on a Saturday was rare. But he was only here, he explained, to pick up his new Thinsulate ski gloves he'd forgotten.

"We've got weekend family lift passes—the powder's fantastic, I hear." Her boss slid on one of his new gloves to show her. "What they're thinking is that after the scumbag left him alone there, the kid started a fire in a wastebasket to keep warm. Altogether charming family, I must say, a real credit to the community. You're going to talk to that chiseler of a contractor, right?"

"Billy Clauston's not a chiseler, Chip."

Chip worked his fingers to loosen the glove. "Darlene, take it from me: You can't trust these tradespeople any farther than you can throw them. We need to be ordering more zombie books—my kids can't get enough of them."

Zombies. The black glove on his hand bothered her. At her story hour this morning, Darlene took pains to ensure there would not be an empty chair. But no matter how closely she gathered the children about her, Ganaego's little black and ethnic faces, in Darlene's imagination there stood, isolated, an unoccupied chair. She had not seen the boy's mother recently—her name was Jessica Schumacher, that much she knew—so it must have been the father, whom she'd only seen from a distance, who had been bringing him. About the child she knew nothing. He was shy, never spoke, would not respond to her questions, seemed to have no friends. But he liked her stories, or, if Darlene wasn't even entirely sure of that, she was certain that he followed them. As she dramatized her Aesop fables at her flannel board, sticking and unsticking her animals, she would feel the boy's cornflower-blue eyes on her, gravely weighing these remarkable matters of which she spoke. But apart from these few superficial details, she would have told you—had you asked—that Derek Driscoll, except for not being as squirmy as the other little boys, was no different from the rest of the children. But that wasn't true. They knew that now.

Squatting in the G. C. Murphy?

About the weather, Poppa, unfortunately, had been correct. After story hour, Darlene watched pillowy flakes beginning to sift down. For the moment you could count them, but even in the twenty minutes she spent tidying up, the storm intensified. Not so worried about driving in poor weather on local commutes, she *was* daunted by the prospect of sixty snowy miles of unfamiliar country roads. But the weather was only an excuse. Even if she left the hairdryer behind, wasn't the fact that she had purchased such a lame gift clear indication of how ridiculous a person she was? She squinted at people through her thick glasses, her hair fell across her forehead in straggles, her features were coarsening, she had become frumpy, a foolish, frumpy woman. Despite her crack to Chip about writing a paper, she and Fanny hadn't even started; all they'd done was talk about a paper. Fanny had published. She and Dominic moved in a rarefied orbit, he a professor of Afro-American studies, she head of the undergraduate collection, they were grown up and sophisticated. And the thought that she herself might someday join the august assembly of those who have contributed to the trove of human wisdom, that she might be cited and catalogued by a fellow librarian—to Darlene that would mean the world. But it was absurd. To think that a librarian from a town no one ever heard of could author a scholarly paper? Fanny was a dear, dear person and meant well, but she was only humoring her. The snow was irresistible: It solved everything.

Fanny, taken by surprise, was disappointed. "Not snowing—bright sunshine!"

"Because it's coming up from the south." Darlene didn't know that, but storms, especially wet laden ones, frequently bowled up the Ohio River Valley. But no matter where the storm was coming from or going to, it was a betrayal. This was Fanny's *birthday.* She could picture Fanny in her kitchen: jeans, rag socks, olive-oil spotted sweatshirt. Darlene apologized and, as was her nature, apologized a second time.

"Don't be a big silly." Fanny loved to coo at her. "We'll postpone, what the heck."

"What about next week?"

"Next week? Oh no, recruitment duties. When else are you free?"

How about the rest of my life? Darlene wanted to cry out. "Week after?"

Fanny groaned. "I was afraid you were going to say that. We're not usually this busy?"

"I don't have my calendar here." To her lie Darlene gave a bouncy lilt. "Why don't I give you a buzz on Monday when it's not so darn hectic?"

~ ~ ~

Death in the 5 and 10

Inserting the phone in its cradle, Darlene becomes aware of silence. Usually, she only notices the stillness of her secluded office to revel in it. Today silence descends with a gluey viscosity: It's as though she's suspended in amber, estranged from time. She tarries at her desk until well past noon, then collects her manila file with information about the new compressor, deposits it on Chip's desk, and leaves without saying goodbye to anyone. Exiting the parking lot, her wipers laboring against the snow, she turns right, instead of left, and creeps her car down Roosevelt, drawing into the curb before Savage's Hardware and Sporting Goods, across from the G. C. Murphy. Scraps of burnt wood and shards of glass lay scattered across the slushy street, along with what incongruously resembles the aftermath of a party: coffee cups, donut boxes, water bottles, pop cans. Before a ribbon of yellow tape three people have congregated, shoulders hunched against the driving snow. Although the rear wall of the building remains, the front, sides, and roof have collapsed into the basement. Charred timbers and anonymous bits of plumbing poke out from mounds of bricks and glutinous plaster, and high up, on a small raft of flooring attached to the standing wall, a bed frame dangles. Over everything a pall of smoke hovers, mingling with the falling snow, and even in here, in the closed car, the sickening smell of waterlogged and scorched wood reaches Darlene. Most conspicuously, of the long red sign with the big gold letters that had spanned the store no evidence remains. Nothing left would remind you of the busy mercantile life that once transpired here, that this had been a place people sought out to supply their wants and ornament their lives.

Ladies for lunch!

Darlene recalls—one final time—the tropical parakeets, then turns her gaze on the bed suspended over the smoldering rubble. Where did they sleep? Did they cook here? Did they race the child around the old display tables? Play hide-and-seek in the dressing rooms? Did the father intend in September to register the boy in school? What address was he going to provide? *15 Yarn and Bobbins Lane?* Why would you leave a five-year-old child alone in an abandoned building? To go drinking? How far beyond the parameters of the human community must you have strayed, how deep into despair must you have fallen, to do such a thing?

From here, she cannot see Rafferty's. But it is only a short walk down the avenue past the vegetable market that no longer exists, the milliner's, long gone, the tobacco shop, gone, the old Company Store, boarded-up, then Max Fischman's Jewelry and Small Appliances, in the process after Max's death of being liquidated, then the bank with its grand columns and barred windows, the municipal building, the State Liquor Store, to come at last to glowing Rolling Rock and Pabst Blue Ribbon signs, one in each small window, that bracket a grated door.

Before which she pauses, daunted.

Ganaego's row bars enjoy a well-deserved reputation for danger. Not overcoming her trepidation so much as going on despite it, Darlene pushes the door against where it has eternally scraped the floor and enters. It is as if she were stepping back in time: *Has anything changed?* The narrow room illuminated by advertisements from beer companies that yield the fugitive light that men who drink in the afternoon prefer, the silence of those men, their isolation one from another, their bleak introversion. But it is the smell—the fetid soup of sour malt, crumbling plaster, rancid cooking grease—that carries back memories. The only affair she ever had, sordid, humiliating, and mercifully soon truncated. He was manipulative, used people, laughed at the damage he inflicted. But even so, the experience gave rise to an anguish that has ever lingered.

Except for those three weeks she has slept every night of her life alone.

Darlene resists looking at the bartender, for fear it *is* the same man. But no, no one, not even in Ganaego, could be that stuck in time. This bartender is a heavyset man with pig-tiny eyes and a shaggy mustache. He folds his meaty arms across his black shirt and stares at her, until she selects a stool, maybe the same stool she sat on the night she told the other bartender that she had stuffed his clothes and shoes in a box and shoved it into the hall.

"Dewar's," she's learned to say. "Little bit of water, no ice." As he places a pasteboard coaster and tumbler of whiskey before her and collects her five-dollar bill, she asks, "Is he here?"

"Who?"

"Derek Driscoll's father." The bartender switches his big head irritably. "He comes in here," she presses. "He spends his days in here, right?"

"Don't know nothin' about it."

"He *was* in here—when the fire started, right?" She lifts her voice to his retreating back. "Did he even bother to go watch the fire that killed his son?"

A stool scrapes. Her chest tightening, Darlene watches a young man—a belligerent, slouchy boy in a plaid hunting jacket—amble up to within a few feet of her. Curling his lip cowboy-fashion, he accosts her. "Whacha want with Driscoll?"

He's even younger than she at first thought: Is he underage? "Are *you* a friend of his?"

"Ain't saying I am, ain't saying I ain't."

The bartender's black-shirted mass drifts back. "Lady, maybe you better go, huh?"

Ignoring him, she addresses the young man. "Well, if you ever make up your mind and decide you *are* his friend, then you ask him two questions for me. *First,* you ask him if he ever read to that little boy. I know he liked to be read to, I know that for a fact."

"Lady," the bartender interjects, "this—"

"I'll go when I'm ready!" She keeps her focus on the young man, who, in the meantime, has hooked his thumbs in his trouser loops as if they were tools he doesn't know what to do with. "The second question you ask Derek Driscoll's father is *this:* Why didn't he ask for help? Why didn't he ask *me?* I would've mothered that child for him, I would've been a good mother."

The young man, without having anything even remotely close to a conceivable answer, smirks clownishly. Darlene, finished with him, turns to the bartender, whose mustache bunches angrily up under the strawberry fruit of his nose. She pushes her untouched glass across the bar. "I don't want this," she tells him.

~ ~ ~

Her car windows are socked in with snow. Darlene slams the door behind her and searches for her phone. A dowdy, overweight woman closing in on menopause who can never find anything in her purse. She's trembling, but not from the cold. She pats her glasses dry with the tail of her blouse, jabs the phone buttons, and whimpers when Fanny answers.

"Is it too late to change my mind?"

"It's snowing like mad! You're not on the road, are you, sweetie?"

"Fanny, I want to come, if it's all right? To work on our paper? But you've probably made other plans, I'm sure?"

"No, we haven't made any other plans. But it's dangerous—they're saying we might get fourteen inches."

"I have to ask you something first. Do you and Dominic really want me to come? It's your birthday—you must want to be alone?"

"Darlene, sweetie, are you all right?"

"Do you want me to come?"

"Yes, yes, you silly pooh, I—*we*—want you to come. We want

you to come and share my birthday, we *do!*"

"I have a terrible gift for you, Fanny? It's horrible."

"Goodness, you are in a state. Why would I care what your gift is?"

"Because it is. And you have to forgive it in advance—or I won't come."

"Sweetie," Fanny purrs, "your gift to me is *you*. But I'm worried: Are you sure it's safe?"

"I'm the daughter of a Polish turkey farmer," Darlene answers, as if it were a solemn declaration she is making. "I know how to drive in the snow. But I want to start on our paper, Fanny, I really, really want to start."

"And so we shall!" Fanny cries out. "I'll clean off the kitchen table. On this table many a good paper has begun."

~ ~ ~

Climbing out to brush the snow from her windows, Darlene understands that before she leaves she needs to call Billy Clauston, too. She can't stop at Billy's *and* make it to Fanny's. And neither can she fob off on Chip the inadequate compressor, even though that's what he deserves. To do that to the library? No, she cannot do that. But even before she calls Billy, there's something else.

An hour of storytelling could not compensate for such a life. How bewildering, how terrifying, the boy's existence must have been. But in a life that appeared to offer little in the way of safety and comfort, her story hour, she hopes, brought Derek Driscoll some momentary escape. When he would succumb to a particular mishap or misadventure her flannel beasts had fallen prey to, the child would blink both his eyes slowly, his gaze intensifying in consternation. She hopes her storytelling helped. But to be honest, as she crosses the littered street, the sidewalk deserted now, to stand beside the yellow tape, her head bowed in the lowering snow, Darlene doesn't know.

She thinks of an unloved child lying in the basement of a mortuary, no one to touch him, no one to hold him in their arms, a child alone in darkness.

You can't know, she thinks, how could you?

Spare Parts and
Bloody Bones

Memorial Day Weekend 2010

Twice now she'd been to the recovery room. The first visit had been standard medical policy, checking in on her patient. That Pleasance Stubbs, an elderly woman she'd known for a long time, had not yet awakened should have raised—and did raise—a level of concern. It was early, however, and the operation, a total hip replacement, a revision, had, by all accounts, gone uneventfully, just under three hours.

"She did fine," Aliz had reassured Pleasance's husband, a shy, pale, recessive man named Arthur who rose—sprang to his feet—when she'd stepped into the waiting room.

"She should've never tried moving that buffet. I tol' her that, Doctor."

That the contumacious eighty-three-year-old woman's refusal to control her weight or moderate her activities contributed to the excessive wear that brought about this second procedure were indeed significant. The woman irritated her. Frankly, Pleasance Stubbs had long irritated Aliz Kovacs. But all that she had let pass, replying neutrally, "She's going to have to learn to slow down."

"Oh, you know her." Arthur Stubbs had smirked as if they were sharing a private jest over their backyard fence. "No use telling Pleasance nothin'." He hesitated. "I don't want to push, but can I go in to see her, Doctor?"

How unassertive was that? Husbands were gaily shooting movies of their newborns emerging blood-smeared and purple from birth canals; grandparents crowding into examination rooms; whole families clustering about shadowy X-rays, nine-year-old heads wagging sagaciously. It was the *Era of the Customer*, Ganaego Hospital's Chief of Staff proclaimed, unintentionally echoing Jimmy Boswell's ubiquitous slogan anyone who had grown up in Ganaego had long taken as gospel, *Jimmy's Buicks—It's Your Money, Ain't It?* The thought of Jimmy, her erstwhile lover who was waiting for her today on his boat, brought her a moment of rueful ambivalence, but this much Aliz Kovacs, who could be said to have only incidentally grown up in Ganaego and who had little use for slogans and nine-year-old advice-givers, *was* clear on: The deference this mild man, fingers to his lips, afforded her she appreciated. She was aware of how people, especially men, reacted to her authority. "Soon, they're very busy," she said, as if to both reprove and excuse the staff. "Don't worry, she'll be awake in no time."

But even then there lingered a doubt. The quicker Pleasance Stubbs surfaces, Aliz had thought, striding away, the better. *Revision Operation*—an apt description, and always fascinating to travel back over your own ground, recognizing the decades-old cicatrix along the skin and within the leaden sedated body the scar tissue across the gluteus maximus, then making of the heavy muscle a second separation, lifting it away to reveal one's handiwork, the stainless steel femoral and damaged polyethylene acetabular prostheses. Well, at least, the latter would be updated with a ceramic fixture, and the violated flesh—what choice did it have?—would once again commence knitting itself back together. True, innovative, less invasive techniques were becoming more common, an anterior rather than a posterior approach, riskier but resulting in less muscle contusion and a speedier recovery. But that procedure required specialized

Spare Parts and Bloody Bones

equipment to which backwater Ganaego Hospital would not commit the resources. And, truth be told, so many hundreds of times had Aliz performed this tried and true procedure that she regarded the necessary updating of her own skills to undertake such a change of practice with a certain disinclination.

Why bother? would be the way Jimmy Boswell would respond, gunning his cabin cruiser under the dirty bridges that spanned Ganaego's dirty river. *If it ain't broke, why fix it?*

Indeed, the procedure was time-tested, her prior work and today's above reproach: dislocating the joint, removing the failed prosthesis, fitting and cementing in place the new implant, closing the wound. No, it was Lunner, the anesthesiologist, who worried her. A playboy, floral shirts, expensive shoes, always a story to top yours— she distrusted the fellow. Solazar was the superior anesthesiologist, but the holiday, gateway to America's summer, loomed, and Martin Solazar, as had most of the staff, had long vanished—to his backyard grill, to his tomato patch, to his fishing worms, all the things, even fifty years after immigrating from Hungary as a child, Aliz still did not understand about her adopted country. Had Paul Lunner over-medicated?

And this was not the day's only open question.

When she had, going up to her office, checked her voicemail, there had been a peculiar message: someone identifying himself as Lieutenant Oliver Brown from Creighton, several towns downriver. He claimed to have information possibly relating to her father. Peculiar for certain, because her father was presumed deceased long ago somewhere in Europe. She had no living immediate family, and so, doubtless, the call was a mistake—or a scam. MDs were prey to con artists. And when the summons had come from the nursing staff that brought about this second recovery room visit, she put Lieutenant Brown out of her mind and rushed down.

Pleasance had surfaced in intense pain, complained of dizziness, and vomited. She was disoriented and needed to be forcibly restrained to keep her prone. The danger of dislocating the hip was severe. Aliz again reassured Mr. Stubbs, now seated beside his wife, who had grown even paler. Is *he,* she fretted, going to faint? She leaned over to speak to her patient. "Pleasance? You're doing great. But we need you not to move, do–you–understand–that?"

The old woman, eyes two primordial seas of confusion, surged against her restraints and bellowed like a fish peddler, "Homework a day late gets docked one full letter grade!"

Arthur leapt to his feet. "What's up with her? She keeps thinking she's teaching! She hasn't taught school in over twenty years!"

I know, Aliz almost said, remembering the third-grade teacher, fifty-six and still vigorous, weeping in her office at Aliz's adamant judgment: *Retire or face potential crippling.* She had been a very young doctor then, sure of herself, quick and determinative in her opinions. Perhaps she had come down too insistently on Pleasance, but the woman *had* abused the first hip replacement, the right, and then, after her reluctant retirement, abused the second, the left, and was now on her third operation. Aliz, suppressing memories that went back even farther, murmured, "If she could handle the farm boys from Rose Township, she can handle this." Ducking out of the alcove, she hissed to a nurse, "Page Dr. Lunner."

"All you're going to get is his answering service."

"He's gone—*already?*"

"He and his wife have an evening flight," the nurse defended him. "His son got them tickets to the Dodgers-Rockies game tomorrow."

When would she learn? Aliz, shaking her head, reviewed Lunner's notes. He had used Servoflurane, then switched to Desflurane. The vertigo and nausea were serious enough to warrant concern, but would pass. More troubling, given the patient's age, was the disorientation. Seizures, although remote, were a possibility. Aliz started the paperwork to have Pleasance transferred to the ICU and prescribed an antipsychotic and sedative. By now, she was definitely uneasy. Small-town Ganaego Hospital lacked a dedicated ICU physician, but a little known secret was that probably its brightest staff member occupied one of its least commanding positions. Aliz took the elevator to the first floor. Since the late-seventies, Rupa Mudaliar had worked in the emergency room, many nights had *been* the emergency room, the saffron and yellow saris beneath her white jacket and the vermillion bindi in the center of her forehead disconcerting the suspicious steelworkers and their families whom Dr. Mudaliar good-naturedly stitched up.

Aliz did not need Rupa's consultation, it was a little friendly company she sought more than anything else, but she was happy enough to take her colleague's concurrence: sedation and observation. The Indian woman, ruddy face prettily framed by her snow-white hair, looked up at the blond, sharp-featured Eastern European woman: Western Pennsylvania, a singular place to meet and form a friendship. "Do you vish to leave, Aliz? I vould be happy to keep an eye on your patient?"

"I was supposed to meet a friend, but that's all right."

"It is no trouble?"

"No, no, I wouldn't think of it."

Dr. Mudaliar, smiling mischievously, steered an imaginary pilot wheel. "This the millionaire? Mr. Zoom-Zoom?"

Was anything in this town not public knowledge? Embarrassing enough at fifty-nine to even *have* a boyfriend, even worse to have a boyfriend on the hospital Board of Directors (well, not everyone would agree that was a bad thing) named Jimmy—that was his authentic given name, the name on his birth certificate. *Zoom-Zoom* was the name he'd given his boat. It was a wonder he hadn't christened all four of his children Zoom-Zoom.

"I'll buzz if I need you," she said dryly.

On the elevator up to her office, her pager burred in her pocket. In the screen gleamed Jimmy Boswell's cell number. Letting herself in the darkened office suite and then her office, she called as she thumbed through Pleasance Stubbs' records.

"Jimmy, I'm sorry, I'm probably not going to make it. Can I call you tomorrow?"

Behind him she could hear his stereo: *Eine Kleine Nachmusik.* For an uncultured man, Jimmy Boswell had surprisingly good taste. Music was what they talked about the day they met at a hospital function. But tonight, jilted and all alone on his luxurious boat, Jimmy whined like a sulky child. "Aliz, sweetheart, you're not the only doctor of record in Ganaego? I've got two of the most beautiful steaks you ever laid eyes on. Dry-aged, twenty-nine bucks each— Aliz, you could send these steaks to college! Gee whiz, how much longer you gonna be?"

He professed he wanted to marry her, and although that was out of the question (he wasn't serious, she wasn't listening), she did like Jimmy Boswell. *Sending steaks to college:* He amused her, teased her out of her gloomy introspection. But she was, at the moment, in no mood for being indulged. "I've got a patient in distress and my goddamned anesthesiologist's gone to the baseball game! This place is like a morgue, and may turn into one. I'll call tomorrow!"

No, *this* was the worst: to be dating someone who said *Gee whiz!*

~ ~ ~

Sometime ago she had set Pleasance Stubbs' records aside. Nothing new was to be gleaned here, and she now put down the journal she was reading to ponder the pad of paper with Lieutenant Brown's number. A computer check informed her that the number was legitimate. Could this man in Creighton really have information regarding her father? Impossible. It was past eight. Tuesday she'd call and find out. But then, perhaps because she was fidgety, she went ahead and left a return message on Lieutenant Brown's voicemail, acknowledging his call.

Three people: three theories. Although her mother had not been present that afternoon at Lake Balaton, she had absolutely no questioned that she knew what had happened. Estranged from their father and furious with him only the way someone in love can be, she declared that Vidor, remorseful over his infidelities, had drowned himself. And lord knows, gray-eyed, slim, handsome, a womanizer long before her mother attempted to redeem him, their father, a morally frail man, was capable of such a senseless and spiteful act. Jan, on the other hand, two years younger than Aliz and unfortunately, as it turned out, of no firmer character than his father, claimed that Papa, who had taken Jan with him into the bathhouse and then bafflingly disappeared, had been abducted by the secret police. And that was possible, too: Vidor Kovacs, minor party functionary perpetually in debt and involved that summer in a repugnant ménage â trois, might have finally gone too far and antagonized the wrong people. In Hungary in the 1950s, people did disappear from the face of the earth.

But Aliz never believed either her mother's or her brother's theories.

It was she who'd waited outside the bathhouse that warm Sunday, wet swimsuit rolled in her towel, squinting (astigmatic, even then) imploringly at the door. She could smell the lake, Balaton's silky, salty waters that were infused with a soup paste of minerals: sulfates, magnesium, calcium carbonate. The pungent scent lingered in the cotton of the towel, in her hair, on her skin. Desperate people, seeking cures, drank the stuff—which, then and now, appalled her. *August:* The late-afternoon sun sent long strands of rufous light through the square. Dust coated the leaves of the plane trees. At her feet lay great scabs of brown bark. A man strolled past walking a miniature dachshund. He stopped to let her stroke the tiny panting animal and pointed out that his pet had one brown eye and one blue eye. What was taking Jan and Papa so long? Finally, Jan in his short pants appeared, bewildered. Had Papa come out? He hadn't. Of that, Aliz—bashful and frightened to be alone, racing through her change—felt confident. Jan dashed back inside, the soles of his leather shoes clattering in the corridor. In a few minutes he reappeared, his panic more pronounced. Again he ran back inside, and now, this final time he exited, tears streamed from beneath his glasses. A vendor who sold colored ices took them under his protection. A search was undertaken; the police were summoned; their mother called.

"He ran off," seven-year-old Aliz, shattered by her father's betrayal, announced. And neither had she ever doubted her theory. "Fled across the border, assumed a new name, became a drifter, a *bum.*"

But wouldn't he have been caught trying to cross? Dr. Aliz Kovacs, fifty-two years later methodically plowing through the stack of medical journals on her desk and resisting the headache building behind her eyes, would agree that arguments could be raised against all the hypotheses. People don't vanish into thin air. If Vidor, in misery over squandering his wife's affections, had drowned himself, eventually his body would have washed up somewhere, wouldn't it? His clothes, his camera, his shoes—where did *they* go? If the secret police had seized him, wouldn't some word as to his fate have eventually reached them? Wouldn't somebody have seen him interrogated, met him while imprisoned, witnessed his execution?

Honestly, given how passionately she had also loved him, had her father reappeared with any excuse Aliz would have, every bit as much as her mother, forgiven him. How could you not? To love Vidor was to love life. Why else had her mother—an otherwise independent,

Spare Parts and Bloody Bones

clear-eyed woman, someone who had subsequently undertaken to flee Soviet-occupied Hungary with her two children—clung to her fantasies to the day she died? But if Aliz's theory was correct, it was, in effect, this calculating and cruelly engineered betrayal whose poison had seeped into her brother, eroding his confidence and undermining his childhood and adolescence—and *that,* that Aliz would never forgive. Nor would she ever trust a man again. Jan's overdose was ruled accidental. Most overdoes are. But in thirty years of grieving she never doubted that it had not been an accident. And indeed, when her beeper sounded, bringing her out of a fitful doze, she thought it was the telephone and Lieutenant Brown and refused to answer it. A second later, realizing her error, she looked at the beeper's display, saw it was the ICU, and raced for the door.

Pleasance had awakened hallucinating again. The episode had occurred during one of the husband's fifteen-minute visits. Pleasance, snapping out of a deep sleep, had seized Arthur's wrist and demanded to see his hall pass. It had so unhinged the poor man that he had shrieked, bringing the nurse scurrying.

"For crying out loud," the nurse complained, "you would've thought he was being murdered. Should I increase her medication?"

Pleasance had slipped back into sleep. Her respiration was normal, blood levels unexceptional, vital signs stable. Aliz would rather not increase the dosage, but would like Pleasance to get a full night's rest. "Nothing else unusual?"

"I was just *in* here. I think he poked her, that's what I think."

She went out to the waiting room. Arthur Stubbs, having been chased from his wife's room, sat, or, rather, slumped in a chair, his socked feet curled over one another and resting on his shoes. His withered face was splotched from his leaning on his palm. Did they have no children to spell him? She couldn't recall, then, a beat later, came the answer: Pleasance Stubbs' children, Pleasance had stridently proclaimed, had been the multitudes of Ganaego's nine-year-old savages that she transformed into civilized beings. Pleasance even shared her mission with her tiny pupils: Aliz could attest to that. As soon as Arthur spotted Aliz, he struggled to his feet.

Had the man been in the military? "Long night for you," she said softly.

"They said I could turn on the boob tube"—he inclined an indifferent shoulder toward the darkened set—"but it's all junk. Stupid movies and buying shows, you know?"

"I could find you some more magazines?"

"Nah, Pleasance's the reader." He stared hard at her. "This ain't right, what she's doing, is it, this teaching stuff? She never pulled any of this funny stuff before."

"It's not uncommon," Aliz reassured him, "for people—older people, especially—coming out of anesthesia to present with some disorientation. If you're going to stay all night, you should at least get some coffee? The cafeteria's closed, but there are vending machines. In the basement."

"Figured there must be."

"I mean," she apologized, "it's dreadful coffee?"

"Better'n nothin'." He turned in a complete circle. "Hey, you want some? I'll bring you up a cup? My treat." They both, at that moment, occasioned to look at his stockinged feet. He grinned sheepishly. "I got ferocious bunions—big as acorns."

There were holes in his socks. She looked away in distaste.

"You said they was in the basement," he clarified. "The machines?"

"But you can't take the elevators. They're locked out of the basement at night, I don't know why. There's a stairway. But it's not easy to find. It's sort of in the back?"

"Don't you worry. Pleasance couldn't find her way out of a paper bag, but when it comes to directions"—Arthur tapped his nose—"I gotta schnozz like a bloodhound."

Somehow she doubted that. Picturing Arthur Stubbs blundering around the Radiology Department, she said, "Why don't I show you?"

Even a few minutes of enforced small talk could make Aliz squirm. Being trapped in passing social situations with strangers, sitting next to a yakker on the plane, even as she closed out patient visits she would find herself casting about for something to chat about, weddings, births, the weather. The thought of spending ten minutes with this man seemed intolerable. But she watched helplessly as Arthur turned a second aimless circle and sat to wiggle into his broken shoes. Together they rode the elevator to the lobby in silence. The nurse's comment about Lunner and his baseball game came to mind, but what did she know about sports? Jimmy came to mind. But Jimmy Boswell's wickedly potent Manhattans, his CD changer with Wolfgang Amadeus Mozart and Felix Mendelssohn, the amber glow of the complicated controls of his swanky watercraft—all that, to Arthur Stubbs, would be as exotic as an article in the *British Journal of Surgery* on which she might seek his comment.

"Do you have a hobby, Mr. Stubbs?" she suddenly asked.

Her own question astounded her, but Arthur took it as a perfectly natural inquiry. "I fix things. Pleasance's always on my case because I'm bringing things home and fixin' them."

"What kind of things?"

She led him down a flight of gloomy stairs into the basement and then into a small galley, where a battery of brightly blinking vending machines stood. The little room was warm from the various motors and units. While she fed a dollar bill into a machine and collected a cardboard cup of insipid tea, Arthur fumbled with his change, sorting through it carefully. Aliz glanced away, suppressing her impatience, then became increasingly annoyed at his painstaking study of the coffee machine's multifarious options.

It all tastes the same! she wanted to scream.

Clutching his cup at last, he turned. "I see they got the kind with chocolate?" He awarded her his conspiratorial smirk. "Pleasance's *addicted* to that stuff." He looked around searchingly. "Don't suppose there's lids anywheres . . . *Ah!*" He retrieved two lids from a fixture on the side of the machine. "Just gotta know where to look." He capped his coffee to his satisfaction and waited for her to cap her tea, then added, "Toasters, toaster ovens, old radios, even TVs—things like that."

She looked at him nonplussed.

"Things I fix."

"I'm sorry, I forgot, yes, so?"

He peered at her with a sort of parental expression. "You ain't staying here just because of Pleasance, are you? That would be terrible, it's a holiday weekend."

"Of course not, I have a lot of work to catch up on."

"Because I'm sure she'll be all right and everything?"

Why do Americans go to experts and then tell the experts their business? If she lived on this continent a hundred years, this she would never comprehend. She was tempted to snap at this ignorant man, *Your wife may never come completely out of the anesthesia. She may be impaired— permanently!* "I'm sure she will," she said firmly, reclaiming her ground. "We just need to keep an eye on her."

"Oh, my thoughts exactly." Arthur guffawed noisily. "Just spare parts and bloody bones—that's all we are anyway."

"Excuse me?" Aliz wasn't sure she'd heard what she just heard.

"That's what old Doc Schmutzler used to say. He was before your time."

Aliz compressed her lips. "I remember Dr. Schmutzler." She turned her back on him to leave. "Sorry, I need to get back."

As they rode the elevator up, the uncomfortable silence returned. At a loss, Aliz asked, "So, you fix things?"

"You would not *believe* what people throw out." Arthur spoke with a righteous anger. "Sometimes I pick up a piece of wood or metal somebody's shit-canned—sorry, throwed away—and I just stare at it, you know, just stare and stare at it." He scratched the top of his coffee against the stubble along his cheek; it looked to be a kind of sage gesture. "And then suddenly—*boom!*—it'll hit me."

"What will hit you?"

"How to use it! How this piece of throwed-away metal or wood could be put to good use—somewhere in the house or in the car? Oh, I'm real smart that way, figurin' out new uses for old things. You need a toaster, by any chance?"

"Thank you, I'm fine."

"I got more toasters than you could shake a stick at?"

How far did she have to go with him? All the way back to the ICU? She rebelled. As the elevator doors opened at the fourth floor and he stepped back politely waiting for her to exit, Aliz said all in a rush, "No, no, go on, I'll be down later. Just don't wake her when you go in."

"I didn't wake her before."

"No, no, I know, but just the same, she needs to sleep."

"Oh, absolutely," Arthur concurred. "Sleep's the best medicine."

Maintenance in Ganaego Hospital was as fickle as the staff. The elevator doors, for some reason, would sometimes close and suddenly open, then close and suddenly open. Not always, just sometimes, and now, as Aliz stood on the elevator and Arthur stood beyond it, the doors opened and closed spontaneously once, twice, a third time, then stopped midway. Aliz, embarrassed, infuriated, appealed with a mute shrug to Arthur, who said, "I could probably fix these."

~ ~ ~

In her office, first thing, she dumped the cup of tepid tea into her zebra plant.

On her voicemail was a second message from Lieutenant Brown. At one-thirty in the morning? Cognizant that she was displacing her irritation—Lieutenant Brown had done nothing wrong—Aliz nonetheless punched Call Return intending to inform this police person, whoever he was, to please leave her alone. Expecting to get his voicemail, she got him instead. "Bless you, you must be a night owl too." The lieutenant started right in, as though they were about to become dear friends. "I know you gotta be busy, doctor, so I'll keep it short. Do you know a Zoltan Balcazar? Hungarian, gentleman in his early eighties, lived here in—"

"Lieutenant," Aliz cut in, "what does this have to do with me?"

"Getting to it, ma'am. Now, ordinarily, we don't get involved in these sorts of investigations. But there were some loose ends that didn't sit right. No known next of kin, but, okay, common enough, but the people who knew him didn't seem to know much about him either, even though he's lived here practically forever. And then, once I started poking around, I found other things, fraudulent Social and so on, and so I—"

"Lieutenant," Aliz interrupted again. She had suffered one garrulous fool tonight, she would not suffer another. "I have a patient who is experiencing some difficulty. You said you'd keep it short?"

"Beg pardon, ma'am." Lieutenant Brown sounded chastened. "So here's the scoop: I have reason to believe that this Zoltan Balcaza might have been—and I emphasize that *might*—a Vidor Kovacs. Originally from Hungary, Keszthely—hope I'm pronouncing that—"

"You can't be serious?"

"Come again?"

Aliz apologized, then went on. "I'm sure the police mean well, but just because there was a Vidor Kovacs in Keszthely—and yes, there *was* a Vidor Kovacs in Keszthely—doesn't mean he's somebody named Zoltan something or other in Pennsylvania? Vidor Kovacs disappeared five decades ago—in *Europe.*"

"That may be, ma'am, I'm not saying we've got this thing nailed one hundred percent, but among his things we found some letters and pictures and whatnot. No one could make head nor tail of the letters, but you folks in Ganaego are blessed with a humdinger of an assistant librarian. That gal, she put us in touch with someone who could translate them, and we started working it back. They're from a Krisztina Kovacs. Do you—"

"He had my mother's letters?"

"Was there a problem, I mean, in the marriage? They were separated?"

"Lieutenant, that's neither here nor there. What I want to know is how did this strange individual get his hands on my mother's letters? I'm assuming they're very old? He must've found them somewhere, I have no idea, but, yes, I can see the source of your confusion now."

"Well, that's right, too," the lieutenant agreed. "He could've picked them out of the trash or found them in a secondhand shop, whatever. And some of them do go way back, like you said? But not all of them. They end about eight years ago. Did something happen then? Here, lemme toss you another poser: You matriculated from Ganaego High in 1971, right? He had snapshots of your graduation ceremony."

"Graduation ceremonies are public events—anyone could have pictures like that."

"I *understand* that, ma'am. But he also had a lot of newspaper clippings. You graduated from Mead College, right? Then medical school?"

"This is ridiculous!" Aliz was outraged. "It sounds like I've been being stalked. Lieutenant, I think I've heard quite enough about this old man. If you could just return my mother's letters, that would be fine."

"One of the clippings was your brother's obituary. Ma'am, *please:* We may be all wet here, but, given the ambiguity, I really *do* need your cooperation. We have not interred the body. Can I ask you to come over and ID it?"

"*Again,* Lieutenant, I would like my mother's letters returned, if you please. But I have no interest in going all the way to Creighton to view some strange man's remains."

"What about JPEGs of the deceased? Can I at least *send* them to you?"

"All right, send them!" Aliz snapped. "So we can finally cross this possibility off your list! Why some *bizarre* person got such a perverse fixation on my family I don't know, but I *do* know that a man gone missing in Hungary in 1958 doesn't magically reappear in some Podunk town in Pennsylvania in 2010. How long did you say this person lived in Creighton?"

The lieutenant's sharp intake of breath she had no difficulty hearing. "You know, Dr. Kovacs, we didn't have to do this? We could've just buried this poor old sot? But if it amuses you, people can trace Zoltan Balcazar to the year he rebuilt Ester Von Rosenberg's porch and chased away the rabbits that lived under it—that was in 1964. But anyway, I'll be more than happy to email you the pictures and be shut of it, too."

Shaken, ashamed of her temper, Aliz called the ICU and was informed that Pleasance had had no more episodes and that her husband had volunteered to replace the burned out bulbs in the waiting room. She could go home, get a few hours sleep, perhaps lose the headache, and return for morning rounds. Instead, Aliz turned off the buzzing fluorescent lights and settled at her computer. She opened a draft of a paper she was co-authoring.

Anything to make the night pass.

Half an hour later Aliz clicked on an attachment in her email application, and in the darkness of her office her father's face materialized. Eyes closed, features preternaturally subdued as death will do as it withdraws vitalness from flesh; nevertheless, it was her father, and his long-lost presence, glowing like a vision, transfixed her. Was she sure? *Positively?* Granted, had she passed this old man in the street she could have easily failed to recognize him. If you aren't alerted to the possibility of something, even the obvious may escape you. But if you were wholly absorbed, as Aliz was now, you could deftly reverse time's alterations: tighten the jowls, reshape the nose and ears, clear and smooth the complexion, reduce the puffiness under the brows. But even without the repainting provided by her imagination, she would recognize her father, Vidor Kovacs, she would *see* him.

Nothing's changed, she thought.

But that was not true. What had changed was that one mystery had been replaced by another. Victor had not drowned himself, had not been executed. He had abandoned them, yes, as she had always insisted, but then, unfathomably, lived out his life not ten miles away. *Why?* The letters from her mother that ended enigmatically to Lieutenant Brown eight years ago ended because eight years ago her mother had died. Why had her mother never told her? Never reunited the family? Yesterday, had you asked her whether she could have been deceived by her mother in something so momentous, she would have laughed out loud. She and her mother had been close. To be near her was the main reason, after her residency, that Aliz had returned to Ganaego. Had *Jan* known? Known and never told? Her brother had pushed her away, as he pushed everyone away, but, still, Jan had never shown the least evidence of guarding such an enormous secret, and she doubted that.

Her graduation: Why had he not, that night of all nights, made himself known? She had been the Valedictorian, had delivered an address. Creighton was not a place she had occasion to frequent often, but she drove through it and every now and then poked around an antique shop there. Had she passed him on the sidewalk? Sat beside him in a delicatessen? *Was* it political? The tentacles of Communist Hungary reached deep into people's lives, and paranoia can persist long after whatever engenders it dissipates. Was it shame? Vidor Kovacs had been a man who loved gaiety and courted intrigue, who gloried in a scandalously lived life. What had happened? What had gone wrong? Her father's face, shrouded in death, hovered eerily over Aliz's paper-strewn desk, luminous, inexplicable, silent as a mask.

~ ~ ~

When her mother the summer of 1962 took Aliz to the Ganaego School Department to register her, she should have been, according to her age, enrolled in the fifth grade. Because she was so shy and backward and her English so rudimentary, she was placed in third. One morning that fall the nonresponsive, solitary pupil was asked by Mrs. Stubbs what the day's date was, and she did not know. She was sent to stand in front of the class and interrogated again and again for the date of the day. To the delight of twenty-seven jeering third-graders, Mrs. Stubbs thundered, "Stop feeling sorry for yourself! Take responsibility for your life, child! Shush your whining and look around! You will find everything you need!"

On the wall had been a calendar.

For Aliz Kovacs that had probably been the most important lesson in her life. For humiliating her so savagely, she had never forgiven Pleasance Stubbs, nor had she ever failed to credit Pleasance for shocking her out of the trauma, the self-pitying lassitude, that had gripped her since the abandonment of her father and their immigration to a new country. Decades later, at six-fifteen on a warm sunny holiday weekend, Dr. Kovacs stands over the old woman as she emerges from the morass of medicated sleep.

"Pleasance," she asks, "how–are–you–feeling? How is the pain?"

A moment that balances between good and evil, a calculation to be of this world or of another, registers on the seamed, blanched face and in the glassy eyes, then the dry voice rasps, "Where's Arthur?"

"He's outside, I'll get him. So, are–you–feeling–better?"

"I want to paint the kitchen."

Not good. Aliz, silently cursing Paul Lunner, places a restraining hand on Pleasance's shoulder. "You'll need to rest up a little before you start painting walls."

Fury grips the patient; she shakes free of the doctor's touch. "I don't intend to paint a thing! All I intend to do is pick the color! Where *is* he? That man is never around when you need him!"

In the waiting room Aliz leans over the snoring Arthur, then recollects. She takes a step back and says gently, "You hoo? You hoo?"

It's not precisely one entirely fluid motion that brings Arthur Stubbs to attention, rather a series of disjointed marionette-like motions, but as he lands more or less intact on his stocking feet, he yelps, "Yes, ma'am!"

"She's going to be fine," Aliz tells him. "I think she has some chores lined up for you? But listen here: If a piece of furniture is to be moved, Mr. Stubbs, *you* move it."

~ ~ ~

In the hospital parking lot Aliz roots in her purse for her phone. Summer this ultimate weekend in May has indeed ushered itself in. Languorous warmth pours down, stranding the few automobiles scattered across the sprawling asphalt expanse as though they were lost to their roofs in a tidal wave of light. The blooms of a nearby tree perfume the air. "What was your father like, Jimmy?"

She fears she has awakened him and that he will be grumpy. But grumpiness is not a salient Jimmy Boswell trait. Not much different in this regard from Arthur Stubbs, he readily answers her incongruous question. "The old man? He'd patch a leaky radiator with a wad of chewing gum and unload the car on a minister, then turn around and buy a truckload of pork butts for an orphanage. With him, you never knew."

"But did he love you, Jimmy?"

"He was a gruff son-of-a-bitch, but, yeah, he loved us. Never laid a hand on his kids."

"Didn't run out on you? Didn't mysteriously disappear? Didn't spy on you?"

"He catted around some, but, nah, Pop took care of his own. Full of questions today, aren't we? You all right, Aliz?"

"Do you love your children and your grandchildren, Jimmy? You do, don't you?" As soon as she says this, Aliz regrets it. "I'm sorry, Jimmy, I wasn't thinking."

"No, no, that's all right, Aliz, don't worry. It's been a year since Terry's death. The family's never going to get over it—*I'm* never going to get over it, I'm the one who bought him that red Miata—but we have to talk about it, we have to go on. Yeah, I love my katzenjammers and my grand-katzenjammers, and I'll tell you that even though not a single up-and-coming Boswell seems remotely interested in carrying on the car business."

"Did you sleep on *Zoom-Zoom* last night, Jimmy?"

"What'd they feed you in the caf? You lost your patient, didn't you, Aliz?"

"You're getting to know me, aren't you, Jimmy? No, everything's fine, but thank you for asking."

"And you're okay?"

Aliz Kovacs considers that. "Jimmy, I don't know . . ." Once again, she imagines her father at her high school graduation. How close had he dared to come? In the crowds of families milling about, hugging each other, had he slipped past, brushed her gown? Had he risked smiling at her? *Spare parts and bloody bones:* She would, Tuesday, visit Lieutenant Brown and apologize to him, and she would lay to rest her wandering father beside his wife and his son. She would collect Vidor's few things and sift through them and perhaps uncover some clues. But somehow it did not matter as much, unraveling this second mystery. He had not abandoned them, had not abandoned her. He had, in his own fashion, watched over them, watched over her. She was not pretty, not in the manner she understood men liked women to be pretty: fragile, tender, accommodating. She had little use for that kind of thing. But her solitariness, especially these past years, had come to weigh on her.

"I need to go home, Jimmy. I need to pull down the blinds and turn off my beeper. Later, I'll need to come back here for a little while. But if you want to do something tonight, I'd like to? It doesn't have to be fancy. I don't need college-educated steaks, but I'd like to sleep on the river tonight, unless you're busy . . . ?"

Sometimes birds will land on the arms of Jimmy Boswell's radar, an expensive piece of equipment he has no need for, and calmly go round and round. But all in all, Jimmy Boswell and his radar do precious little harm, perhaps even some good. "Aliz," Ganaego's most successful car dealer declares, "I'll pick you up at seven. Maybe we can find us a blue-collar fish for dinner."

Red Box, Red Box

Spring 2015

It was the third time: He knew what to do.

When Tyler Hodge sent Bartkiewicz and Smolin back into the store with their teetering dollies, ordering them to stack the packaged chops in Paolo Colorusso's cooler to the butcher's satisfaction, Teddy shoved a fifty-pound box of case-ready sirloin to the edge of the trailer. He leapt down and lugged the box over to Tyler's BMW and secured it in the unlocked trunk. As the assistant manager's car registered the weight of the expensive steaks, Teddy pressed a palm down on the trunk lid to close it with a soft click. The first time he'd had to be told twice before he grasped what he was expected to do and wondered how Tyler intended to reconcile the bill of lading with Colorusso's inventory.

"Because Paolo's cool," Tyler explained that night when Teddy had shown up at his house as instructed. "Three of us, that's it. No freelancing, no amateur stuff. You punch out, not a carrot in your pocket that doesn't belong to you." He handed Teddy a telephone-book-sized Porterhouse steak, an item that seldom ended up in the buggies of baggers and shelf-stockers. "Keep your trap shut and do as you're told, capeesh?"

Tyler Hodge, twenty years Teddy's junior, wore a Rolex Submariner that nestled cozily in the dark hair of his slender wrist and bragged that he possessed a photographic memory. And Tyler would, in truth, astonish new checkout clerks by rattling off the PLU of practically any fruit or vegetable the T&V carried. A young man on the make, someone, to borrow his own words, *screwing his way through his twenties*—meaning, Teddy supposed, not only women but the businesses that hired him—Tyler hadn't bothered to ask whether Teddy wished to join him in petty theft. But he understood how things worked. Hadn't he been doing what he had been told ever since someone escorted him to the alley behind one of the countless grease shops he'd worked in through *his* twenties and thirties and now into his forties and removed his front teeth for him with a torque wrench? His mother, bless her, bought him new teeth, and the one particular of which Ted Bachelor, Jr., could reliably attest to was that this second set of choppers he had no intention of parting with.

As he scrambled up into the trailer, Smolin came wheeling his empty dolly crazily through the dock, waving a plump arm. "Teddy, you got a call! It's an emergency!"

Tyler was irked. "I told you to help Colorusso."

"But it's an *emergency!*" Smolin sang out again.

Tyler transferred his annoyance to Teddy. "Go. I'll babysit these jerks."

Teddy hurried through the store. The T&V had a strict policy: No cell phone use during work hours. Not that that policy crimped him much, since his son, making tugboat noises, drowned his phone in the bathtub some months ago. He climbed the stairs to Rollie Schuster's office, the loft with the big open window where decade after decade Virgil Ferrara had stood, arms folded across his chest, gazing impassively over the sprawling store that he and his brother had built into one of Ganaego's most prosperous businesses. You can bet your boots, Teddy mused, accepting the phone from Nina, Rollie's secretary, that when the Ferrara brothers ruled the T&V nobody was tucking prime beef into his trunk, not if he valued his neck.

It was Lily, Teddy's wife. "You gotta come—now, right away!

Noah had an attack!"

"Come where? Where are you?"

"At the hospital! It's his *brain!*"

"He fell?"

"He didn't fall, just come—*now!*"

Teddy handed the phone to Nina and met Rollie, T&V's new manager, huffing up the stairs. A big, flat-footed black man, shambling and stolid, Rollie, who should have been enjoying his retirement by now, liked to bring his morose, moon-shaped face down close to his employees and share their tribulations. Stealing Tyler from Foodland had been, he claimed, his biggest coup. After hearing Teddy out, Rollie patted him on the shoulder. "Take as much time as you need, son. Our prayers are with you."

Rollie, Teddy was thinking as he raced through the late-afternoon parking lot, really should meet Lily sometime: They'd have a lot to talk about.

~ ~ ~

The T&V and hospital were not ten minutes distant from each other. The emergency room receptionist brought her fist down on a large red button and buzzed Teddy into the examination rooms, where he discovered his wife and youngest child in one of the alcoves. Teddy looked at Lily, who appealed to him in anguish, then at his son, who seemed relatively fine. They had the boy—all of seven and doing great, Teddy and Lily had been assured, in his special needs class—in a blue flannel gown. An IV in his arm was administering what looked to be a saline solution. He probably should have been lying still, not twisting his head from side to side to goggle at the blinking and beeping instruments, but short, cherubic Noah, eternally intrigued by the mysteries of the world, was irrepressible: You'd need a rope to tie him down.

Teddy, puzzled, rubbed the boy's bristly hair. "Hey, guy, what's

Red Box, Red Box

going on?"

He brought a forearm against his son's kicking legs to stay them and pulled Noah's grabby hands from his glasses. He'd had a daughter from his first relationship, a daughter now entering her thirties and well into the passions of her own life, and then a first baby with Lily, Emmie, and then Noah, with whom Teddy had formed a peculiarly close bond, perhaps because of the challenges the child faced. He'd had an uncle who was retarded, probably the same Down Syndrome. And because of his Uncle Rags then, retardation never spooked Teddy, as it sometimes did others.

"Don't touch him," Lily cautioned. "Not on the head."

"You said he didn't fall, right?" If Noah had suffered some sort of cranial injury, the hospital, it seemed to him, would have wrapped his head or at a minimum cushioned and braced it. Teddy readdressed the question to his son. "You go headfirst off the monkey bars?"

"Nooooo," the boy giggled.

"Walk into a tree limb? That's what I used to do."

"This is no laughing matter." Lily, as expected, was pretty much in pieces. She was brittle, a furtive, suspicious woman. "It *was* during recess, but he didn't trip, it wasn't like he was running or anything. The monitor said he saw him, he was all by himself staring at a downspout on the corner of the building—you know how he does that?—and he just crumpled over."

"That's what they said—*crumpled over?*"

"That's not all! They couldn't wake him up—he was out of it."

"So, they called the ambulance?"

"No, I brought him here. They just figured he got dizzy in the sun or something."

"So, they called you then, the school?"

"Yes, yes, will you listen?" Lily glared at him. "They said to come and get him. As far as they were concerned, all he needed was a day home watching television."

Teddy swallowed before he spoke. "They could've been right, you know? Low blood sugar, something like that?" Teddy pinched his son's nose. "You eat all your oats this morning, mister?"

"Oats," Noah agreed. "Oatsoatsoatsoatsoatsoats—"

"Noah, stop it!" Lily put a hand to his lips. "You know I don't like it when you do that."

"He's all right." Teddy defended his son. "They had a name for that, something . . ."

"Well, I don't like it—whatever it's called. And I don't think it was just a fainting attack, I think it's epilepsy. We know that's a possibility."

"Well, yeah, but anybody can faint. There's a guy at the—"

"Rather than playing doctor," Lily snapped, "why don't we wait for the real doctors!"

She turned aside, dabbing at her eyes. When they were told that the baby would not be normal, he urged her to have the abortion, pleaded with her. He knew what they'd be getting into: his uncle who had to be scolded every day of his life to wash his face and change his underwear, who, in profound bewilderment at his mother's funeral, became hysterical when they lowered the coffin lid. Lily was twelve years younger than he, thirty at the time, they could have tried again. But Lily Anne Campbell, raised fundamentalist, would not hear of such a thing. Teddy cupped his wife's arms from behind and squeezed them, hugging her as she shook. "You're right," he whispered. "What have they told you?"

She sniffled. "They waggled their fingers back and forth in front of him and made him follow with his eyes. They asked him what his name was and Emmie's, then they pricked his toes with a pin to see if he could feel it. Six of them, they were all jammed in here gawking at him like he was something they found on the curb. But

Red Box, Red Box

the Indian one—you know her?—she's the main one. She said they'd do a CAT scan, and that's what we're waiting for. It's a tumor, that's what they're thinking."

"Did they say that? That they think it's a tumor?"

"Why won't you ever listen to me? They don't *know!* They're going to find something in his brain, I just know it."

"Why don't I talk with her, the Indian one?"

"Why don't you *pray?* That would be a better use of your time."

Lily had always—in her own way—borne witness to her faith, but with every passing year her religion seemed to leave her more unhappy. Teddy grimaced, then hugged his wife again and hurried off. Rollie Schuster—who in Teddy's half-year at the T&V had serendipitously taken a liking to him—might urge him to take as much time as he needed, but Rollie Schuster, as good a man as he was, was not going to pay a bagger who wasn't bagging. On his second trip around the central station, Teddy intercepted the doctor exiting an alcove.

"Mr. Bachelor," she said jovially, "that leg of yours, how is it?"

"You remember that?"

Dr. Rupa Mudaliar the tag pinned to her lapel said. He'd never known her name, even though the foreign physician had been a fixture in Ganaego's emergency room as long as anyone could recall. A full head shorter, Dr. Mudaliar beamed up at him. "Left, am I not correct? And your daughter, the nasty cut above her eye? So now, it appears ve are to have the pleasure of meeting your young son, too?"

"You think it's a tumor? That's what my wife says?"

"Ve don't know that." Dr. Mudaliar wagged her pen back and forth. "It is a possibility, yes, but only one among many."

"I think he just got dizzy and fainted? He likes to stare at sparkily things, he's a—"

"Your young Noah is an unusual child, I understand perfectly.

He carries the gift of an extra chromosome. Vas not your uncle much like your Noah?"

"You knew him, too?"

"And his sveet mother." Beneath her white physician's coat the doctor wore a flowing pastel gown. "The day Mr. Rags drank the rancid cherry syrup." She lay a dark hand on Teddy's sleeve. "Please, Mr. Bachelor, try not to fret. This episode may be, as you say, no more than heat exhaustion, a minor fainting spell."

It was well over an hour before an attendant came to fetch them. Being pushed on a gurney through the corridors of the hospital, Noah, ordered to lie quietly beneath the sheet, grew panicky when the elevator doors closed on them. Teddy saw the sudden fear seize his son, the widening of his overly round eyes, the small pointed chin trembling.

"Daddy, am I gonna die?"

"No, no, you're not going to die." Beneath Teddy's hand, the bones of his son's shoulder seemed twig-like, as fragile as the bones of a bird. "All they're going to do is take some pictures of your noggin." He tapped the boy on the forehead. "We're going to frame them and put—"

"Would you please stop touching his head?" Lily whispered.

Teddy, aware of the attendant's pricking up his ears, whispered back, grinding the words between his teeth, "It's all right, Lily. He's not about to explode."

"Mommy says," Noah continued on with his thought, his eyes revolving to take in the enclosed space of the elevator and the tremors of the car as it descended, "I'm going to go to hell when I die."

"I never said that!" Lily shook a finger at him. "That's a lie!"

"It's–all–right." Teddy lay a restraining hand on his wife's sleeve and stroked his son's shoulder. Some doctor, along the way, had pointed out the telltale flecks in his son's irises, hugely pleased with himself for making that discovery. "You're not going to die, you're going to be fine."

"I don't know what gets into him," Lily said. "I never, *never* said such a thing!"

~ ~ ~

After that first relationship guttered out in a trailer whose wheels were permanently mired to their axles in a former goat paddock, an eight by fifteen tin can that reeked of mold and seeping kerosene, he drifted from woman to woman, job to job. You don't solve your problems, Teddy had come to believe: Either they solved themselves or they walked out the door. To be a bagger and shelf-stocker at forty-nine is to have come to little in life, but he gave himself credit for putting groceries on the table of that first woman and supporting that love child until she graduated from school, as he went on putting groceries on the tables of all the women thereafter who solved their problems, usually, by walking out the door.

Some left notes, some didn't.

Noah's CAT scan proved negative. Teddy, trying not to stare at the maroon spot in the doctor's forehead, heard Dr. Mudaliar out, her verdict that, "Ve can find nothing anomalous. If you vish, we can admit him and conduct more extensive testing, particularly for epilepsy?" When asked if that was necessary, the doctor shook herself noncommittally. "Unless or until something else occurs, I vould prefer to describe it as a transitory event." Teddy hugged his skeptical wife and quickly helped his son into his Superman shorts and his britches. The sooner they got out of there, the better. But even so, they did not get home, after collecting Emmie, until seven-thirty. A phone message provoked another sharp exchange.

"You're not going out?" Lily cried. "This is a family in crisis!"

"Half an hour."

"Is this more *meat?* Why is your boss giving you all this meat?

It doesn't make sense."

"Lily, please." Teddy, thin and sallow like his parents, never a man who craved hunks of red meat, who never craved hunks of anything for that matter, jingled his car keys irritably. Lily was a secretary for Keezer's Insurance. She earned more than he did, but not much more: Theirs was not a family that could turn aside windfalls. "Tyler has a manager's relationship with the wholesalers. It's a perk he gets. They comp him freebies every once in a while. And since I help him out at the customer service window, he sometimes likes to pass along his good luck to me."

Lily ran an institutional-size can of spaghetti around the opener. "I don't believe it," she said over the grind of the motor. "Nothing's free in this life, except God's love."

Wholesalers' comps had been his invention, a way to account for coming home with a twenty-five-dollar sirloin in your arms. But Teddy had his own misgivings: Petty theft does not buy foreign sedans and expensive watches, and thieves, petty or otherwise, seldom make grand successes of their lives. He took little solace from Lily's religion, but did recollect from his short-lived Sunday School career that the guys hanging to either side of Christ were thieves.

Getting out of gangs, however, is harder than getting in them.

"No way, out of the question," Tyler said, brushing aside Teddy's resignation. "Trust me, everything's coming up roses."

You could grow weary of people telling you to trust them. They were standing in the assistant manager's bachelor kitchen, not so upscale as his clothes and automobile, but at least the Formica counters weren't blistering. "I don't have to know a thing, I can turn a blind eye," Teddy reassured him. "I'd just rather not be part of it anymore."

"I'm glad you're here, I need a ride." Tyler, reaching for his sport coat, patted the pockets as he slid it on. "Across the river, ten minutes."

"Tyler, I've got a sick kid?"

The assistant manager loaded a blood-stained package into Teddy's arms. "Let's go, my kid sister's got my car."

Beneath the old bridge the river shifted past in wavy patterns, glimmering. Every time his eyes fell to the package between them, Teddy rued the first time he'd complied with Tyler Hodge's request. Half-asleep, he assumed that his boss's order to load the heavy box of porterhouse steaks into his trunk was legitimate. He was probably going to deliver them to a restaurant or hotel. That fantasy lasted all of a heartbeat when Tyler snapped at him for sauntering back to the trailer, *Get up here, asshole! Keep your mouth shut!*

Of course he was not going to deliver those steaks to a restaurant, and neither was Tyler delivering steaks to anyone tonight. He directed Teddy down Ashport's single main street to the end of the commercial district, where the avenue rose up into the developments and women hung their laundry off their balconies and their husbands still wondered what happened to their jobs in the steel mills. Tyler had him turn down a side street, then into an alley.

"Here," he said, "keep your motor running."

Tyler scrambled out and disappeared half a block up into a door with a lone light bulb burning above it. Pizza joint? Bar? These last blocks of downtown Ashport were hardly more than government offices and thrift stores with broken chairs in the window. The longer Tyler was gone, the more nervous Teddy became. You could also, the thought played across his mind, grow dead listening to people telling you to trust them.

Or maybe just swallow your front teeth.

The door he was staring at opened, throwing a ball of light into the night. Tyler, not running but moving determinedly, coat tails billowing beside his hips, strode up the alley and swung himself in the car. "Beat it," he commanded. "Drive, baby, drive!"

He was exuberant, flying. No one forty-nine and seldom, if ever, exuberant, could fail to see it—plainly, unmistakably—in the younger man's face, the radiance of his eyes, the working of his jaw, lips wet and gleaming, tongue visible in the hollow behind his teeth: Tyler Hodge didn't look all that different from Noah when the child passed a large, noisy packet of gas. Definitely not delivering steaks. When Teddy pulled into Tyler's drive, he attempted to tender his resignation a second time. Tyler cut him off.

"Just leave it rest, will ya?" The young man yanked a roll of banknotes from his pocket and uncurled a hundred-dollar note. "Bonus," he said, "for being such a good doobie. You should buy yourself some nice Idaho potatoes to go with that steak."

~ ~ ~

He checked in on both Emmie and Noah before coming to bed. Noah, asleep, thumb a plug in his mouth, and Emmie, assigned to study an article in the *Chronicle* about the momentous political events taking place in Ganaego next week. Fearing that his daughter sometimes got lost in the family's woes, Teddy sat with her.

"Is he going to be all right, Daddy?"

She was fair-haired, fair-complexioned, an honor-roll student. He looked into her troubled eyes. Sometimes he worried about Emmie more than he worried about Noah. "He's special, your brother, but there's nothing wrong with him."

"Mommy said she's keeping him home tomorrow."

Teddy pressed his lips together, holding his tongue. *When did I,* he wondered, *become an adult?* "I suppose, I guess, if that's what she wants?"

Lily was in bed, but awake, when he came in. She kept her back to him. "I don't know what you brought home," she announced, "but we're not eating it. You might as well throw it out."

Teddy let that pass. "He could go to school? Wouldn't it be better to—"

"There's *something* the matter with him! *You* can't see it, *they* can't see it, but *I* can. I'm not going to work tomorrow, he's staying home with me, and that's that."

"All right, all right, a day home won't hurt him."

"If you think he's okay, if that's *your* opinion," Lily said loudly, spitefully, "then what you might want to do is get down on your knees and thank the Holy Savior for that."

They had met at low points in their lives. Lily, estranged from her West Virginia family, he, home from surgery and sucking his dinners through a straw. They were both moody, fatalistic people. He'd never met a woman with whom he could sit for hours without speaking. But Noah's birth had tested them. It was wrong to call their marriage bait and switch, but on both sides a whiff of resentment lingered. Teddy sat on the bed. "Lily, I'm not going to pray to your god."

"He's *every*body's god."

"Not to the Chinese he isn't, not to Rupa Mudaliar."

"Who's *that?*"

"Nobody, forget it."

Lily thrashed in her covers. She went out of her way to lift herself on an elbow to turn to him. "Are you going to get on your knees and thank your heavenly father—or aren't you?"

"No," he said reaching over and turning off the light.

~ ~ ~

The next morning Rollie searched him out. Teddy and Smolin were in the aisles restocking. "How'd you make out yesterday? How's your boy?"

Rollie liked to relate his personal story of success to his employees. He liked explaining how devastating the closure of the steelworks had been for him and his family and how, out of desperation, he'd borrowed a hundred dollars and started a business selling potatoes from a trailer directly across—as it turned out—from the store he had now come to manage. When he told Teddy his inspirational story, Teddy, somewhat incredulously, asked, "You didn't happen to have a partner named Ted Bachelor, did you?" Rollie, suddenly recalling and connecting the name, had thereafter taken a protective interest in the son of one of his first potato-stand partners.

"Noah's fine, thanks for asking," Teddy told him. "Just a little drama to spice up our lives."

Rollie, clearly in the last job of his life, his last chance to grab the brass ring, was perpetually beset by the investors who had bought out the Ferrara family and questioned why the store could not seem to turn the profits that Tommy and Virgil had once raked in. Lifting his eyes, Rollie gazed, annoyed, at Misha Smolin, who had taken it upon himself to rearrange the macaroni shelves. Frankly, if you asked Teddy, the T&V had grown tired. The store carried an abiding odor of stale produce and purple meat, of floors scrubbed but never gotten quite clean. Rollie returned his sorrowful expression to Teddy. "Tyler's late, I can't get a hold of him. Why don't you cover the customer service window? It's not like him not to call, I have no idea where he is."

In bed with a high-end hooker?

~ ~ ~

The answer to Tyler Hodge's whereabouts came, first, from a checkout clerk on break whose husband was a police captain and then from all quarters of the store as employees, flouting the T&V's policies, spoke excitedly on their phones. It was Nina, charging down from the office to locate Rollie, who flew by Teddy's window to inform him.

"They found him in his car!" Nina's face was flour-white; she looked like she might be sick. "In the DPW garage. He was shot—in the *head!"*

No freelancing, no amateur stuff. So, who was the amateur, after all? Teddy ran his tongue over his store-bought teeth. How much that had hurt: birdcage of wires in his mouth, reconstructive surgery, months of excruciating pain. Yes, but, as it turned out, how paltry a tuition fee he'd had to pay to grow up. *That's* when I became an adult, he decided. But hardly did he have time to dwell on Tyler Hodge's fate—and the mind *would* go there, even as one tried to keep from imagining the gruesome scene in that public garage— for another worry worming its way into his consciousness, a worry emphasized by Paolo Colorusso.

You seldom found the old butcher far from his meat counters. He leaned across Teddy's window to whisper in a rasp, "The great mastermind, the brains of the outfit. You got any idea what's shaking?"

Teddy opened his palms and shrugged. "I guess we should figure the cops are going to come sniffing around."

Paolo Colurusso's biggest thing in life had been every July helping parade a plaster saint through the brick streets of Ashport, until his church, its roof riddled with leaks, was closed by the bishop. Blood studded the cuffs of his butcher's jacket. "I had a sweet little concession going before he showed up. *Brains!* Splattered over his dashboard, his brains. I don't know nothin' neither, and it ain't Kojak I'm worried about."

All they had on him—whoever *they* might be—would be his car. And in a shadowy alley, half a block away, how likely was it that his car had been tagged? On his lunch break, however, Teddy prudently drove to McKinnon's Mobil. Pumping gas here when he was 17 had been his first job, and, despite never gaining the full blessing of crusty Ralph McKinnon, McKinnon's was one of the few employers with whom Teddy had left on good terms.

"I need another car," he told Danny, Ralph's nephew. "Clean swap, whatever you got."

Danny pulled his head from the engine compartment of a pickup whose finish over time had come to resemble gray suede and scowled at a fingernail lifted from its quick, a pale crescent in black grease. He shook his head.

"I'll trade down," Teddy said. "I don't care."

Since what he was driving was a thirteen-year-old Ford Escort, a hand-me-down from his father, he had little bargaining room. What he did have, though, was a hundred-dollar bill.

"That'll do it," Danny said, sucking his injured finger.

~ ~ ~

He was late getting back to the store. Scrawled on the telephone pad in the customer service office lay a note, *Call your wife.*

"He had a seizure!" Teddy could hear the hollow sound the shell of the car made around Lily, the rush of wind by the windows. "I heard a thump! Like something fell over and then a little scream! When I went in, he was on the floor, twitching all over!"

"Where are you?"

"Following the ambulance! He couldn't *breathe!* This is your fault! This sickness runs in your family!"

Lily was notoriously inept at driving while talking. Teddy persuaded her to end the conversation. On his way up the office stairs two steps at a time he encountered Rollie on the way down. "Do you have to leave today"—the manager groaned—"of all days?" Then answered his own question. "Of course you do. Run along, we'll manage."

"I'm sorry, Rollie."

His boss looked to be at his rope's end. "Colorusso quit, you know that? Just walked off, and I can't find his records. But go, we'll manage." As Teddy turned, Rollie touched him on the shoulder.

"Son, when you get back I wanna talk to you."

Vexed, his mind elsewhere, Teddy mumbled, "Sure."

Rollie clapped his hand on Teddy's shoulder and lowered his big head. In his teeth were strands of the corned beef he liked to nibble from the deli counter. "I'm gonna need some help. I've been told I got ninety days to turn this place around. I want you to work directly under me. We need to stir up some excitement. Maybe with this big visit we got coming next week, we can do something around that—host some events, get ourselves in the news? This Tyler stuff's got me so rattled I can hardly think, but anyway"—Rollie gave him a friendly shove—"go, go, your son's more important than ten stores. We'll talk when you get back."

~ ~ ~

Perseverate. The nurse educator's technical term floats back: *oatsoatsoatsoats.* His Uncle Rags used to drive people mad. In the T&V, when Rags, fifty-five years old and making motor noises as he pushed the buggy for his mother, spotted the graham crackers he loved, he'd start shouting *Redbox!redbox!redbox!redbox!* Grandma Nettie had warped her life around Rags, from the day the unfortunate child was born to the day she died and passed on the burden of her firstborn son to her second.

In the hospital lot Teddy parks beside his wife's car. Sometime soon lies another inconvenient conversation: Why is he suddenly driving a Plymouth? In 1962 JFK swept up Roosevelt Avenue in a motorcade ushered through the tumultuous crowds by forty motorcycle police, sirens wailing. A day Ganaegoans still talk about. Teddy's parents, long divorced, still talk about it: That was the day his father proposed to his mother. Next week Barack Obama is to visit Ganaego. Fifty years from now what will Ganaegoans talk about? Teddy reconsiders an earlier judgment of his: Getting his face bashed in did not mark his coming to adulthood. That still has not occurred and, who knows, maybe never will.

But even so, what has he learned so far, along the way?

That what you expect growing up—a steady if soul-draining job in the steelworks, Little League mitts for your kids, money to lavish on birthday parties—is no longer there and will never again be there. That way of life, that safety, is gone forever. What else has he learned? Oh, yes, you can shoot off your mouth once too often and be rewarded with a torque wrench for lunch. And Lily, what has he learned about Lily? Lily might yet join the procession of women who solved their problems via the door, but he doesn't believe that will happen. Lily is different: She needs him, and, despite the irksome entanglement of her white bearded god in their marriage, the truth is he needs her, too. And some little boy whose life will never make much sense to him needs them both.

Red box, red box.

Author's Afterword and Acknowledgments

At night the skies over the mill towns trembled like lamps whose bulbs had come loose in their sockets. In the passageways between the row houses and duplexes, orange and green shadows wobbled against the eaves, and grains of fly ash tumbled across the shared porches. *Black sugar,* we called it, and even in surrounding villages nestled in the knobby hills you had every morning to broom your porch and brush away the black sugar that speckled your sills. You could always smell the sprawling complexes that lay in long embrace of our oil-sheened rivers, the iron and steel mills, the chemical processors, the power plants and foundries, the lead smelters and slag yards: a burnt match and coal gas odor that clung to your clothes and followed you indoors from room to room. And you could always hear the tortured industrial complaint: the tall orange feathers of natural gas venting into the skies with a roar, the hoarse bellows rising from the throats of the Bessemers, the clangor of the pipe mills and piccolo chatter of the machine shops, the spit and fizz of escaping steam, the morose, admonitory horns of the tows on the river—and the whistle. The whistle you heard every day, Christmas, Easter, Memorial Day, Independence Day, and yes, even on Labor Day. More shriek than whistle, the imperious ribbon of sound that echoed through the hollows and sent the men streaming into the smoky brick streets like so many flecks of fly ash themselves. When the long strings of coal trains bowled down our steep-shouldered valleys, the frames of our houses shook and our bedroom windows hummed in their frames. Paydays the sidewalks were thronged, and vacant parking spaces were rare. As you traveled from store to store you might meet half the people you knew and you might hear a dozen languages. On those halcyon days the row bars did a gangbuster business, the markets overflowed with shoppers, and, if you needed shoes, that's when you got them, payday shoes.

You will not locate Ganaego on any map. Its housing plans do not conform to any known town developments, and its flights of wooden stairs up the steep-shouldered hills and its residents and families exist only in my imagination. Families like the Bachelor-Zobarskases, the Fischmans, the Begleys, the Stubbses, the Kovacses, the Schumachers, and the Pickering-Namarian-Woldings, whose generations have been with me for decades. During this long process of writing and rewriting to get their stories right, to find truth in fiction, I have had the patient assistance of numerous readers. I wish to thank Sloan Nota, my wife and always first reader. Her comments always cut right to the heart of things. Likewise, the insights over the years of my writing friends, Michael Colonnese, Paul Bellerive, and Kevin McIntosh, have spared me innumerable mistakes and infelicities, and I thank them sincerely. I wish to thank Margot Livesey, gifted writer and teacher, under whose wise guidance our seminar at Sewanee Writers' Conference workshopped "Ralphie's Clarinet," helping me to focus Audrey's story. And I wish to thank Joe Taylor, Director of Livingston Press, for selecting the story collection as this year's Tartt First Fiction Award winner and for ushering the manuscript through the long path to publication.

About the Author

Robert McKean's *The Catalog of Crooked Thoughts* was first-prize winner of the Methodist University Longleaf Press Novel Contest and was published in 2017. The novel was also named a Finalist for the 2018 Eric Hoffer Award. A recipient of a Massachusetts Cultural Council grant for his fiction, McKean has been nominated three times for Pushcart Prizes and once for Best of the Net. He has published extensively in journals such as *The Kenyon Review, The Chicago Review, Armchair/Shotgun, 34th Parallel, Kestrel, Crack the Spine,* and *Border Crossing.* For additional biographical detail, please see his author's website: *www.robmckean.com.*